Deliverance From Evil

Deliverance From Evil

Blaise Apoldite

This is a work of fiction. Names, characters, places and incidents either are the product of the author's imagination or are used fictitiously, and any resemblance to any actual persons, living or dead, events, or locales is entirely coincidental.

This book was printed in the United States of America.

To order additional copies of this book, contact:
Xlibris Corporation
1-888-795-4274
www.Xlibris.com
Orders@Xlibris.com
68323

CHAPTER ONE

AUTUMN HAD ARRIVED somewhat unexpectedly in the historic, colonial New England town of Marion. The temperature started to drop in the higher elevations as distinctive shades of leaves were falling off deciduous trees and getting swept up by cars traveling along the interstate. Granite formations reflected the sunlight and displayed their unusual yet marvelous contour that bordered the hillside.

It was the first week of September, and the new millennium was approaching. Y2K was the topic of discussion throughout most of the country. The feeling was one of panic. Corporate America was squandering exorbitant sums of money to secure their computer technology from collapse. It turned out to be nothing but scare tactics and a lot of useless propaganda. I'm sure there was some economic motive behind all of that nonsense.

Summer vacations were over. The children had returned to school, and the roadways were less traveled. Birds had ascertained their new home and congregated near the river, searching for breakfast before venturing out. Some flew high above the water and with their keen sense of sight suddenly accelerated toward the river, engulfing their prey. They were feasting on the remains of what was once a robust, ten-pound catfish. They devoured its flesh so rapidly that within minutes all that remained were tiny skeletal fragments, and as the wind picked up, the scattered bones were released into the water.

The evergreen trees surrounding the town were impeccably landscaped. Myriad colors glistened as I drove along the placid country road. Soft clouds remained dormant in the distance. The more I stared at each one, the more I found each cloud to be what I imagined. I'd see a child inside her mother's arms waiting to be fed or a very large ship setting sail among the dark blue skies. And– if I really concentrated, just maybe – the face of God would reveal itself somewhere in that visible white mass of water high above the ground. At that moment, I was convinced that I would never find a more picturesque atmosphere filled with such grandeur.

The evening sky was illuminated as though billions of celestial diamonds were sprinkled across the universe. It was Utopia from east to west. As I drove with the top down, I could feel the gentle breeze against my face, blowing through my thinning hair. The temperature steadily declined. My dark brown eyes had become completely filled with saline fluid that trickled down to my chin.

I momentarily inspected my facial appearance by flicking the light switch and glancing in the mirror located in the sun visor directly overhead. I was now staring back at a man in his early thirties, with slight wrinkles atop his forehead, who feared the unwelcome arrival of premature aging. I perceived it to be a curse. Punishment for all of my sins committed on this imperfect earth. Somehow, I believed I could avoid it through repentance or atonement. Of course, I soon realized there was nothing I could do to stop its fury.

I gazed into the sky while zealously inhaling the aroma of the ocean air coming from the opposite direction. I drove that night along vacant roads in anticipation of exploring a new world. I was consumed with life in the big city. Leaving New Jersey was one of the best decisions I had ever made – or so I'd thought. Saying good-bye to low-paying jobs and high unemployment rates was easy. Jobs were few and far between. The real estate market was not considerate of first-time buyers. Since when does a house valued at two hundred thousand dollars sell for over a half-million? I pondered, as though I were that naive.

As the population swelled, so did the standard of living. Property taxes skyrocketed, and the increase in auto insurance left many residents skeptical about the future of the Garden State. It wasn't long before demonstrations were held outside the Capitol Building. Protesters rallied on the State House steps in Trenton, arguing for auto reform.

"We need lower rates!" a woman yelled.

Others shouted, "stop the bleeding and oust the corruption!"

There were hundreds jammed firmly like sardines, pacing back and forth, wearing that look of smugness, making every effort to get their point across. They carried signs with aspirations so that those driving down State Street would take the time to read them and become concerned about their plight.

"We want the governor to address our issues," they chanted persistently. Some time later, the governor's aide came out and delivered a speech to the crowd, advising them that their concerns were being handled with the utmost solicitude. This was just a ploy to keep the people happy and hopefully send them on their merry way. I was cognizant of their frustration. All they wanted was to see the light at the end of the tunnel, but it was a great distance from where they were standing.

They found little support from onlookers who probably didn't even care about their state's economic condition. I was certain these people earned enough money so that they could turn a blind eye. I didn't and so I'd felt compelled to remain long enough to see just how democracy played a role in government. Believe me, I was fed up with political antics. I was in dire need of a job myself, and it didn't look like anything was going to change in the near future.

"I'll take anything at this point; just give me health insurance," I said in desperation, when registering at one of many temp agencies. I started to doubt my confidence. I knocked on every door, but none of them seemed to open. Not even a crack. I knew it just came down to luck, and I was hoping to catch my first break.

"I'm sorry but, I don't have anything that fits your qualifications," I was told by nearly every agent who received my curriculum vitae. It just didn't make any sense. I was at the wrong end of the spectrum. I had the education, but lacked the experience. I had a simple question for these wealthy, avaricious corporations. *How do you obtain experience if no one hires you?* Everyone praised the recent economy, but no one paid any attention to the unemployment rate that had been on the rise for the last three years.

Financial experts had predicted the arrival of a recession, yet little had been done to create long-term employment for citizens in New Jersey. Maybe one reason for this was corporate downsizing and the desire to leave the United States to do business in a foreign land where labor was cheap and profits were enormous.

As a recent college graduate pursuing a master's degree from an unknown school, believe me, I had my share of doubts about exhausting any more funds on academic interests. *Whatever happened to all of those great positions that followed graduation? Where did those job fairs go? Is anybody looking out for the young prospects of tomorrow who were promised employment based upon their qualifications?* I thought to myself while glancing through the want ads that were in the Sunday paper.

As the years went by, I was inclined to believe that a change in lifestyle was forthcoming. I needed to create my own opportunity. Remaining passive about the entire situation was down right futile. I needed to become an active participant in my future. Remaining in my state of domicile was not a way of accomplishing that. It was time to turn over a new leaf. Get a different outlook on life. Get out of the monotonous lifestyle I had been so damn accustomed to. Inadvertently, I had discovered a new environment, one without any smokestacks, chemical plants, or skyscrapers. Before I'd realized it, I was six hours from home.

While driving down the narrow road that ran parallel to the Massachusetts Turnpike, I had thoughts of moving to New England. But, as I looked in my rearview mirror, I observed what appeared to be lights in the distance. I continued to drive, yet the lights got closer, and of course, a police car approached. Sure enough, I had to pull over.

"License and registration," the officer said angrily. "I pulled you over because you were doing seventy-eight in a sixty-five," he continued. He shined his flashlight inside my car, and after concluding that I was not inebriated, nor possessing instrumentalities of criminal activity, he took a hurried look at my identification and insurance card.

"You got to be careful and slow down around here," he said, handing the materials back to me.

"I'm sorry, Officer. I wasn't paying attention to the speedometer," I told him. He walked back to his car and ran my license plate number through the computer. I sat there waiting for him to return with just a warning and a smile.

Act courteous and respectful, and he might cut me a break, I thought, with all the confidence in the world. Wishful thinking would not work this time. I was handed a citation in the amount of $85.00.

I moved into a tiny apartment within close proximity of the New Hampshire border. It had one bedroom with a small kitchen and a living room half the size of the kitchen. There was paneling on the walls that needed an immediate make-over. I sought permission from the owner of the building and decided to paint the walls instead. I ripped off the wooden panels and could see the prior damage caused by other tenants.

There was a huge, gaping hole in the center of the wall, and loose Sheetrock gradually fell to the floor like a fine, powdered sand. It looked like someone had put his fist through it after a domestic dispute erupted. The carpeting was torn and had cigarette burns all over it. The prior tenant must have smoked like a chimney. The bathroom sink didn't drain properly and the toilet was constantly overflowing. The stench was enough to make you lose your lunch. I was on the first floor, which meant my apartment would always be infested with insects. I bought the most powerful spray to eliminate bugs, spiders, and centipedes, but it was of no use.

After weeks of complaining to the landlord and getting no feedback, I finally took matters into my own hands. I called the best damn exterminator in all of Middlesex County and got rid of those annoying creatures once and for all. Then, I did something I thought I would never do. I sent the owner of the apartment complex the bill. Then, he retaliated by raising the rent the following month. I threatened to make a complaint at Rent Control and to sue him for damages.

Once he found out I was in law school, he backed off and accepted the amount of rent I had been paying him originally as stated in the lease. Sometimes, I regretted not leasing the studio on the second floor, but I think I would have suffered from claustrophobia. Hell, I couldn't complain. The rent was definitely worth it. Where else could I find an apartment for just $500 per month? I was strapped for money. I relied on loans to get me through law school. My rent was being paid from my life's savings. And it didn't amount to all that much.

The town of Ardmore was well known for its affluent homes and businesses. It had thrived over the years, especially with respect to commercial real estate. Corporations, banks, and small businesses, had flooded this neighboring town. It was also known for its outstanding educational system, including one of America's best private schools. But the land that used to occupy this prestigious town had been replaced by commercial buildings, malls, and retirement homes. Developers bargained with local planning boards and were given the green light to construct numerous subdivisions throughout Middlesex County.

More expensive homes had been built even though fewer people had been moving into the area. Those that did migrate to Middlesex County settled in the city of Landsdale. As the population grew, so did the rate of crime. Theft, robbery, burglary, and drug sales had dominated the city. Big businesses and entrepreneurs had no choice but to leave Landsdale as they lost significant profits and customers. A once prominent city that contributed so much to economic capitalism was now given the label of "America's car theft capital of the world."

About 15 years ago, a law school was formed in the town of Ardmore. It was named the Merrimack School of Law. Originally, the school was built in Boston and remained there for about six years before Dean Marshall decided to relocate. The school was well-known in the New England area for providing students with a strong legal education.

We were now in our fifth week of class, starting the first semester of law school and beginning to stress over the amount of work and reading involved. As I sat in the back of the room, I didn't utter a single word. I was just hoping I didn't get called on. But the odds were no longer in my favor. Almost every name from the student list had been called. It was only a matter of time before I had met my fate. I remember sitting in Room 206 when my Property instructor had begun class.

"Dillon Fletcher?" he asked looking at his roster.

"Oh shit, that's me," I muttered.

I stood up and began to recite the facts of the case. If I were any more nervous, I would have thrown up right there on top of the table. My pulse was beating so fast that I could feel it in my chest. My palms were sweaty and clammy, and I felt as though I would faint. The room appeared to be spinning out of control as though I had Vertigo. *Get hold of yourself,* I said to myself, grabbing hold of the edge of the table and on the verge of a breakdown.

I envisaged the faces of one hundred students scrutinizing me. The anxiety had started to build. The fear of failure had manifested itself. After discussing the factual background of the case for about ten minutes, I thought that I was finished, but the instructor just kept grilling me over and over again. This so-called Socratic method was enough to make me pop anxiety medication so often that I felt like it was candy released from a pez dispenser.

"Did you read this case?" he asked sarcastically.

"Yes, I did," I responded with little self-assurance.

"Then what is the issue the court is deciding? I want you to phrase it with the word *whether*," he said, becoming angry at the way I drafted my question.

"Whether the interest conveyed violates the Rule Against Perpetuities?" I stated.

"And what did the lower court hold?" he asked, strolling around the classroom while latching on to his meaningless disquisitions in search of his next guinea pig.

"It found that the conveyance of the interest did not violate the rule because the transfer involved a charity," I replied.

"What was the appellate court's reasoning for affirming the trial court's decision?" he asked pontificating.

"I – I have it here, somewhere," I said, as I began to stutter. I shuffled through my papers trying to locate the information. I could sense the hostility and impatience on the part of the professor. He sighed after removing his glasses that were two sizes too big and then glanced around the room hoping someone would contribute to the discussion by responding with the correct answer. Moments later, I found the answer scribbled on a sheet of paper that had a coffee stain on it. I looked in the direction of the instructor and ambitiously replied, "the court reasoned that there wasn't any need to invalidate the transfer because charitable organizations were involved, and this type of interest had a specific designed purpose, that would be frustrated if there was a restraint on alienation."

"Sit down," he answered.

I didn't know if I was right or wrong or if the instructor was just plain nutts. In any event, my 15 minutes of shame (that seemed like an eternity) was nonetheless, finally over. I breathed a sigh of relief. I was safe for awhile at least in that class. But I still contemplated dropping out of school. I didn't feel that I belonged there. When class was over, I exited the room and was approached by a young, attractive woman near the stairway.

"Nice job," she remarked.

I was astounded that she really thought I did well. I was certain, however, that I made a complete ass of myself. She was quite statuesque, a towering five foot-ten to be exact, with beautiful dark brown hair that extended slightly beyond her shoulders, and gorgeous, sparkling blue eyes that reminded me of the Caribbean. I saw her height as an advantage, even though I was about one full inch shorter. Her legs were long and the rest of her body was well-proportioned. Hell, I wanted to screw her right there on the steps.

Of course, it was her soothing smile that attracted me at first. The hallway was not well lit, but it didn't have to be. Her eyes were radiant – so bright I bet I could see them even if it was pitch-black inside the building. If words couldn't describe how I felt at that moment, then surely the apparent bulge in my pants would have helped to explain it.

"I'm Kerri – Kerri Cafferty," she exclaimed.

I then introduced myself and shook her well-manicured hand, noticing she wasn't wearing a wedding ring. As we walked outside toward the gazebo, we were surrounded by an array of fresh flowers and a small path constructed as a shortcut to the parking lot. It was at this point where we exchanged phone numbers. She smiled as I became impatient, encountering difficulty in programming her number in my cell.

"Here, I'll do it," she said, pressing the keys with her long, delicate fingers.

When I arrived at my home in Marion, that was only two miles from the school, I fixed myself some dinner and then took a shower. By the time I had read all of my cases for my classes the following day, it was approaching midnight. It was time to turn in. I needed a good night's sleep in order to be fresh for my 8:30 writing class. As I reclined in bed, I couldn't help but think about Kerri.

Is she seeing anyone? I wondered. I pondered whether I should ask her out and considered waiting a little while longer. I glanced over at my alarm clock, that displayed 12:34 a.m. I shut my eyes and drifted off to sleep. Tomorrow was another day.

I awoke to the sound of police sirens and an ambulance that pulled into my apartment complex. I would have overslept, since the alarm clock in my bedroom had apparently stopped due to loss of power during the night. I put on the radio and heard the DJ announce the time. *"Good morning, Boston. It's going to be a gorgeous day with high temperatures reaching eighty-five degrees and low humidity."*

It was just past 7:00, and I barely had time to eat breakfast. I grabbed a snack and a banana from the table before heading out the door. One thing was for sure; law school made me a better cook. Living alone for three years and having to prepare all of my meals made me realize how spoiled I used to be. Talk about taking something for granted. Now I was forced to fend for myself or starve. There weren't any leftovers in the refrigerator, so I had to get accustomed to making meals on a consistent basis. That lasted for a few months, and then I changed my diet. I tried an alternate route – fast food. This saved me more time studying. The downside was I gained 20 pounds in my first year, and my cholesterol shot up an additional 50 points. So much for trying to save an extra few hours.

I arrived at school well before my scheduled 8:30 class and had time to chat among friends. I was speaking with another classmate in the cafeteria when I happened to see Kerri enter.

"Good morning, Dillon," she said in her soft, ingenuous voice.

"Would you like to study with me sometime this week?" I asked.

"How' bout if I come over to your place tonight around five-thirty?" she suggested while grasping her case briefs for class.

I told her 5:30 would be perfect. Besides, it gave me time to clean up the clutter in my apartment. I had dishes in the sink for over two weeks. And stuff in the refrigerator had started to get moldy.

As we left the cafeteria, we were approached by Shane Baxter. He was an obnoxious sort. He made it his business to ask students about a particular case, even though he had never read it himself. This guy was a downright lazy son of a bitch. He was the epitome of an underachiever. His only priority in life was to feed his eating addiction, that had been exacerbated ever since he entered school. He weighed about 215 pounds; that was immense in comparison to his five-foot-five-inch frame. His conduct was disreputable. Students disfavored him because he rarely studied and always wanted somebody's outline, because he didn't make his own. He never briefed his cases and was often unprepared when called on by the professor.

"Did you read this case, Mister Baxter?" the instructor asked. It was obvious the professor knew the answer to this question but didn't want to make any premature assumptions by failing to give the indolent student the benefit of the doubt.

"I'm sorry, Professor, I forgot to brief this one," he replied hoping to climb out of a huge hole that he had just dug for himself.

"Well, you know the rule, sir; pick up your things and leave," the professor told him.

The instructor wasn't going to waste his time or anyone else's. It was more efficient just to remove a student who had nothing to contribute to that class. I think Shane was thrown out of class twice for being unprepared.

He had the brilliant idea of showing up at study groups to obtain his information, but students grew tired of his shenanigans and decided not to share information with him. He lacked basic common sense, but tried to compensate for it through his vociferous voice. It wasn't long before the students implicated him in hiding research books in the library.

He was caught on camera taking case law books and statutes and placing them in an undisclosed area. After a disciplinary hearing was held with the assistant dean and two faculty members, he was expelled from law school. It was the best thing that ever happened to the legal profession. This guy would have ended up an ambulance chaser who felt no shame in passing out his business cards inside the lobby of the courthouse.

The Board of Bar Overseers would not have hesitated in disbarring him within the first month of his being sworn in. Students were filled with such gratitude after hearing the news, that they went to a local bar to celebrate his departure.

Then there was Skippy Olsen. His real name was Chester. The students called him *Skippy* 'cause he intentionally missed most of his classes. Everyone thought that he was the biggest retard at Merrimack. Olsen was wrong in every class in which he opened his mouth. He was the subject of ridicule at study groups. Average students loved him because they used his lack of intelligence as a barometer toward their own success in law school. He couldn't possibly score better than anyone else on an exam. That's what I had thought along with three hundred other smucks. Ironically, the little shit managed to fool the entire student body. It turned out that he stagged the entire episode to screw up the grading curve. In other words, he faked being an idiot. Most students thought that he would end up in the lower 25 percentile based on his consistent absenteeism and total display of ignorance regarding the law. They detrimentally relied on this assumption during final exams. Three years later, the cunning soon-to-be lawyer would give a speech at graduation. Students were left speechless when his name was announced as the recipient of three academic achievement awards including graduating with high honors.

Law school was about analyzing legal theories and memorizing judicial holdings. I'd soon found out, however, that the only thing I needed to remember was $C=JD$.

I sat on the sofa watching HBO until Kerri needed to be buzzed in. I couldn't wait to see her. With all the prior bad relationships I had been in, I was just hoping to get passed first base.

When I opened the door, she greeted me with her potent smile. I could have kissed her at that moment.

"Come on in and make yourself at home," I told her.

As she brushed past me and sat on the sofa, that was in dire need of repair, I caught the scent of her perfume. It had a vanilla fragrance. She was wearing a short green corduroy skirt, a white long-sleeved shirt, and three-inch sandals exposing her newly-polished French pedicure. She looked stunning, and she wasn't even wearing make-up. I wore my newest pair of khaki trousers, which I had purchased half off at a clearance sale. I made certain that I came across as being a good host and asked her if I could get her something to drink.

"Any beverage will do," she said, finding a comfortable position on the couch. I brought her a fresh glass of iced tea and sat beside her as we began studying our notes. At first, I was disinclined to sit next to her, as her beauty would have intimidated even the most audacious men. We had been studying for approximately three hours.

"Do you live around here?" I'd finally asked while inching my way closer to where she was sitting.

"I live on Walnut Street, three blocks from Bader Hall. I'm originally from Long Island and came out here five years ago," she replied before taking another sip of her beverage.

She had an exquisite two-bedroom apartment that was surrounded by an affluent community of suburban homes. It was located on a quiet cul-de-sac. The Township had a Shade Tree Commission that was responsible for the planting and maintenance of evergreen trees along the sidewalks.

The interior of her apartment was commodious and quite contemporary. Portraits of early 18th century artwork hung from the walls, and the fireplace in the living room would bring solace to anyone who appreciated its architectural design. Her rooms were anything but disheveled. She had decorated them warily, providing each with its own separate and distinct identity. She loved pets and was disappointed when the landlord handed her a lease that prohibited dogs and cats.

Kerri came from a wealthy family. Her father ran a successful business at an automobile dealership. Her mother was a nurse at a hospital in Massapequa, Long Island. Her parents continued to reside in Huntington.

Kerri was a dazzling woman. Her attractiveness, however, stemmed not only from her physical appearance, but her alacrity at learning. Describing her as anything but pretentious would have been devoid of any truth and downright scornful. She had graduated magna cum laude from New York University with a major in molecular biology and also received her Master's degree in applied sciences at Fordham. She was the recipient of a partial scholarship to Boston University School of Law, but declined to attend. She had waited a few years and decided to enroll at Merrimack.

We both discussed the fact that we desired to become attorneys in our senior years at college. She wanted to focus on environmental law and became involved in community activities, assisting in clean-up efforts and the amelioration of air quality and energy conservation. She was a member of the Environmental and Oceanic Studies Program at NYU. I told her of my interest in becoming a public defender. Of course, that led to a debate.

"Don't tell me you want to represent murderers?" she asked, flipping the pages of her case law book.

"Somebody has to; so why not me?" I responded.

I knew what her next question was going to be.

"Would you represent child molesters?" she asked, this time raising her voice slightly and rolling her eyes.

I discerned that I had struck a nerve with Kerri. My defense to her statements regarding representing criminals did not persuade her. It was evident that she had no desire whatsoever in becoming a criminal defense attorney. All of the chatter gave both of us an appetite, and it was probably a good idea to end the debate anyway.

CHAPTER TWO

MAUREEN HENSLEY HAD to be the most promiscuous woman I had ever met. The word around law school was that she had slept with every male student on campus. Maureen slept with some for free and others for a small fee. Usually no more than $200. She was at the low end of prostitution. No wonder some students were increasing their loan amounts for tuition. You could tell when she was looking for a good time. If she weren't seeking sexual gratification, she was lighting up a cigarette outside the building. She smoked only Marlboro Lights. But she lit up more than the evening sky.

She was a chain-smoker, up to at least four packs per day. And it had started to affect her general appearance. Her face looked older and more wrinkled, as if she had been exposed to sunlight for long periods of time. Boy – was she thin, and my first impression was the poor woman was battling an eating disorder, possibly anorexia. I really never saw her dine in the cafeteria, so I had to believe the rumors that she had a conflict with her weight.

Maureen was not the type of person to be committed to a relationship. The pitiful woman had issues. She gave new meaning to one-night-stands. Intelligent enough to attend law school, but not smart enough to practice safe sex. Maureen never used protection and demanded the same from all the other men she'd slept with. Her philosophy was simple: If you put on a condom, she'd put you out the door. Like so many other students, I, too, was surprised she had even been accepted into the program.

Unfortunately, her body was discovered in the Merrimack River sometime in November of 2000. Evidently, she was raped, and then the killer dumped her pathologically, thin body into the river. The only evidence found near the river was part of a bracelet with her last name engraved on the back. Autopsy reports concluded that she had been dead for about two days. Police did not have any leads or primary suspects, however, the Ardmore Police Department did visit the law school to question students who had any information that might assist in solving this heinous crime. Any male student at the law school could have been a suspect. I'm willing to have bet that more than half of those horny *esquires to be* managed to get that eccentric whore in the sack.

Dean Marshall informed students about cooperating with police and distributed handouts detailing the events that had transpired. The police were filled with doubts and were not sure how to approach this case.

"I believe this is a killing where the perpetrator knew the victim," stated Sgt. Watson of the Ardmore Police Department after being questioned by the local press. "What we don't have here is a random killing of a twenty-seven-year-old female. We are conducting a full investigation and working with local police departments to gather any leads."

A man appeared at the police station a few days after the report of the killing and told them that while he was running alongside the river, he had observed a male in the distance getting into his car and leaving but didn't think anything of it at the time. The jogger could not describe the man due to his distance from the scene and because it was later in the evening.

Almost four months had gone by, and police were still without any information. Over ten miles of the river had been fully searched with the help of investigators and local police departments. Dogs had been sent out in an attempt to aid police in facilitating the investigation. It had become a frustrating and tiresome experience. Any newly discovered evidence would be difficult to encounter as it was approaching the first week of February, and snow had fallen throughout the New England area. Family members of the victim pleaded with police and local authorities to keep the investigation open.

Maureen was a very intelligent woman when it came to academics, but she had a serious problem with drugs. Some days she missed class because she was just too strung out to attend. She experimented with everything from marijuana to more serious drugs, including cocaine and ecstasy. She relied on her friends to deliver the harmful substances she so desperately needed.

"Maureen was addicted to cocaine during her teenage years," her mom told police, as her fragile hands trembled and she fought to hold back tears. Her mom also stated to police that Maureen had terminated her pregnancy a few months earlier. "She just wasn't ready to be a mom," her mother added, snatching the box of Kleenex on the small table in the living room. Police were becoming more and more frustrated as they lacked any credible evidence to link to this crime.

Then about a month later, while rummaging through her deceased daughter's clothes, Maureen's mother came across a picture of a man with a phone number on it. Thinking it might assist police, she phoned the precinct and spoke with the captain. It turned out that the name of the man identified in the photograph was Derek Martin, a bartender in the town of Landsdale.

Derek was a very handsome and well-dressed individual. He stood about five foot eleven, with dark brown hair, and he weighed approximately 180 pounds. If there was one thing he was good at, it was picking out extravagant clothes. He shopped only at popular name brand stores. He wore expensive shoes, mainly Bruno Magli.

He enjoyed flirting with women but sometimes went too far, where his comments could have been construed as offensive, even unscrupulous. He had never met Maureen's parents because

Maureen was afraid to tell them the man she was dating was African-American.

Her father would have had a coronary if she came home with any man who wasn't white. He told her if she ever thought about marrying a black man, he would disown her. It's not like they were hardened racists. They didn't despise black people – they just thought it would be best if every race remained separate, but equal. If the topic of black people came up in conversation, the Hensleys would refer to them with the utmost respect, calling them Negroes and not the other "N" word. They just couldn't see the possibility of an interracial relationship involving their only daughter. Maureen's parents were very strict when it came to dating, but they had their prejudicial views as well.

Luckily, Maureen had developed her own mind-set, ignoring her parents' preconceived requests. She was attracted to black men, period. In fact, every man she had gone out with since high school was African-American. You would always hear Maureen out on the soccer field chatting with her friends about getting laid by a black man and how she would never allow herself to be screwed by an inexperienced white boy. "Black men are bigger," she'd relate to her female classmates. She never could bring herself to tell her parents about Derek. She knew it would cause friction and ruin the family. She managed to conceal this unpleasant situation for almost a decade. Unfortunately, her parents had to discover the truth following her death.

Derek admitted to police about having an ongoing sexual relationship with Maureen. He also provided information that he had supplied her with narcotics within the last three years. Derek was becoming agitated by the fact that the police believed he was a potential suspect.

"Should I call my lawyer?" he asked, concerned that he might be in trouble.

"No, that's not necessary," responded Officer Brown. "You're not a suspect. Right now we just want to question you about the crime," he said.

Derek responded, "I have nothing to hide. I had sex with her, that's all. Nothing happened. I didn't kill anybody."

The police asked him to submit to a DNA test.

Derek paused momentarily and then replied, "What for?"

"It's police procedure," replied another officer, who placed a pen inside his shirt pocket.

Results from the examination revealed that his DNA matched that found on the victim. Law enforcement had a hunch he had something to do with Maureen's murder. Derek was, in fact, the last person to have been with Maureen prior to her death. He did not have an alibi. He could not establish his whereabouts on the day she was killed. Police were hoping he might screw up and give them a reason to arrest him.

Sgt. Watson decided to keep a close eye on Derek and set up a surveillance to track his steps. While Derek was at work, the police, after obtaining unlawful consent from the landlord, entered his apartment to conduct a full search, looking for anything to link him to the murder. A few diskettes were left out on top of Derek's computer table. Officer Cowell inserted them into the hard drive and opened each document.

Cowell found pornographic pictures that were downloaded from the Internet. Later, he detected Maureen's screen name on Derek's buddy list when he signed on using Derek's screen name and password which were automatically stored. While all of this was going on, a few other officers went to the home of Maureen's parents and requested consent to view documents and photos from her computer.

Police found that even though Maureen's screen name appeared on Derek's computer, Derek did not use his primary screen name when communicating with her. Police, finding this odd, contacted the Web site and discovered that both Maureen and Derek were communicating online in some form of a chat room under the presumption that Maureen did not know the person with whom she was corresponding. Officer Cowell then asked, "why would Derek change his screen name in order to speak with Maureen? Something just doesn't add up. It appears as though he was trying to hide something."

Police concluded that Derek used a different screen name in order to lure Maureen to an undisclosed area where he would then rape and kill her. They received records of all the communication that had transpired online between Derek and Maureen. Oddly enough, it appeared Maureen never discovered Derek's on-line identity. He used numerous screen names when making contact with other website users as well.

Maureen was communicating with other men about sexual fantasies, and perhaps the police assumed Derek had become insanely jealous, thereby developing a motive to kill her. Police telephoned the magistrate at 3:37 a.m. and went to his residence to obtain an arrest warrant.

They arrived at Derek's apartment forty-five minutes later and approached the door, announcing, "This is the police, Derek Martin. We have a warrant for your arrest!" When they heard no response, they decided to push in the door. Inside they found him asleep in his bed and a bag filled with marijuana near his alarm clock. He awoke as police were placing handcuffs on him and reading him the Miranda warnings. One of the other officers searched the immediate area and found two hand guns between the mattresses. One was a – 22 and the other a – 57. Derek didn't have a permit to carry either one of them. Police immediately seized the weapons.

"I didn't do nothin, I already told you!" he yelled. "You've got the wrong man, I'm fuckin' innocent."

Derek was escorted to the police station wearing blue jeans and sandals.

"I want to see my lawyer right now," he added. Once arriving at the station, police began fingerprinting him and taking his mug shot. Derek was now considered a murderer and a rapist.

CHAPTER THREE

DEREK MET WITH Brendan Schneider, his defense lawyer inside the jail right around lunch time.

"Good afternoon, Derek. My name is Brendan, and I will be representing you in this matter." Derek responded, "I didn't do it. I keep telling everybody that I had nothing to do with Maureen's murder. They found some nude photos on my computer, and that makes me a murderer?" he asked, ridiculing him.

"The judge is going to ask you how you plead," said Brendan.

Derek became agitated, stating, "I plead not guilty. I am not responsible for that woman's death, period."

"Okay, Derek. You understand that if you plead not guilty, there will be a trial?"

"I understand," he said, "but this is crazy, man. I didn't kill nobody."

Arraignment was scheduled for the following Tuesday. Derek pled not guilty, and the judge scheduled the trial for some time in March. Brendan immediately filed a motion to suppress the weapons, the marijuana and the photos found in Derek's apartment, but all motions were denied. Apparently, the judge thought there was sufficient evidence to move forward with the trial. I thought for sure the evidence would be considered tainted and in violation of Derek's Fourth Amendment rights under the exclusionary rule. It was clearly fruits of the poisonous tree, but the judge didn't see it that way.

Voir dire proceedings were held inside the Landsdale Superior Courthouse adjacent to the federal building. Realizing that the case had brought a great deal of publicity to Middlesex County, Brendan decided it would be in Derek's best interest to have the case moved to another venue. His motion, however, for a change in venue was denied by Superior Court Judge Timothy Crawford. It really didn't matter where the case was tried. Derek couldn't get a fair trial anywhere in Massachusetts due to the widespread media coverage.

After a slight delay, the trial was scheduled to begin on Wednesday, March 10th, 2001. The prosecutor was Raymond Sciarpa, who was the assistant district attorney in the county of Middlesex. He had over 20 years' experience in conducting criminal trials.

He was tall with bushy, gray hair and in his mid-fifties. He could have trimmed his oversized mustache, that covered the majority of his face, but others found it added to his character and made him appear somewhat more intriguing. His demeanor represented a man with immense austerity, and he never lacked an ounce of integrity.

He had graduated with high honors from Harvard Law School. He was a member of Law Review and had written several articles on the constitutionality of capital punishment. He began his career as an associate attorney for the prestigious firm of Bauer, Gorman and Fortay in Boston. His job at the firm was to handle potential claims involving class action lawsuits. This was Sciarpa's biggest case and it ended up putting him on the map. One morning, one of the senior partners dropped a file on Sciarpa's lap while Raymond was talking on the phone. The case involved a plaintiff who was adamant about suing a defendant, drug manufacturer, operating under the name, *Wilgex Inc.* The defendant failed to adequately warn the general public of potential deadly side effects of a newly-marketed substance called *Sex-Blo.*

The drug was designed to increase sex drive and help men maintain an erection for longer periods of time. In some rare cases, the drug also enlarged penis size by as much as 15%. (The hell with the side effects!) There were also negative peculiarities present in the prescription medication. Evidently, the manufacturer knew or should have known that the medication also increased heart rhythm and caused abnormal arrhythmia in patients with pre-existing cardiac disease or those with frail immune systems. In just over eight months on the market, the drug was responsible for 14 fatalities and 39 myocardial infarctions.

He was now one of the top personal injury lawyers in Massachusetts. His face appeared in every legal magazine in New England. Now he could afford the advertising and it was just too easy for him to get clients. He made every other lawyer out there jealous; not to mention regretful that they had gone to law school in the first place.

Sciarpa was brilliant at using legal principles to advance his case. He could recite the law in his sleep. No defense attorney wanted to face him because his record in prosecuting criminals was impeccable. Raymond did not favor plea bargains. He believed if the defendant committed the offense, then the defendant should be tried for that offense.

Raymond was overly confident, carrying a sense of arrogance with him into the courtroom. Nothing excited him more than a grueling cross-examination. He would practice his interrogation at night when everyone was asleep. He liked reading his notes out loud. It helped him to easily identify his mistakes or to make changes if something didn't quite sound right. Over the years, he had perfected his cross examination. He was a veteran esquire. His secret to success – Fear. Leave the adverse witness feeling like a fish out of water. Dead in his tracks. Gasping for air while on the stand.

Derek was being tried for first-degree murder: a deliberate, intentional, and premeditated killing of another with malice aforethought. Brendan attempted on several occasions to get the charges dropped, stating insufficient evidence to prosecute and lack of probable cause. Raymond, however, would not cooperate with Brendan's requests, and the first-degree murder charge was not withdrawn.

Brendan was a rookie attorney working in Haverford, Massachusetts. He graduated from Suffolk Law School in 1998. He was also the class president. He didn't want to be. His name was voluntarily placed on the ballot as a write-in. It was accomplished by 240 classmates who selected him for the prestigious position by writing his name on a piece of paper and placing it inside a small red box. The votes were tallied at the end of the week. Brendan had more write-in votes than the two main running candidates.

Brendan was of average height and quite handsome. He was on the slender side and his wife had been encouraging him to gain weight after he had recovered from a stomach flu a few weeks earlier. His hair was always parted perfectly. Even on the windiest of days, his hair remained stationary. Brendan looked much younger than his actual age of 29.

He had a solitary practice where he rented out an old two-story building on Claremont Street, that was once a thriving tailor shop. The owner of the building gave Brendan a discount and only charged him $850 rent per month. He felt sorry for him. The owner knew that Brendan was just starting out and had outstanding loan obligations that had to be paid. He was looking at well over $100,000 in legal debt. Brendan's only experience in trial litigation had taken place when he was a law clerk for the Hon. Richard Morganstein in Suffolk County Superior Court. Now his first major case happened to be a homicide. He would have to handle it on his own. There were no senior partners or associates from whom he could beseech assistance. The only opinion that mattered was Brendan's. That's what he got for putting up a shingle right after graduation.

It was 9:00 a.m., and the courthouse parking lot was filled to capacity. Reporters from *The Boston Globe*, *Boston Herald*, *Landsdale Tribune*, and local news stations gathered around the front of the newly-constructed building awaiting the arrival of Derek Martin. He appeared with his lawyer and was escorted into the courtroom. Derek wore a dark gray striped suit with a vest and was accompanied by his mother and sister, who sat behind him.

The victim's family sat on the opposite side of Tanya and her daughter. Maureen's parents kept staring at them with great animosity. They were convinced that Tanya's son had murdered their only daughter. They blamed Derek not only for the murder but also for allowing Maureen to become addicted to drugs and other harmful substances. At times, it sounded like the father had mumbled something under his breath. He was disconcerted over the entire incident. If someone could have read his mind, it was probably saying, *Go on up there and strangle that son of a bitch.* And I'm sure Mr. Hensley had thought about it. He could barely remain in his chair. And if he wanted to attack the defendant, it wouldn't have been that difficult. The only court officer was standing all the way on the other side of the room. Mr. Hensley had a clear shot at Derek. He could have gotten in a few punches before the officer would have been able to pull him off the alleged predator. But he also would have been arrested and held in contempt. It just wasn't worth it and he realized that. He was placing his trust in the hands of twelve jurors to make the right decision and put away the man that he thought was responsible for killing Maureen.

Derek was quite nervous as he constantly wiped the sweat off his forehead. Even though it was only the beginning of March, it felt like mid-August inside the courtroom. The court clerk entered and stated, "All Rise…the Honorable Timothy Crawford presiding."

She then called out the case of *Commonwealth v. Martin.* "Be seated," said the judge. The judge looked in the direction of the prosecutor and asked him if he was ready to begin.

"Yes, Judge, the Commonwealth is ready," said the prosecutor.

"Very well. Why don't we begin with opening arguments, Counselor."

"Good morning, ladies and gentlemen of the jury," said Sciarpa. *"I appreciate the fact that all of you took the time out of your day to be here and serve as jurors. This will be a long and tedious trial. There will be a lot of information presented during the trial that you need to be aware of. I ask that you pay close attention to all the witnesses who take the stand and testify before you throughout these proceedings.*

Now, the Commonwealth of Massachusetts has charged the defendant, Derek Martin, with first-degree murder. This means that there is present an intent to kill accompanied by premeditation and deliberation. The Commonwealth will show that the defendant had such intent and premeditation to commit such a wanton and wilful act. He had a motive for killing the victim, Maureen Hensley.

It appears the defendant was jealous that the victim was having sexual encounters with other men whom she had met over the Internet. Becoming angry at the fact that he believed she had been cheating on him, he decided to use an alias screen name to track her whereabouts and then lure the victim to this secret location. He would then rape her with intense force and after killing her by means of asphyxiation would then dump her body into the river. Police discovered the victim was raped, and the results of a DNA test demonstrate that the source of semen was traceable to the defendant. This is a human being with no feelings and no remorse for his actions.

This is a selfish man who enjoys watching innocent people die. Pay close attention to the police officers who will testify as to their investigatory findings. You will hear tragic accounts of how the defendant strategically planned this entire incident from beginning to end. Make no mistake about it, ladies and gentlemen, the man seated at the defense table is a ruthless killer. He was heavily involved with drugs and even administered drugs to the victim.

Police will testify that they found evidence and other instrumentalities of crime at the defendant's residence. Clearly, the defendant knew the victim. This was not a random killing. This was a carefully executed scheme to violently commit the most heinous offense known in our society. The defendant had the intent to kill. He'd thought about it for some time. He had the opportunity to reconsider his actions and reflect upon his behavior. But he made the wrong decision. His selfish rage led to an innocent woman's death.

After hearing all the evidence and testimony from police officers, investigators, expert and lay witnesses, you will find that this man, Derek Martin, is guilty of the crime of murder in the first degree. Thank you."

"Mister Schneider, if you are ready, we will listen to opening arguments from the defense," said the judge.

"Thank you, Your Honor," responded Brendan. *"Ladies and gentlemen of the jury, the Commonwealth of Massachusetts has charged my client, the defendant, Derek Martin, with first-degree murder of the victim, Maureen Hensley. Yes, it is true that the defendant knew the victim, had sexual relations with her, and did, in fact, supply her with various drugs.*

These factors by themselves do not establish a motive to kill. Are we saying that every drug dealer or user is a murderer?

The defense will show that even though the defendant knew the victim and communicated with her on-line, it does not demonstrate with sufficiency that he developed a motive for her killing. The Commonwealth of Massachusetts cannot show any link between the defendant and the victim other than prior sexual encounters.

There is no evidence that the defendant had ever acted in a violent manner toward the victim. In fact, he had never demonstrated dangerous propensities toward anyone. He has no prior criminal record. The defendant is a bona fide citizen who works at two jobs. He is well liked, and his reputation in the community is that of a benefactor.

As you will see throughout this trial, the defendant is a peaceful and loving man who demonstrates strong compassion toward those closest to him. The defense will show that after all the evidence is in, the defendant will be acquitted. Thank you."

The Commonwealth called its first witness, Lenore Reece. Lenore had been friends with Derek for about five years. They became acquainted while working together at a restaurant. Lenore also had purchased drugs from him in the past.

She smoked pot most of the time, but when she was filled with mettle, she experimented with coke, thereby snorting it through her corroded nasal cavity. Over the years, she had lost a great deal of her faculties, and her ability to recall remote instances was greatly diminished by consistent drug use. She was skinny and pale-looking, as though she had been battling a terminal disease.

"Please state your name for the record," demanded the prosecutor.

"Lenore Reece, sir," she replied, trying to keep her eyes opened. It appeared that she was strung out herself. It was difficult for an effective direct examination to take place where the witness called by that party shows up at trial with drugs in her system.

"How long have you known the defendant?" Sciarpa asked.

"We have been friends for about five or six years," she replied.

"Where did you meet the defendant?"

"I'm sorry?" she answered. "I didn't here you."

"I asked you . . . where you had met the defendant?"

"Yes, we met at a restaurant. I was a waitress there," she added.

"When did you learn the defendant experimented with drugs?"

"He told me at his apartment that he used to smoke marijuana, snort coke, and I think he tried LSD a few times. It was LSD and all sorts of stuff like that."

"Did you also use drugs with the defendant?" Sciarpa asked glancing toward the jury box and wishing he could run a blood test of his own witness just to see what the hell she had ingested into her skeletal body.

"Objection, Your Honor. Miss Reece is not being tried in this case," said Brendan, in an angry manner and with a look of disappointment in his eyes.

Judge Crawford sustained the objection, and the prosecutor continued his questioning of the witness.

"Has the defendant at any time during your friendship displayed a violent disposition?"

"Objection, leading."

"Sustained," said the judge.

"How did you meet Maureen Hensley?"

"I never met her," the witness replied.

"Did the defendant ever mention her?"

Brendan could have objected to that line of questioning as well, but overlooked it.

"Yes. He mentioned that he used to be good friends with her, and they had an ongoing relationship."

"Please describe their relationship as best you can."

"Well, I know they were friends for a long time. If you're asking me whether they were intimate or not, I'm not sure. Derek is a private person."

She paused and gathered her thoughts. Then she looked toward the jury box where she gave them a close-up view of her bloodshot eyes and replied, "He keeps to himself, so I wouldn't know his personal affairs."

"What did you think when you heard the news that Maureen had been killed?"

"I felt horrible, you know. I mean someone died. Damn. I felt so bad. And I knew Derek was very upset," she told him.

"Did you ever suspect the defendant may have killed her?"

"No, sir, absolutely not. Derek is a great person. I know because I am his friend," she replied with her mouth gaped so that it was easy for Sciarpa to count all of her fillings.

"Were you with him on the night that Maureen was killed?"

"No," she said raising her voice and confusing Sciarpa momentarily.

"So you didn't actually see the defendant that night?" he asked.

"No, sir, I did not."

"Do you find it odd that the defendant cannot recollect where he was on the evening of the murder?"

"Objection, Your Honor. The state is asking the witness to formulate an opinion about the defendant's memory."

"Sustained."

"Have you ever heard that the defendant made sexual advances toward anyone?"

"No, sir, I did not," she answered, before awkwardly banging her head into the microphone.

"I have nothing further," Sciarpa replied.

"Mister Schneider, would you like to cross-examine the witness?" asked the judge.

"Yes, thank you, Your Honor. I just have one or two questions, Miss Reece.

"Did the defendant ever engage in violent behavior toward you?"

"No."

"Do you think he could be capable of murdering anyone?"

"No, sir, not Derek."

"Thank you, Miss Reece. Nothing further, Your Honor."

She stepped down and was assisted by the court officer who had escorted her to the lobby. I'm sure he thought that before Lenore went home that evening she was going to make an impetuous visit to the "*drug store*" in the back alley of her neighborhood. The judge took a twenty-minute recess and then reconvened.

CHAPTER FOUR

A FTER RETURNING FROM a brief recess, the prosecutor was going to call another witness, but Judge Crawford instructed that the trial end early due to a major snowstorm that was heading toward the Boston area and points north. For several days, meteorologists had indicated the possibility of a Nor'easter striking down over all of New England, bringing blizzard conditions and gusty winds exceeding 50 miles per hour.

The majority of court personnel departed the building by noon after the Governor of Massachusetts declared a state of emergency. The Department of Transportation responded quickly, sending out over one hundred sand trucks to all major highways to ensure the safety of travelers.

As nightfall approached, the wind began to intensify and snowflakes the size of golf balls fell to the ground. It appeared that most people in New England were used to such exorbitant amounts of snow as they nonchalantly drove their cars on slick and frozen roadways.

While Bostonians are accustomed to heavy amounts of snowfall, I have yet to become acclimated to their style of winter. I would rather remain indoors at all costs. Besides, I find repose to be most beneficial during a snowstorm. Nevertheless, I do find most impressive those undaunted individuals who venture out while knowing the danger and risk involved. Then, of course, there are those who travel in sport-utility vehicles convinced of their immunity from such treacherous conditions in that they can somehow avoid sliding on the ice or getting stuck in mounds of snow.

The trial was delayed for approximately four days while the courthouse parking lot and sidewalks were being cleared. By the time the storm left the New England area, the total snow accumulations were estimated at three feet. This made driving an unusual task. Children, however, failed to appreciate the danger. Many decided to walk to the nearest park where hundreds were snow boarding and riding their sleds. Some courageous teenagers left their homes in Danbury and went down to the lake to play a game of hockey.

A young boy named Ralph was skating on the northern end of the lake with his friends. They decided to set up a hockey game on the ice. While they were playing, one of the boys hit the puck too hard and it went into a wooded area. The boys went to look for it in order to continue the game.

As they were trying to gather their thoughts as to which direction the puck may have gone, Ralph came upon something and blurted out, "Oh, my God, let's get out of here!" and ran in the opposite direction. The other boys went into the woods and spotted what appeared to be a decomposed corpse. The boys ran home shocked and frightened as they attempted to describe to their parents what they had just witnessed.

The police were summoned to the immediate area. Upon arriving, Officer Downs, who was dispatched to the scene, stated to his fellow officer, "This body must have been here for months." It was completely charred, and making out any facial identification was highly improbable. In fact, parts of the corpse were no longer attached to the victim. Police believed that the body was that of a young female due to skeletal size and bone density.

The remains of the victim were brought to the pathology lab at Tufts University Medical Center. The medical examiner was able to obtain the identity of the victim through dental records. Her name was Maria Edwards, a twenty-seven-year-old college student, who attended the University of Lowell. She was in her third year and had been studying to be a nurse. Autopsy reports indicated that the victim had been dead for approximately three months.

When the information was passed on to Sgt. Watson, he immediately stated, "This is a signature crime and Derek Martin is the killer." Watson immediately notified the prosecutor and assistant district attorney about his findings. The prosecutor now believed Derek was a serial killer, and the possibility existed that other missing women may have fallen victim to his sadistic murders. The prosecutor wanted him charged with first-degree murder of Edwards.

Once the news of another killing reached the newspapers, there was pandemonium throughout Ardmore and nearby towns. People began protesting in the streets, arguing for the Commonwealth to charge Derek not only with both murders but to seek the death penalty as well. That would not be possible as Massachusetts abolished capital punishment in 1984. Sciarpa met with defense attorney Brendan Schneider, stating his intentions to charge Derek with the second murder.

"You have no proof that my client killed anybody," said Brendan without displaying the slightest amount of intimidation.

"How do you explain the similarities between the two murders?" asked the prosecutor who was attempting to discredit his adversary's statement.

"Maybe what we have here is a copycat killer on the loose," replied the defense attorney.

"So you do admit that Derek is guilty of at least one crime?" asked Sciarpa.

Brendan, growing impatient with his adversary, stated, "I'm not admitting anything. What I am saying is that Derek didn't kill these people, and someone else did; maybe the killings involve the same person, maybe they don't, but my client didn't do it. Show me a scintilla of evidence linking my client to either murder."

"I will save that for the trial, Mister Schneider," said the prosecutor, as he gathered his briefcase and exited Brendan's office.

Kerri was going to be busy for the next few weeks helping one of her friends move into an apartment. I had some time off for spring break and thought it would be best to go home and visit with family. She was kind enough to drop me off at Logan International in Boston. I purchased a ticket from Continental Airlines and flew to Newark Liberty International Airport in New Jersey, where I was met by my family.

To celebrate my arrival, we decided to take a trip to Atlantic City the following day. By the time we reached the Garden State Parkway, there was a traffic jam that stretched over ten miles. It took nearly four hours to travel from our home that was less than one hundred miles from the casinos.

We arrived at our favorite casino at approximately 2:30 in the afternoon. I withdrew two hundred bucks from a nearby ATM that charged ridiculous fees. Then I sat down at one of the black jack tables where smoking was prohibited. Seated next to me was a young woman, who had over one thousand dollars worth of chips in front of her. Interestingly enough, she'd kept winning. And not because the dealer busted, but simply because she kept being dealt face cards. I was lucky if I saw one. All I had were deuces and fours. I squandered half of my money in less than twenty minutes and headed for the bar. I could have ordered a free drink from one of the cocktail waitresses on the floor, but finding one was more difficult than expected.

Time seemed to fly by as I sat there putting quarters into the video poker machine. I always found it humorous that casinos never display clocks on the wall except near the restaurants where they are seating people with reservations. Speaking of reservations, we decided to have dinner at the buffet restaurant on the second floor. The lines outside the restaurant stretched as far as the escalators leading to the casino.

Not again, I thought. I wasn't about to wait a minute longer. I was famished, and watching everyone fill their plates did not alleviate the situation. We were waiting for a table for four people. Of course, we wanted to be seated in the non-smoking section, so that meant waiting an extra half-hour.

Finally, the hostess wearing an inappropriate mini-skirt and flashy high heels brought us to our table, and the waitress went to get our drinks. We ate until we couldn't physically walk back to the buffet line. On this particular day, we were gluttons, and I definitely paid the price. It was my own fault. I didn't need to eat seven varieties of desserts. On my way out, I stopped at the gift shop and purchased a box of antacids.

Following dinner, my brother and I decided to head back downstairs and try our luck at Blackjack. After about 45 minutes, my brother went outside in order to catch some fresh air on the boardwalk and also to obtain a few phone numbers from single women looking for excitement. Even though I would have loved to buy a woman a drink at the Hawaiian-style bar located right on the beach, my priority was to win enough money to pay back some of my law school debt. I sauntered through the casino floor with my ATM card in hand. I made another quick withdrawal of $200 and advanced toward the high-roller section. As I was walking toward the roulette tables, I noticed a familiar face. Without saying anything at first, I stared in disbelief.

"Professor Guillard?" I asked, as he was strolling passed the coin redemption center. He then looked in my direction and approached me wearing a Boston Red Sox sweatshirt. I always referred to him as the absent-minded professor. I don't think he even knew half of his students names. Well, maybe all of the female ones. One thing that I was certain of was that the lascivious pervert couldn't tell his ass from a hole in the ground, but he graduated law school and got his doctorate, and that's all that really mattered. Aside from that, I found him to be boring and confused. His face was drawn, and he wore those outrageous glasses that had lenses larger than hubcaps. I thought this style faded after the 70s', but apparently no one bothered to tell him.

"Dillon, is that you?" he asked with a confused look. He probably couldn't see two feet in front of him.

"Yes, professor," I said.

"How are you enjoying your vacation?"

"Just relaxing. Are you staying in New Jersey long?" I asked, but didn't really care one way or the other.

"Well, my wife and I leave tomorrow. I have to attend a meeting at the law school on Thursday. Are you taking any summer classes?"

"Yes, I'm taking Environmental Law."

"Oh, good for you," he said. He paused for a moment and then asked, "Have you been paying attention to the murder trial of Derek Martin?"

"Yeah. I guess everyone thinks he did it."

"I don't know. I mean, they haven't questioned any other suspects."

"Are there any other suspects out there?"

"I don't believe this guy did it. Anybody could have done it. I think the prosecution's case is going to be weak."

"Did you know Maureen?" I asked.

"She was a student of mine about a year ago. She would drop by my office for extra help from time to time."

I had to wonder just what type of help he provided. His door was always closed and I never heard any communication taking place especially after a female student entered his office.

"I heard that she was quite promiscuous," I informed him.

"I don't doubt it. She had many boyfriends. Hell, if I was single I would have screwed her," he said, jokingly.

I was positive that he had already done that. I noticed his hand was wrapped in a bandage and the cut looked rather fresh.

"What happened to your hand?" I asked staring at the gauze.

"Oh, I cut it at home with a knife."

"Oh, that's too bad. Well, enjoy the rest of your vacation, Professor."

"You, too, Dillon. It was nice seeing you again."

I have to admit there was always something uncanny about Professor Guillard. He seemed aloof at times, but then on other occasions he was more personal and direct. Rumors spread around the school that he was having marital problems with his wife of 25 years. He was always out of the house. He was spending less and less time with his significant other. Busy doing this and doing that – he basically abandoned his wife. Deserted her. Sometimes he would stay out all week-end and not even call to ease her worried mind.

Apparently, his wife suffered from alcoholism and had been admitted to a clinic several times. That may have been one of the reasons for his consistent departure. I'm sure that he had contemplated divorcing his wife. It was obvious that he had an attraction toward younger women. He would eat lunch with his female students instead of sitting with other members of the faculty.

He taught Contracts, Environmental Law, and the Internet. He was considered by some to be one of the toughest graders in the school. Students enrolled in the Internet class because Guillard discussed topics like pornography, chat room privacy, wiretapping, and e-mail fraud. He brought to class photos of naked females from real Web sites to show the importance of protecting private citizens and children from sexual predators and at the same time upholding the First Amendment in permitting viewers to have full access to these obscene depictions, excluding child pornography, of course, which is not protected.

Curious as to the investigation of the murders, I went to purchase *The Boston Globe* to inquire about the trial. Judge Crawford apparently had pneumonia and was hospitalized for two weeks. The trial was delayed approximately one month.

After the judge returned to work, and reviewed the documents left on his desk by his astute law clerk, Kyle Davenport, the prosecutor met in his chambers and spoke about the possibility of charging Derek with the second murder, as well. Judge Crawford did not find that the evidence was sufficient to warrant a finding that Derek was involved with the murder since police lacked any information and had no possible leads, even though both crimes were quite similar in their execution. Therefore, Derek would be tried only for the murder of Maureen Hensley.

CHAPTER FIVE

S CIARPA WAS FURIOUS at the judge's findings. He argued that aggravating circumstances existed and that the presence of a serial killer had been established.

"Your Honor, these killings are similar in every way," Sciarpa said.

"Counselor, I have already told you that you have failed to demonstrate with sufficiency any evidence to the contrary," remarked the judge.

"Will you consider the police reports?" he pleaded.

"No. There is no need to review these records based on what you have presented here today. I will not allow you to charge Derek Martin with this subsequent crime."

It was now the seventh week since the outset of the trial, and the Commonwealth was calling its next witness, Sgt. Watson of the Ardmore Police, to testify as to his findings regarding the murder of Maureen Hensley. Then it was time for the defense to cross-examine him.

"Good afternoon, Sargent Watson. I would like to begin with a few preliminary questions about your experience in handling this case. How many years have you been on the force?" Brendan scoured.

"This is my twentieth year," the officer said in a proud voice.

"How many murder scenes would you say that you have investigated?"

"Oh, a lot. At least fifteen, maybe more."

"How long have you investigated this case?" Brendan asked while his fingers were grasping a few papers on the table.

"About four or five months."

"Uh-huh. I see. Could you please describe the intricate details of your investigation?"

"Sure. On or about November tenth, 2000, we were summoned to the Merrimack River in Marion where we discovered the body of Maureen Hensley. Part of the investigation involved taking pictures of the scene, obtaining samples of hair strands, dental records, and DNA of the victim. We also looked for fingerprints or anything that helped aid the investigation."

"Could you describe what happened to the victim prior to her death?" asked the defense attorney.

"Yes, we believe that she was raped sometime before the murder," Watson informed him.

"When did you believe that the defendant was a suspect?"

"We found that the defendant was communicating with the victim a few days before she died and that he at some point met up with her. After we received the lab reports, we discovered the defendant's DNA was also found on the victim."

"Do you mean the defendant's semen was found on the victim?" Brendan asked.

"Yes," Watson replied convincingly.

"What do you believe was his motive?" Brendan inquired.

"We believed that he became jealous of the fact that she had been communicating with other men whom she had met on-line. Perhaps he thought she was having a sexual relationship with them and he decided to kill her."

"Have you found any physical evidence linking the defendant to this crime?"

"No, we didn't find any murder weapon or object used to kill her. DNA test results, however, did reveal that the defendant had sex with her, and that gave us probable cause to arrest him."

"No weapon, and you want to show that the defendant is the murderer? Isn't it true that the police had no real or direct evidence whatsoever to arrest Mister Martin, and you based probable cause solely on sexually explicit communication involving the victim?"

"Objection!" yelled Sciarpa.

"Overruled," the judge answered allowing the witness to respond.

"No, we found other evidence that linked him to the crime."

"Are you referring to the drugs found in his possession? So basically, you want to convict a man based on circumstantial evidence?"

"There are several factors that led us to believe we arrested the right man."

"Nothing further," Brendan answered with a slight grin while turning toward the direction of his adversary.

Brendan succeeded at what he intended to do. He laid the facts on the table and then used that evidence, or lack thereof, to impeach the witness. Part of being a good defense attorney is to make the witness appear foolish or catch the witness off guard. Establish even the slightest doubt and hope the jury runs with it.

Brendan was just hoping he could get the jury to keep an open mind, evaluate the evidence in a reasonable fashion, and if they did, when it was all said and done, Derek would be a free man.

———————

It was approaching four-thirty in the afternoon, and Judge Crawford decided to end for the day. He kept a busy schedule. If he wasn't presiding over numerous criminal cases, he was attending legal seminars and giving public speeches about improving the legal profession. If a law student thinks he's out of the woods after graduating and passing the Bar, think again. Each state mandates that licensed attorneys who are members of the Bar in that jurisdiction enroll in so many courses per year in order to keep up with any changes in legislation.

Derek was not happy with Brendan's handling of the case and demanded a new lawyer. Brendan explained to him that withdrawing from the case at this juncture in the trial would be detrimental to his interest. Derek explained that he wanted to take the stand and tell his side of the story, but Brendan attempted to dissuade him at all cost.

"You can't testify because the prosecutor will eat you alive!" Brendan yelled.

"I am not going to jail for something I didn't do," replied Derek, who was growing impatient with Brendan's failure to accept his demands.

"Look, if you want to guarantee your conviction, take the stand and let the jury see you as a murderer. If the prosecutor gets you on the stand, there's no telling what he might ask. I can't help you once you're up there. You're on your own at that point."

"And if I don't testify, then what? Who will hear my story?"

"Derek, I told you before, the Commonwealth has nothing to offer. Everything the prosecutor puts forth from this moment is circumstantial evidence. The jury will have a hard time finding you guilty because there are too many if's and maybe's. Why put yourself in a worse position than you are in right now?" Brendan asked.

"Can you be absolutely sure that I'm gonna get off of these charges?"

"Of course, nothing is absolutely certain, Derek."

"See right there. You can't stand here and tell me that I would be any better if I just sit at the table and keep my mouth shut while they spread lies about me and destroy my name."

"I'm not risking this entire case by watching you get on the witness chair and make a fool of yourself."

"So now I'm a fool, huh?"

"I don't mean it like that."

"You just said it."

"I meant that if you tell your side of the story, it will still be interpreted differently. The prosecutor is well-trained. He has been around the legal profession for over two decades. He's tried a shit-load of these cases. He can make you say something you didn't want to say. He will make it look like you've been caught in a lie. Once the jury thinks you lied, you can say good-bye to your freedom. Don't piss off the jury. They don't want to be there to begin with. If they think you're wasting their time, they will let you know."

"What about my family?" asked Derek.

"What do you mean?"

"Is my family going to testify?" Derek inquired with enormous incredulity.

"I think it is to your benefit to have your mother and sister testify to show the jury your good character traits. I would not attempt to go beyond that."

"Fine. You're the lawyer. I just hope you're right."

"Don't worry. I know what I'm doing," Brendan replied with assurance.

Brendan left the courthouse and drove back to the office to finish working on his other files.

CHAPTER SIX

AFTER A SLIGHT delay, the trial continued and Raymond Sciarpa called his next witness, Amy Harper. Amy was called to testify against Derek, alleging that he had harassed her on several occasions while at work. She was barely over the age of majority, but looked much more mature for her age.

She was strikingly beautiful and turned heads simply by entering the room. Her face was a natural, golden brown. She never applied self-tanning lotion or went to tanning salons. You could tell she pumped it out at the gym when you got a close view of her forearms. She took very good care of her skin. And if you had a leg fetish, she'd be the one that you'd want to have rock your world. But Amy wasn't that type of girl. She demanded respect from all of her customers and made it clear when some of them overstepped their boundaries and tried to get her in the sack. Sciarpa approached the witness stand and began his line of questioning.

"Good morning, Miss Harper."

"Good morning, sir."

"Could you tell me how you and the defendant had met?"

"Yes, I was working at the restaurant as a waitress and he was a cook."

"Now, did you have a problem with the defendant immediately after he began working there?"

"No. I would say that I was there about three or four weeks before any trouble started."

"How would you define trouble? Was there a confrontation?"

"Well, first off, Mister Martin started making sexual comments, and then it became more physical as time went on."

"Could you please describe the physical nature of the defendant's acts?"

"Sure. He would sneak up behind me when I was in the kitchen bringing the orders in, and he would grab me, sometimes touching my butt and sometimes fondling my breasts."

"Did you mention this to anyone in a supervisory position?" asked the prosecutor. "Not at first. I let it go, but as time went on, it became unbearable and I didn't want to put up with it anymore."

"So then you complained about it?" asked Sciarpa.

"Yes, I went to my staff manager and told him what was happening," Amy replied.

"What did he intend to do about it?"

"He said that he would talk with Derek and hear his side first."

"Eventually, was Derek terminated from his position?"

"Yes, he was," Amy said.

"Thank you, Miss Harper."

"Mister Schneider, would you like to cross-examine the witness?" asked the judge.

"Yes, thank you, Your Honor. Good morning, Miss Harper."

"Good morning."

"How long have you known the defendant?"

"About three years."

"Are you stating to this court that he harassed you throughout the three-year period?"

"No, it was on and off."

"Could you estimate how many times the defendant made physical contact with you while you were employed at the restaurant?"

"I can't say for sure, but it had to be at least ten or twenty times."

"Ten or twenty times that he touched you inappropriately?"

"Yes, he would rub up against me, too. He just didn't come out and touch me directly. He made it look like it was done accidentally."

"Do you think it was done by accident?"

"No, no way, not that many times."

"How large of an area is the kitchen?"

"About ten or fifteen feet."

"How many people do you believe could fit inside the kitchen area without making incidental contact with another co-worker?"

"I don't know, maybe four or five."

"Have you ever made contact with another person while entering or exiting the kitchen?"

"Objection."

"Overruled."

"I'm sure I made contact, but it was not done on purpose."

"How do you know the defendant did it on purpose?"

"Because he would make comments to me right after he touched me."

"Isn't it true that you wore a mini-skirt to work one day?"

"Objection."

"Overruled."

"Yes, I did."

"Well, why would you do something like that?"

"Because I had to attend a family dinner that evening and I didn't feel like rushing home to get dressed."

"Are you sure you didn't wear it for attention?"

"Objection!" Sciarpa shouted.

"Sustained."

"Isn't it true that you were attending a dance recital and not a family dinner?"

"Objection! Counsel is attempting to impeach the witness on a collateral matter." Sciarpa looked as though he were about to pop a vessel. The veins in his neck were visible even from the back of the courtroom.

"Sustained!" yelled the judge.

"I have nothing further, Your Honor," said Brendan.

Ms. Harper stepped down from the witness stand, and Judge Crawford ended the trial early since he had a legal seminar to attend.

The next day, Brendan arrived at the courthouse early in order to speak with Derek about testifying at trial. Brendan informed him that he believed the prosecution did not have sufficient evidence to prove beyond a reasonable doubt that Derek had, in fact, committed murder.

Derek wasn't persuaded by Brendan's comments. He insisted that he be permitted to take the stand. Since this was a criminal trial, the right to testify belonged to the defendant, and the attorney could not prevent such a privilege. Therefore, Brendan would have to adhere to Derek's demands.

During the next few weeks, nine other character witnesses would be called on behalf of the defendant. All of them were impeached either with prior inconsistent statements or by their own convictions. Derek didn't make it any easier for himself by associating with hardened criminals and repeat offenders. This would drastically hurt his case.

Judge Crawford entered the courtroom around ten in the morning and directed his question at Brendan.

"Are you ready to call your next witness, Counselor?"

"Yes, the defense calls Tanya Martin to the stand."

Tanya was probably in her mid-sixties but never disclosed her true age. Her attitude was don't ask – don't tell. On this particular day, she wore her most expensive outfit, which she had retrieved from her relatively large bedroom closet. It was reserved for special occasions like family celebrations or church, but Tanya was quite the fashionable woman and didn't think twice about wearing it to the trial.

It was a stylish two-piece designed by Kay Unger. She wore it with great spunk even though she was extremely overweight. Tanya had been battling diabetes most of her adult life and suffered from hypertension. It was definitely genetic. Her father had died from complications of diabetes, and her mother had passed away after enduring years of congestive heart failure.

As she approached to take the stand, she glanced over at her son and smiled. She needed a little help climbing up the two steps and was assisted by the bailiff. Then she made herself comfortable and pulled the microphone close to her so everyone in the courtroom would hear what she had to say.

Ms. Martin was an emotionally strong woman, and she was proud of her two children. She was glad to be given the opportunity to tell the jury about the man seated at the table. Her view was that her son had been given a bad rap from the beginning and never had a chance to attack those false allegations. Now he had a voice. Someone who spoke from experience. Someone who knew the defendant better than anyone. Brendan knew of Tanya's health problems so he didn't want to interrogate her for a lengthy period of time.

"Hello, Miss Martin." How old is your son?"

"He is twenty-seven."

"When did your son graduate high school?"

"Oh, about ten years ago," she acknowledged while tossing around in the chair until she felt comfortable.

"Has he been in any kind of trouble since high school?"

"No, not that I can recall," she told him.

"Do you love your son?" Brendan asked.

"Yes, very much," she answered.

"Can you describe your relationship with your son over the years?"

"Well, he was a very good boy growing up. He never was in any kind of trouble. He never was arrested or anything like that. I always taught my children to respect others. My son is a good-hearted individual. He is honest and very generous. I don't know of anyone really who ever had something bad to say about him."

"Do you think your son could be capable of murdering another human being?"

"No. Absolutely not. I know my son and he is not a killer. I didn't raise no killer. My son is a churchgoer. He doesn't have time to hate. Our family spends most of our time in the house of the Lord. You won't learn how to hate there."

"Thank you, Miss Martin."

The jury was kind of divided at this point. Some believed Tanya's entire testimony, but some were skeptical and regarded her statements as self-serving. There was silence in the room for about 30 seconds, and then Sciarpa rose from his chair and proceeded toward the witness to commence his cross-examination.

"Good afternoon, ma'am."

"Good afternoon," she replied.

"How many children do you have?"

"I have one son and one daughter," she said.

"Did your children grow up in Massachusetts?" Sciarpa questioned.

"Yes."

"Did they attend school in Massachusetts?"

"Yes, they did," she told him.

"Very good. Now, I would like you to be completely honest with me; do you think you can do that, because you have sworn under oath to tell the truth."

"Yes, I will."

"Good. Can you tell me if you are aware of a time when your son was involved in a fight at school?" he asked, although he already knew the answer.

"Objection, relevance!" yelled Brendan.

"Overruled," said the judge.

Apparently, this minuscule piece of evidence should not have been admitted over Brendan's objection. First off, it was too remote in time. Secondly, it did not involve an arrest or conviction. And finally, it did not pertain to a false statement or dishonest act. Nevertheless, the prosecutor wanted to offer it to show the defendant had a dangerous propensity to become violent by referring to specific instances of misconduct.

"Yes, I believe he was involved in a fight when he was in high school, but I'm not sure what grade he was in," she told him.

"Okay, that's not important. Now, do you know what the reason was for your son fighting?"

"I think it had to do with another girl," she said.

"Was any disciplinary action taken against your son for fighting?" he asked.

"Yes, he was suspended a few days," she said.

"Do you know who started the altercation?"

"Yes. It was my son," she replied.

"Thank you, Miss Martin."

So much for Derek's reputation of being an obedient child. It doesn't look good to have a mother testify on behalf of her son and then have her integrity be called into question. I'm sure she didn't mean to avoid her son's fighting on direct, but juries don't like to see witnesses change their stories. You only get one chance with a jury to tell the truth. Lie once and the consequences could be severe.

Brendan then called Derek to the stand. As he approached the witness chair, no one from the jury made eye contact with him. It was as though his guilt had already been determined. Some members of the jury decided they had heard enough and didn't even listen to the defendant's testimony. This was Derek's last chance to tell his side of the story. If he was going to be acquitted of the charges then he needed to be completely honest with everyone in that courtroom.

"Good afternoon, Mister Martin."

"Good afternoon, sir."

"How long had you known Miss Hensley?" Brendan asked.

"About eight years," Derek replied.

"Could you describe your relationship?"

"Yes, we were friends."

"Were you intimate?" asked Brendan.

"Yes, but we didn't consider dating or living together."

"Did you ever make sexual comments toward anyone?"

"No, I did not," he answered.

"How long were you employed at the restaurant?"

"About three years," Derek told him.

"What did you do there?"

"I was a cook and ran the dishwasher," he replied.

"When did you meet Amy Harper?" asked Brendan.

"About three years ago," said Derek.

"When did you realize she didn't like you?"

"She complained that I was harassing her at work, which wasn't true."

"What did she say that you did?"

"She told my manager that I was making sexual comments or jokes and touching her inappropriately."

"Did you make these comments or touch anyone inappropriately?" Brendan asked while peering in the direction of the jury.

"No, I complimented her."

"How did you compliment her?"

"I told her she looked nice. If she wore something attractive, I pointed it out in a good way. I wasn't rude."

"Could you give us an example?"

"Yeah. Like if someone was wearing a new outfit I would be like – that outfit looks really good on you. No one ever came to me and said they thought it was offensive."

"Do you think she could have misunderstood your intentions?"

"Objection, leading."

"Sustained."

"How did you perceive Miss Harper's feelings toward you?"

"I think she's overreacting and blowing this whole situation out of proportion."

"Did you tell police that you couldn't establish your whereabouts at the time of the murders?"

"Yes," Derek answered.

"Do you remember now what you were doing that evening?" asked Brendan.

"I may have been home watching TV, I'm not sure."

"Did you use an alias screen name when communicating with Ms. Hensley?"

"Yes."

"Why did you do this?"

"I didn't want her to know it was me because I was talking about private matters."

"So you did it because you were embarrassed?"

"Objection, leading," replied Sciarpa.

"Sustained."

"Did you rape Miss Hensley?" Brendan pressed further.

"No, sir."

"Did you have anything to do with her murder?"

"Absolutely not."

"Did you love her?"

"Of course," replied Derek.

"Nothing further, Your Honor."

It was now time for Raymond to cross-examine Derek. He had waited a long time for this moment. Sciarpa showed no mercy toward defendants on trial for murder or rape. He was well respected in the legal profession, and prosecutors glorified him. Defense attorneys, however, had mixed feelings. Some argued that Sciarpa had an ax to grind.

He grew up poor in a small town. His mother divorced when he was just six-years-old. His desire to become an attorney began during his teenage years. One day, his mother, Trisha, was walking home from the supermarket carrying her groceries. As she turned the corner, she was approached by two men who demanded money. She gave them her purse and dropped her groceries. One of the men ran away with the money. The other stayed behind and raped her. Both men were found guilty of conspiracy to commit robbery and rape. They were sentenced to a maximum of 30 years in prison.

His mother passed away a few years ago at the age of 87. He still kept her picture on his office credenza. He stood up from his chair and walked over to the witness stand to begin his grueling cross-examination of the defendant.

"Mister Martin, you stated on direct that you made physical contact with Amy Harper at work, but you admitted that such contact was incidental even though it occurred on several occasions. Is that a fair interpretation of your statement?"

"Yes, it was by accident," Derek said.

"How do you touch someone by accident over and over again?" Sciarpa asked attempting to mock his statement.

"Well, like I said before, there is very little room in the kitchen to move around, and it is possible for someone to bump into another person unintentionally."

"Do you suffer from any muscular disease?"

"No."

"Do you have a problem keeping your hands off people?"

"Objection!" yelled Brendan.

"Sustained," replied Judge Crawford.

That was the only time the courtroom erupted with laughter. Even the jury thought Sciarpa's comments were quite humorous. But Crawford wasn't turning his proceedings into a circus. He ordered everyone to remain silent. Then he peered in the direction of the prosecutor and warned him to refrain from making such statements.

"I'll rephrase the question. If you do not suffer from any disease that would make you lose control of your hands, how do you account for the numerous complaints made by several employees, including Amy Harper, who testified right in this courtroom that you walked up to them and touched them in inappropriate areas?"

"I told you it was an accident," Derek replied in anger.

"An accident. You want this court to believe that every time you touched Miss Harper it was by accident. Of course, it was. How long had you known Maureen Hensley?"

"At least eight years."

"You were not married?" Sciarpa insinuated.

"No, we were friends."

"Yet you were intimate on several occasions?"

"We had sex a lot, but we weren't in any relationship. We were not dating."

"Do you own a boat, Mister Martin?"

"Objection, relevance!" Brendan argued.

"Overruled," said Judge Crawford.

"Yes, I own a boat," Derek answered.

"Do you like to fish?"

"Objection, Your Honor, where is counsel going with this?" Brendan inquired.

"Overruled."

"Yes, I like to fish."

"Have you ever fished in the Merrimack River?"

"Of course," he told him.

"Are you familiar with the river?" Sciarpa asked holding up a map.

"What do you mean?"

"Well, how far did you travel in the river from where you live now?" Sciarpa asked.

"I would say about fifteen or twenty miles."

"So you know the area well," Sciarpa said attempting to put words in Derek's mouth.

"I know that part of the river. The river stretches for hundreds of miles. I have not gone that far."

Derek was becoming irritated with the prosecutor and was starting to develop an attitude when responding to questions.

"Wouldn't you say that a person who intends to dump a dead body into a river would have to know the area pretty well?"

"Objection."

"Sustained."

"Did you purchase a sterling silver bracelet for Maureen?"

"No."

"Did you know she had a sterling silver bracelet?" Sciarpa asked.

"I may have seen her wear it from time to time."

"Where is the deepest part of the Merrimack?" he probed while analyzing the sketches on the table.

"I am not sure, maybe twenty miles from here."

"Do you know what the depth of the water is?"

"Maybe thirty or forty feet, I don't know."

Raymond laid the proper foundation to enter an investigative site report into evidence and asked Derek to read part of it: "The body was found twenty miles from where the victim was placed on the boat."

"You see, Mister Martin, the person who placed the victim in the boat knew where he was going because he wanted to be sure he had brought her to the deepest part of the river. Why? He had to be certain that the body would never be discovered. That is why the killer used bricks to keep the body from resurfacing. He was hoping the victim would be eaten by fish, but instead her body was found by fishermen when their lines got tangled. How do we know the victim traveled twenty miles on the boat? Part of her bracelet was found at an entrance to the river twenty miles south. The name Hensley appeared on the back of the bracelet," Sciarpa replied pontificating.

"I didn't kill anybody. We had sex and that was it."

"Why did you use an alias screen name when you went on-line to chat with her?"

"I didn't want her to know it was me because I was saying private things."

"So you basically misrepresented yourself by pretending to be someone else," Sciarpa concluded.

"Everybody does it. Maureen did it when she talked to other guys."

"Did it make you jealous that she was chatting with other men?"

"No way," Derek answered.

"You wouldn't be jealous of a woman who corresponds with other men about sexual matters when you had slept with that woman on several prior occasions?"

"I didn't care because she wasn't my girlfriend."

"Did you love Maureen Hensley?"

"Yes, very much."

"Did you love her so much that you couldn't stand to see her with anyone else and so you killed her?"

"Objection."

"Nothing further."

Judge Crawford instructed the jury that closing arguments would take place on Wednesday and adjourned for the day. Gary Spence, a news reporter for Channel 12 in Boston tried to question both attorneys upon their departure from the courthouse, but neither had any comment.

CHAPTER SEVEN

IT WAS APPROACHING August, and students had to register for internships in order to gain some practical legal experience. I applied to a firm outside Boston that specialized in criminal law matters and was affiliated with another firm in New York. After waiting patiently for a response, I telephoned the office and spoke with their receptionist.

I called Kerri and discovered that she had exhausted numerous hours calling law firms as well. She decided to do her internship in criminal law, which was the antithesis of what she had hoped for. Her primary goal was to represent a corporation whose interests involved environmental issues. Of course, her attitude changed when she realized she was working part-time for Brendan Schneider, the high-profile rookie defense attorney. I ended up taking a position with a small firm in Chester handling commercial real estate transactions.

I arrived at the exam room to take my Evidence test around two in the afternoon. We had three hours to take the test, and I was one of the last people to turn in my exam. Having skipped breakfast and eaten only a bag of potato chips for lunch, I was extremely hungry and became light-headed. I drove across the street to the Winston Tavern to have dinner.

I arrived at the hotel lobby and entered the bar. The bartender brought over a menu, which I glanced at before making my decision. I opted for the cheese steak and fried onions. The Red Sox game was on ESPN. They were playing the Baltimore Orioles and trailing four to three in the bottom of the sixth inning.

"Can I get you something to drink while you're waiting?" asked the bartender.

"Sure, I'll have a Coors draft," I responded.

When the game ended, the bartender changed the channel with his remote and put on the evening news. The top story once again was the Derek Martin trial, that was approaching seven months. Part of the delay resulted from Judge Crawford's brief illness, but both sides kept asking for time extensions.

Kerri was gaining legal insight working alongside Brendan. She had learned how to draft memoranda of law to the court and other correspondence to witnesses and adversaries. Brendan had little time to prepare for closing argument. He had asked Kerri to assist him in drafting his summation, which she had reluctantly agreed to at first, due to her inexperience with trial preparation.

Brendan thought he had a very good chance of obtaining a not-guilty verdict due to the lack of credible evidence presented by the prosecution. The Commonwealth's theory regarding the trial was based on circumstantial evidence, and Brendan's main objective was to poke holes at Sciarpa's analysis. It would basically come down to closing argument and who was more persuasive or convincing toward the jury.

Judge Crawford entered the courtroom carrying his jury instructions book. After he sat down, he asked Sciarpa if he was ready to begin his closing argument. Sciarpa approached the jury box and addressed the jury: *"Ladies and gentlemen of the jury, let me take this opportunity to thank all of you for your outstanding service throughout this ordeal. I know it has been a long and drawn-out trial. I appreciate your patience, especially during times when the trial was delayed. Now more* than ever, your obligation as a juror is of utmost importance. You will have to decide the fate of this man, Derek Martin, who has been charged with the first-degree murder of Maureen Hensley.

You have heard the testimony of credible witnesses who have testified as to Mister Martin's bad character. You have heard police and investigators describe in full detail the results of their findings. This man planned the entire murder. He had the intent to act; he had time to reflect on what he was doing, and he acted purposefully and with malice. Mister Martin had sexual relations with the victim on several occasions. He was the last person to see her alive. He denied having anything to do with the murder. Yet, when questioned by the police as to his whereabouts on the day the victim was supposedly killed, he could not establish his location. He had no legitimate alibi.

This man used the Internet to lure the victim to an undisclosed area where he then choked her to death prior to disposing her body into the river. He went on-line under a different screen name so the victim could not ascertain she was communicating with the defendant. The defendant argued that he used a different screen name because he felt embarrassed, yet he took nude photos of the victim while she stayed at his apartment. Do you really think he was ashamed of what he was doing?

The defendant also claimed that he did not have an ongoing relationship with Miss Hensley; apparently they were just friends. What about the DNA, ladies and gentlemen? Does DNA lie? The defendant's DNA was found on the victim. No other match was found. There were no other suspects in this case. The defendant testified right in this chair that he owned a boat, that he had gone fishing in the Merrimack River in that boat, and that he was familiar with the dimensions of the river.

On cross-examination, I asked the defendant how far he had traveled in the river, and he stated about twenty miles or so. I then asked him what he believed the deepest part of the river to be. His response was about thirty or forty feet. His statements were more than accurate, they were exactly correct. Only a fisherman who travels often in the river could know that information.

The defendant had a motive to kill the victim. His motive was based on the fact that he had become enraged or jealous after discovering the victim was having on-line encounters with other men. This made him angry. He *couldn't go to her apartment because then someone would see them together. He had to take her to a secret location. He couldn't just dump her body into the water because the water may have been too shallow.*

He couldn't risk the body being discovered. So what did he do? He took a big plastic bag and about five or six bricks, and he loaded the victim's body into the bag. He placed it on the boat and traveled about twenty miles to the deepest part of the river where he then threw her overboard. His plan would have worked if fishermen had not discovered the body.

Remember that sterling silver bracelet found near the south entrance to the river? How do you suppose it was placed there? Maureen Hensley could not have dropped it there because she was already dead. There are two possible explanations. It could have fallen off when Derek Martin was placing her on the boat. If it didn't fall off, then Derek took it off her wrist and went to put it in his pocket, but it apparently fell out. We know the bracelet belonged to the victim because her name was on it and witnesses recognized the bracelet as belonging to Miss Hensley.

Ladies and gentlemen, there is no direct evidence linking the defendant to this crime. No one saw the defendant dump the victim's body into the water. There was no weapon or instrumentality found that was used to facilitate this heinous offense. What we do have is circumstantial evidence. This means that there is a chain of inferences that leads a reasonable person to believe that the event actually occurred and that the proposition is more likely true than untrue.

Obviously, the sexual comments made by the defendant to several female employees are not sufficient to infer criminal culpability for murder. The fact that the defendant used an alias screen name to chat on-line with the victim, by itself, would not be enough to find that he killed or raped the victim. Knowing that the defendant had familiarity with that particular region of the river, standing alone, would not be prima facie evidence for murder. I ask you to consider these events collectively. Look at the totality of circumstances. Do not address these occurrences separately. Weigh the credibility of all the witnesses who testified before you throughout these proceedings. Consider all the technical and scientific data, including DNA and other forensics.

After evaluating these instances, you will find, ladies and gentlemen, that the defendant, Derek Martin, sitting at that table is guilty of murder in the first degree. Thank you."

"Mister Schneider, if the defense is ready we will hear your summation," said the judge.

Brendan ascended from his chair and walked in the direction of the jury. *"Ladies and gentlemen of the jury, the Commonwealth has charged my client, the defendant in this case, with murder in the first degree. Mister Sciarpa has admitted that the prosecution has no real or credible evidence to link Derek Martin to any crime. All that the State has is circumstantial evidence. Do we want to convict someone based on circumstantial evidence alone?*

The defendant admitted to making sexual comments to several women. He had sexual relations with the victim. He also stated to police his reasons for using a different screen name when he went on-line. These have no relevance whatsoever. The victim was only a friend to the defendant. She was not his girlfriend. She was free to have sexual relations with other men.

Whether she did or not has not been determined nor should it be considered here today. The point being that if the victim did have sex with other men, why weren't these men considered suspects also? The defense does not appreciate the prosecutor's insidious comments and finds them to be quite offensive. The fact that the defendant went fishing in the Merrimack has no bearing whatsoever on the victim's murder.

The defendant was not the only person to ever ride his boat in the river, and he will not be the last person to do so. The police had no clues whatsoever in this case. They based their probable cause on isolated incidents when, speaking holistically, they are totally irrelevant and of no evidentiary value. Yes, it is true that the defendant's DNA was found on the victim, but this shouldn't be a surprise since the defendant admitted to having sexual relations with her in the past.

This forensic evidence undermines the prosecutor's claim because it removes the possibility of rape. Why would a defendant rape a woman whom he had sexual relations with in the past? It doesn't make any logical sense. The prosecutor speaks about the presence of motive. Where is the defendant's motive to commit murder? What would the defendant gain by killing Miss Hensley? They were not married. He was not a beneficiary under any life insurance policy. They were simply friends.

That is not enough to develop a reason for murder. I'm sure the victim had many other friends. Where are they? Why weren't they being questioned by the police? Did the police only question the defendant because the defendant was African-American? Did they assume he committed this heinous crime because of his race? The victim attended law school for about six months. I'm sure she made many friends while she was enrolled there. But the police didn't question these male students. Isn't it funny that all of these students were white?

Ladies and gentlemen of the jury, consider all the possible outcomes of this case. Think about all of the witnesses who testified and determine their credibility. Look at the evidence or lack thereof. Ask yourself, could this man be capable of such a horrible crime? I think after you answer that question you will find that the defendant, Mister Martin, is not guilty of murder in the first degree. Thank you very much."

The jury was dismissed and led to room 216 in the basement of the court house, where they would begin their deliberations.

CHAPTER EIGHT

THE JURY IN the Martin trial was still deliberating after a week. Alba Moore, the jury foreman tried desperately to persuade other jurors that Derek was innocent, but they were not receptive to her position. "Show me the evidence where he killed her," she argued with another juror. "All we have in front of us is circumstantial evidence. I cannot find him guilty based on that."

"What about the DNA match? That proves he was with her around the time she was killed," replied, juror No. 6.

"It doesn't prove a damn thing. He already said he had sex with her," Alba responded.

"The time frame is irrelevant because no one knows exactly when she was killed," said juror No. 4.

"Exactly," said Alba. "That's why I'm reluctant to find that Derek Martin is the only suspect."

"Don't we have to find him guilty beyond a reasonable doubt?" asked No. 6.

"Yes, but don't you think there is reasonable doubt here?" inquired Alba. "There are too many unanswered questions."

"I'm sticking to my guns. I think the son of a bitch did it," said another juror who was growing impatient with Alba.

"The defendant can't produce an alibi. That eliminates a lot of other potential suspects," said No. 6.

"No, it simply means the defendant didn't do anything that night or didn't see anyone. It doesn't mean he is the killer just because he can't recall where he was," said Alba.

"What is your problem? Do you have a crush on the defendant or something? The man is guilty as sin. This is an open and shut case!" shouted juror No. 6.

"I don't have a problem and I think you are downright rude. I believe he is innocent," Alba stated as she walked around the room. They debated for some time before breaking for lunch.

There was a knock on the door of Room 216 and a young man stepped inside carrying a variety of deli sandwiches. He placed them on the table in the corner away from where everyone had been seated. Court personnel had ordered the food for the purpose of keeping all of the jurors together so the judicial process moved more effectively.

Alba, being the only juror advocating for the defendant, ate lunch by herself while the others sat at another table. When they reconvened forty-five minutes later, none of them were willing to compromise. After three hours of debating and harsh criticism, it was time for the court house to close and the parties would have to wait to reach a verdict. Five days would pass and no verdict.

Brendan remained at his office hoping to receive a call notifying him that a verdict was in. Usually, in a criminal case the shorter the amount of time it takes to reach a verdict the more likely the defendant will be found guilty. Brendan had to feel better knowing that deliberations had almost exceeded one week. Kerri came into his office to tell him that Derek's mother, Tanya, was on the phone and wished to speak with him. "Sure, I'll take it," said Brendan. "Hello, Miss Martin, how are you?"

"Please, call me Tanya. I'm Fine, Brendan, I was just curious if you heard anything?" she asked.

"Nothing, yet, but that's a good sign."

"I hope so. I know my son is innocent," she told him with utmost assurance.

"Don't worry, everything will work out for the best."

"You'll call if you hear anything?" she reminded him.

"Absolutely."

"Thank you, Brendan."

Brendan hung up the phone and finished writing his motion for summary judgment in another case he was working on. He charged a retainer of $5,000, but the majority of funds were used to obtain an expert. He had been representing a defendant involved in an assault and battery case where the intoxicated defendant struck the plaintiff outside a bar.

Brendan would have to put up his own money to continue the case because the defendant had mentioned he had financial problems. It's tough being a criminal defense attorney. You're not well respected in the legal profession and you don't earn an exorbitant salary.

Brendan barely made enough to meet his overhead costs. He had a wife, Alison and two young children with a third one on its way. They lived in a comfortable, averaged-size home in Bedminster, New Hampshire, just a short distance over the border. He had been practicing about two years and worked long hours to earn as much as he could. He was just about to leave work when he received a phone call from his sister-in-law, Patricia.

"You've got to get down to the hospital right away. Alison is having complications!" she cried.

"I'm on my way," replied Brendan, who was horrified after hearing the news. He could barely constrain the steering wheel as he raced to the emergency room. He arrived at Salem State Medical Center where he found his wife lying in bed, white as a ghost with a temperature of 104 degrees.

She was given liquids intravenously to prevent further dehydration. Doctors were concerned about the health of the baby as Alison was in her eighth month of pregnancy. Alison had some type of respiratory infection that caused one of her lungs to fill up with fluid. Dr. Sahns, the head of the OB/GYN unit was called in to assist the staff.

"I am worried about the baby's heart rhythm," he said to Brendan.

"Is it serious?" Brendan asked with great concern.

"I will run some tests to determine if there was any damage," said Dr. Sahns. Due to her condition, Alison's left lung was not functioning at full capacity which meant that the baby would not be getting enough oxygen. The nursing staff worked around the clock and by the next day Alison's condition had begun to improve. She would have to remain in the hospital for a few more days to have tests run on the baby.

Brendan didn't want to leave his wife's side but he had to be in court at 9:00 a.m. Kerri had phoned him on his cell explaining that the jury had reached a verdict. After ten days of deliberations, the jury had determined Derek's fate. Brendan rushed to the court house where he was greeted by Tanya in the parking lot.

"Well, I guess this is it," she said.

"I have a good feeling about this," said Brendan, as he put his arm around her.

They entered the court house and walked through the metal detector. Ms. Martin excused herself to use the rest room and Brendan met with Kerri outside the court room.

"How is your wife doing?" she asked.

"Much better, thanks. They have her condition stabilized. They just want to keep her there a few more days for evaluation and to monitor the baby."

"Oh, I'm so glad to hear everything worked out."

"Yeah, me too. Now I hope this works out for Derek's sake."

They sat in the remodeled courtroom with mahogany benches for about twenty minutes before the jury entered. Then Derek appeared and smiled in the direction of his mother and his sister, Janet. He sat down at the defense table and waited for Judge Crawford to commence proceedings.

The judge advanced into the courtroom and took his seat on the bench. He asked the bailiff to hand him the verdict. After looking it over he handed it back. The judge then instructed the defendant to stand while the jury foreman read the verdict: "We the jury find the defendant, Derek Martin, guilty of murder in the first degree."

Family members of the victim were jubilant after hearing the verdict. Even though Derek remained standing, he was paralyzed with fear at what he had just witnessed. His mother sat in horror overcome with grief at hearing the news. She embraced her daughter and cried out to her son who was just convicted. The jury took ten days of deliberating before finding beyond a reasonable doubt that Derek had in fact committed murder.

Derek's mother demanded an explanation. According to her, a huge injustice transpired and she wanted it to be known prior to her departure from the courtroom.

"How did this happen!" she shouted at the jury.

"Quiet mama," her daughter said, worried about her mother's present health condition.

"No, I'm not going to remain quiet. This is an outrage. My son is innocent, you sons of bitches."

"Ma'am, I will have to ask you to refrain from abusive language," said one of the court officers who was trying to calm her down.

"My son has just been charged with murder and you want me to keep my mouth shut?" she responded with the deepest animosity.

Soon after, Derek was placed in handcuffs and led outside toward the back of the court house. He boarded a van and was transported to the County jail a few blocks way. Brendan immediately made his request to appeal the decision of the lower court. Kerri tried to console Derek's mom who was starting to hyperventilate. Brendan immediately hastened to her aid and requested that an ambulance be summoned but she told him not to bother.

Brendan was outraged with the verdict wondering how the jury could have arrived at its decision. He thought for sure the prosecution failed to demonstrate Derek was guilty under the appropriate standard of proof since all they had to consider was circumstantial evidence. He had time to think about filing a Judgment Notwithstanding Verdict (JNOV) as he drove back to the hospital to visit his wife.

CHAPTER NINE

KERRI AND I agreed to meet for dinner at Il Ristorante d' Abruzzi located in the business district of North Ardmore. It was the first time that we'd seen each other in about a month. When she had first arrived, she'd looked like a beauty pageant contestant strolling to greet me at the table. She was wearing a glamorous black dress with matching bracelets and two–inch pumps. She was a goddess and I was the luckiest man in Massachusetts and probably didn't even know it at the time.

"How are you?" she asked, putting her arms around me.

"I'm fine," I said, giving her an elaborate kiss on the cheek and pressing her delicate skin against me with a firm hug.

"You look really good in that dress," I told her.

"Thank you. I was afraid that I wouldn't fit in it. You know I gained about ten pounds since I started law school," she said, placing her jacket on her chair and taking the seat facing the mirror.

The waitress approached our table and read the specials for the evening. *"We have shrimp scampi with linguine for $14.95, prime rib for $24.50, chicken marsala for $17.95 and broiled flounder for just $13.95. All specials are served with your choice of soup or salad and a* *vegetable. Can I get you anything to drink while you're looking at the menu?"* she asked.

"I'll have a glass of Merlot," said Kerri, dangling the shoe from her right foot.

"Make it two," I replied.

As we sat in the restaurant, we discussed our futures and the possibility of a long term relationship. All I knew was that I was head over heels in love with this woman. I spoke of my intentions. By the time the food had arrived, we had already established a meeting of the minds and were partners going steady from that moment on. She hadn't dated anyone since college and I had recently recovered from a huge heartbreak when my relationship ended after discovering my ex-girlfriend was cheating. I had my suspicions, but I guess I remained in denial.

The facts surrounding my girlfriend's cheating couldn't have been more obvious. She would always answer the phone in another room and tell me it was a private call about work. She canceled dinner plans at the last minute and told me she was working late. One time, I caught her kissing some guy in the parking lot of a supermarket. When I confronted her about it, she informed me that the man was her brother. I don't know many women who like giving their brother tongue. The last straw had to be coming home and finding men's underwear mixed in with mine. Then she had the nerve to tell me she purchased them for me as a Christmas gift, but apparently I forgot. I told her I didn't wear boxers and walked out of the room. A week later, I walked out of her life for good.

I knew Kerri was different than all the other women I had dated. In spite of her overwhelming beauty, she was not a bit conceited. She had a phenomenal sense of humor and her giggling throughout the evening demonstrated it. I had her laughing so hard she nearly choked on her drink.

It appeared that things were starting to work out as I once again began to trust my instincts. I was doing well in school and I had just won a raffle drawing for two tickets to a Boston Red Sox game at Fenway Park.

I will never forget the date the game was played. It was Tuesday, September 4, 2001, one week before the biggest tragedy our nation would ever face. The Red Sox played the Cleveland Indians and I remember how the fans cheered and shouted. There weren't any searches of bags at the stadium nor moments of silence during the seventh inning stretch. It was a time of tranquility and blithe optimism for America.

The threat of terrorism would affect only foreign lands and would not reach our soil. We were immune to such violent and unspeakable acts. Up to that point, our democratic form of government acted as a protective shield from these radical dictators and cowards. Who could have foreseen such destruction and turmoil? The heart of our nation had stopped beating and the only sounds that could be heard were the towers collapsing and the cries of people fleeing for safety. The thousands of people whose lives were lost, including, firefighters and police officers would never be forgotten.

The site of Ground Zero had become a sanctified memorial where family members would return each year on the anniversary of this tragic event to pay respects to their loved ones who perished that somber day. Law school was stressful enough just from its voluminous reading and complex exams. When September 11, 2001 arrived, it felt as though continuing my legal education was pointless. I remember having panic attacks while driving to school. I felt apprehensive and restless at times. Relaxing whether at school or in the comfort of my own apartment became my biggest challenge. I couldn't put the television on because it was a constant reminder of the most miserable experience I would ever come to know.

The nightmares eventually would take their toll. It was about three in the morning and I awoke having a rapid heartbeat and difficulty breathing. I couldn't relax so I decided to drive myself to the local hospital. I was diagnosed with anxiety and given a prescription for Xanax. The thought of another man-made catastrophe dominated my inner thoughts. Having some of my friends share these same feelings alleviated part of the suffering, but it would take months before I felt normal again.

As I drove over the George Washington Bridge into New Jersey, I felt empty inside as I looked in the distance and saw nothing but wide open skies. The towers were gone and life would not be the same. The images would be forever etched in my mind. I remember working in New York City in 1998 when I was interning for the Legal Aid Society. I would leave my house and travel to the New Brunswick station to board a train to Newark. From there, I traveled via the PATH train to the World Trade Center that took about twenty minutes.

I would eat my lunch outside in the promenade between the two towers facing the corner of Vesey Street. Employees from various departments in the towers would share a table with me. I did not know many of their names but I remembered their faces as they came outside every day at 12:30 in the afternoon. They were physicians, lawyers, accountants, financial advisors, marketing engineers, office administrators, and security personnel. I often wonder at times if any of those faces made it out alive. I was fortunate to have Kerri in my life during these turbulent moments.

When I returned to my apartment I saw there were a few messages on my machine. One was from Kerri. I called her back and invited her over just to chill and watch a video. Apparently, she had other plans which I didn't expect, but I was ready, willing and able to go along with them.

She arrived wearing jeans and a sweatshirt. It was somewhat stuffy inside the apartment so I turned up the air conditioning . She placed the video inside the VCR and hit the play button on the remote. I grabbed a box of popcorn and tossed it in the microwave on high for four minutes. As I was viewing the coming attractions, I neglected to check the popcorn and the kitchen had begun to fill up with smoke.

"Oh crap!" I said in horror.

"What the hell happened?" inquired Kerri.

"The damn popcorn burned."

"That's okay, sweetie, we have chips and pretzels right here."

"I know. I was just in the mood for popcorn that's all."

Before I had time to open the sliding door, the smoke alarm was activated. I now had tenants from my building knocking on my door to check that everything was all right. All I wanted was a quiet night with my girlfriend. Thankfully, the alarm went off within a few minutes and we were alone again.

Kerri went into my bedroom to retrieve a couple pillows and returned to the sofa where she lied down. About an hour into the movie, she reached into her purse then dropped a bottle of lotion on my lap intimating a body massage was forthcoming. The lotion had a vanilla scent and was purchased from Victoria's Secret.

"Don't you want to finish watching the movie first," I asked, as I took the cap off the bottle.

"Not really, the movie is kind of boring," she said, as she ascended from the sofa in anticipation of a rub down. I shut off the television and dimmed the lights. I opened the narrow hallway closet and stretched out my hand in order to grab a few candles. Kerri loved the smell of scented candles. I just thought it would be more romantic and sensual if I had lit them solely for this purpose. I was actually quite excited about giving the massage, but I didn't let on and remained disinterested.

Kerri lied down flat on her stomach. I poured a small amount of lotion into my hands and then started on her neck. Gently rubbing the back of her neck over and over, I applied more lotion. She told me exactly where the spot was, "a little lower and to the right; yeah right there. Oh, that feels awesome," she related while closing her eyes and maintaining that expression of contentment that could be found on her velvety, firm lips.

Each time I rubbed harder and deeper until she whispered, "come closer" and raised her head slightly in order to extend a kiss. I slid my hands up and down her long, soft, satin-like, tanned legs and maintained eye contact at all times. I was determined to go all the way and she felt the same. She paused momentarily then turned over as I gradually lifted her shirt and removed her bra. I massaged her 34 B-cup breasts while watching her toes curl.

I could see her nipples becoming firm as she looked up at me with her vivid smile. I then unbuttoned her jeans and watched her climb out of them. At that moment, I was definitely harder than the Bar Exam. We were both completely naked and I was on top of her. She took my hand and placed it between her legs. I thrust my finger up and down her warm body as I kissed her tempestuously.

We rolled around on the sofa until I fell off and hit my head on the end of a small table. I'm sure it hurt but any pain I felt quickly subsided once my eyes were fixed on Kerri. I carried her into the bedroom and we cuddled inside the sheets. A few minutes later, I penetrated her and we both reached orgasms simultaneously. The bed shook as though an earthquake had struck the entire complex. Without a doubt, Kerri rocked my entire world. The kissing lasted until we fell asleep in each other's arms.

CHAPTER TEN

CROWDS GATHERED ON the steps in front of the court house to show their support for Derek. Many held signs displaying "DEREK IS INNOCENT," "FREE DEREK NOW," "STOP INJUSTICE FOR BLACKS." A turbulent group of angry protesters attempted to beset the police, who were in the process of closing off the streets with barricades.

Police were forced to use tear gas and pepper spray to quell the riot. At times, the violence intensified and some young black men were apprehended and arrested for breaking car windows and throwing objects. Police had their hands full in trying to redress the harm. Police departments from outside the city of Landsdale were called to assist in restoring order. By the time the situation was resolved, over twenty-five people were arrested and charged with rioting and assault.

Derek remained in jail and was awaiting sentencing that was scheduled in two weeks. Judge Crawford was well known for administering severe sentences. In 1994, he sentenced a man to thirty years for tax fraud. Derek was worried about the imposition of a maximum sentence. Brendan spoke briefly with Derek when he stopped to visit with him after filing papers with the law division.

"Man, I don't know what the fuck is going on. I am completely innocent. The jury got it wrong."

"Right now we are in the process of getting this appealed," Brendan answered.

"Appeal shit, man. I know those things take years before they get reviewed."

"I understand, but that is our last resort, Derek."

"Do you think I'm guilty?"

"Of course, not. I believe you when you say you didn't do it."

"What is my family going do without me?"

"You have to worry about yourself now. Besides, let's wait until sentencing."

"How much time could I serve?"

"It depends, maybe twenty or you could be sentenced to life."

"Would I have to serve twenty before I get out?"

"Not necessarily. It depends on several factors, but like I said . . . that's not important right now."

Brendan left the jail and drove to Salem State Medical Center to check on his wife. She was moved to another area of the hospital once she recovered from her illness. Dr. Sahns told Brendan that Alison would be discharged in two days. Her due date was October 4th.

The couple agreed that they would take a small vacation following the birth of their child. Alison had wanted to travel to Europe and visit with her sister who moved to Paris several years ago.

"I hope the baby is fine," she told Brendan.

"Honey, don't worry. The doctors are handling everything," he said to ease her concern.

Kerri had a final examination in business associations early the next morning and then had to appear in court for a bail hearing. She was quite busy working for Brendan two days per week and attending to her job at the other law firm. She was earning the respect of all of her co-workers who were pleased with her aggressiveness and motivation in taking on new cases.

She never turned down any work and had always anticipated new challenges from the senior partner. Douglass Gottleb, the hiring partner at the firm, approached Kerri with an offer of employment as a full-time attorney upon graduation and passage of the Massachusetts Bar. She had given it much thought, but decided that her interest was in environmental issues.

"I appreciate all the help and experience this firm has afforded me throughout my internship, but I would like to pursue a different area of the law," she stated.

"I understand and I wish you the best of luck in your future endeavors," said Douglass. Douglass had to attend a meeting in Chicago with the law firm of Gruber and Kessler so he wouldn't be at the office on Kerri's last day. He was working on a case involving the merger and acquisition of a parent-subsidiary corporation. The parties were reluctant to reach any verbal agreement over the phone so Douglass convinced his adversary that he would fly to Chicago to expedite the merger.

When Douglass had arrived at O'Hare International, there was hardly any visibility. He had instructed the cab driver to take him to the corporate office, but the cab driver could not locate the address due to the heavy downpour of rain. Douglass was forced to call the office to notify them of his delay. He had arrived approximately an hour and ten minutes after the meeting began. Present at the meeting were a group of shareholders, the board of directors and the CEO of each company.

"Do we have the records from the secretary of state's office?" asked the CEO.

One of the directors handed him the corporate filing documents that contained information on assets and liabilities. After two days of discussing the matter, an offer of compromise was finally reached and the merger was created with the voting rights of two-thirds of each class of stock from each company.

The weather wasn't much better in Ardmore and I was foolish for not carrying my umbrella as I ran toward my car. I was saturated and cold as I sat in my car waiting for the heat to come on. It was about eight-thirty in the evening and I was craving a cheeseburger and fries.

I drove to the Winston tavern and parked close to the entrance to avoid getting wet. Once inside, I sat at the bar and Debbie, the bartender brought me a beer. She was in her early thirties and moved to Massachusetts ten years ago because she grew tired of the cold weather in Vermont. Debbie was attractive and slightly overweight. But not much. Maybe ten or fifteen pounds. She had curves but they were definitely in the right places. And she had the softest hair. I watched her as she made a margarita for another patron.

"What do you want to watch?" she asked, as she flipped through the channels on the tv. "Put on the Patriots game," I told her.

They were playing the Miami Dolphins at Foxboro on Monday Night Football. New England was trailing 27-24 near the end of the third quarter. It was around eleven when I decided to go home and Debbie was just clocking out for the night. I walked her to the car because the parking lot was not well lit. I didn't know her that well, but I was glad that she trusted me as a friend.

On her way home, she stopped off at a service station to purchase cigarettes.

"Marlboro Lights please," she said to the owner who happened to be dozing off in his chair.

When she got inside her car, she kicked off her flat shoes and drove home barefoot. She had the radio tuned to 97.9 FM, a classic rock station. While she was singing the lyrics, a man hiding in the back seat wearing a ski mask jumped up and put a six-inch blade to her neck.

"Do anything crazy and I'll kill you right here," he threatened.

Debbie remained valorous behind the wheel and adhered to his demands even though she was deeply worried.

"Keep driving until I tell you to stop," he said forcefully.

He instructed her to turn off the highway. They drove for about ten miles until they disembarked upon an old country road with very little visibility. She stopped the car as instructed.

"Don't look at me," he said. Don't look in your rear view mirror. Look straight ahead while I put this on."

He placed a blindfold around her face as she lied still with trepidation. Inside the truck, he had tied both of her hands together. Then, he took her to an undisclosed area that was hidden from the main access road.

When they arrived at the archaic house located at the top of a hill, it was boarded up with viscous plywood and there wasn't any ingress leading to the front. It looked haunted. The house appeared to have been built during the mid 1800s'. The only entrance was through the decayed trap door in the basement located on the opposite side adjacent to the garage. It was kept bolted down at all times.

There were a few windows on the side but they did not provide any light since they were tinted. Once within the boundaries of the tarnished home, Debbie was brought into a dark and gloomy room and placed on a bed.

"Please let me go, I won't tell anybody," she pleaded.

He told her to shut up as he was removing her blindfold. Debbie's vision was hindered because there weren't any lights or windows in that part of the basement.

"What do you want from me?" she asked in despair.

His attraction toward women with dainty characteristics was inebriating. He selected them as though he were choosing a bottle of wine. Yet, his choice was not hastened by his desire to encounter the flawless woman. His planning was persistent as he ruminated his next move. To the outside world, he displayed a conventional personality to accommodate his aspirations while simultaneously dismissing any suspicion brought on by his psychotic behavior.

He went upstairs and locked the door behind him. Debbie heard his footsteps pacing back and forth and became apprehensive of his next move. Then he drove off in his truck. Debbie lied in bed wondering if this would be her last night alive.

CHAPTER ELEVEN

DEBBIE WAS TRYING to remove the dense rope tied to her ankles because it was cutting off her circulation. She couldn't unfasten it enough to slide her ankles through. She remembered he had brought her a glass of water earlier. She kicked the glass off the bed where it shattered on the floor.

Then, she slowly slid her body off the bed and dropped to the floor. While picking up a piece of sharp glass, she cut her finger which bled quite a bit. After about ten minutes of slicing through the rope with just the use of her index finger, her hands were free. She then used the sharp object to cut the rope tied to her ankles. If she was going to make an escape, it had to be soon because she knew he would come back for her. She felt around the basement walls that were made of solid concrete. There were spider webs on the ceilings and vermin in the crawl space. God knows what else was traversing along the damp and sticky wooden floor.

Debbie could not see anything so she put her hands out in front of her in order to have a sense of where she was going. As she approached the furthest wall, she came upon a door that led to a secret room on the other side. As she held out her hands to find her way, she felt what appeared to be a string. Apprehensive at first, she decided to pull on it once she'd convinced herself that time was of the essence.

As she pulled in a downward position, a light came on. It was still somewhat dim in the room, but Debbie could see where she was walking. The room had another door that was closed but unlocked. Debbie turned the knob and walked inside. There she found a freezer in the corner of the room. She opened it and cried "Oh, God, no. Oh God!"

She was horrified at what she had seen. There were human corpses inside that had been wrapped and soaked in formaldehyde. He would dispose of each one in the order that he had killed them. Debbie would be kept alive until he had room in the freezer.

The stench was so strong Debbie had to run out of the room to catch her breath. If she had remained in the room any longer, she might have lost consciousness. It was putrid. She started to hyperventilate. Trying to remain calm, she took a few laggard breaths and regained her composure. Debbie knew that she was going to be next if she didn't find a way out soon. She went in the opposite direction feeling her way around as she looked for an exit and came upon a crawl space. Debbie was jubilant at discovering what appeared to be a safe haven. If she could fit through the narrow space, she was home free.

She removed the metal screen that covered the area and once inside, she found a small window. Since the space was narrow and only a few feet high, Debbie had to slide through on her stomach. She arrived at the window and unlocked the latch. She climbed through the window and was now outside.

Just as she stood up in her bruised and wounded bare feet, she noticed a truck pull into the driveway. It was him. From a distance she saw a man with brown hair who stood about five-foot-nine and weighed about one hundred sixty pounds. He continued to walk toward the house and Debbie quickly ran in a southerly direction toward the country road that was a few miles away.

She knew that he would be searching for her within minutes. He entered through the side of the house and placed his keys on the kitchen table. Then he went to use the bathroom. He did his business and then smoked a marijuana joint. On his return, he unlocked the basement door and went downstairs. He called out for her in the dark. "Hey, bitch where are you?" When he heard no response, he assumed she was ignoring him. "I asked you a question."

As he approached the bed, he took out his flashlight so he could see her. He was startled to discover the victim was gone. He searched the entire basement and went into the other rooms where he found the light on. Now he knew she had found the other bodies.

"Son of a bitch!" he shouted with rage. "I'm gonna fuckin kill you!" he cried, punching the unfinished wall with his fist. He ran upstairs to get his keys and was sweating profusely.

It was about two in the morning, and Debbie had just made her escape ten minutes earlier. He climbed into his truck and proceeded to look for her. Debbie was running toward a stretch of cornfields when she observed background lights. Her adrenaline was at an all-time high. Fearing it was him, she hid by lying flat behind some tall bushes.

When he passed at a high rate of speed, Debbie ran through the cornfields that extended into the next town. He was becoming agitated at the fact that he could not ascertain her clandestine location. After running about one and a half miles, she came upon a road with houses. She knocked on the door and rang the bell in an emotional state of panic, shouting, "Help me, please. Somebody help me!" After waiting a few moments, she didn't get any response and ran down the street toward another house. After ringing the door bell, a man opened the door and she pleaded with him to call the police immediately.

The police arrived within minutes and took Debbie's statement. Debbie had difficulty describing the man who kidnaped her because she hadn't seen him close up and she was kept down in the basement where her view was obscured from the dark. She couldn't tell the police the direction in which she traveled due to being overcome by severe emotional distress. She was taken to the County Medical Center where she had undergone a physical examination before she was eventually released.

It was now about four in the morning, and police began taking photos of the scene and looking for tire tracks and any evidence to assist in capturing the felon. Debbie informed the police of her observations regarding her hostage situation.

"There were bodies everywhere. The smell inside the room was nauseating," she cried.

"How many bodies did you see?" asked one of the police officers.

"I don't know, it was hard to tell, maybe five or six," she said, wiping away tears.

"Could you describe the outside of the house?"

"I can't because he blindfolded me in the car and he didn't take it off until he brought me down in the basement."

The police notified Debbie's parents of what happened and told them they would drive her home in a few hours. They were elated upon hearing the news of her return. The police were not able to collect any fingerprints or hair samples from Debbie's vehicle which was found in an isolated, wooded area.

As Friday afternoon rolled around, Brendan returned to the law office. He met with another attorney to schedule a pretrial conference in another criminal matter. Diane, his legal assistant buzzed him over the intercom.

"I have a woman on the phone who wants to discuss something with you. She said it was very important and it involves the Derek Martin trial."

"I'll take it," said Brendan. "Hello?"

"Yes, my name is Vicky."

"How can I help you, Vicky?"

"I was a juror on the Derek Martin trial and I voted to find him guilty."

"I understand. What seems to be the problem?"

"Well, about two months before the trial when all the newspapers and media were getting involved, I received a phone call at my house from Tobar Publishing. Someone acting as a representative of the company told me I could be paid money for supplying information about the trial. I was informed that a book was going to be written. I discussed the case with her and she promised I would be compensated."

"Why didn't you come forward with this immediately?" Brendan asked, becoming irate.

"I didn't think anything was wrong," Vicky answered.

"You didn't think that disclosing information about an ongoing trial was wrong?"

"No, because I would have found him guilty anyway. I thought he was guilty from the beginning."

"It doesn't matter. You were not supposed to speak to anyone about this trial. Do you realize that my client was prejudiced because of what you did?"

"I'm sorry," she replied.

"This is a prime example of juror misconduct. You had a financial stake in the outcome of this controversy. You were considering your pecuniary and monetary interests. You failed to fulfill your obligation as a juror."

"But sir . . ." Vicky pleaded.

"Please don't interrupt me. This is an egregious act on your part. Throughout the trial, you thought about how you were going to make money from this case. How do I know you even paid one ounce of attention to any of the proceedings? Did you listen to all the witnesses? Did you determine who was credible and who was not? You probably didn't listen to anyone because you had already made up your mind prior to deliberations."

"Mister Schneider, you don't understand. I would have voted guilty anyway. I was one of the first people to say he was guilty at the beginning."

"You did not take your obligation seriously, Vicky."

"I have a daughter who is battling a terminal disease. I don't have a health insurance carrier that will cover the costs of her medical bills. When the woman told me that I would receive money for my story, I had to take advantage of the offer."

"And by doing so, you may have convicted an innocent man. Why are you calling me now? If you think you didn't do anything wrong, why are we having this conversation?"

"I was just worried – in the event that this gets out. I don't want to be in any trouble," Vicky stated.

"What you did is considered serious. You have tampered with jury proceedings and violated your duty. You must disclose to the court your improper conduct."

"What do you think will happen after that?"

"I don't know. I would like to ask you something though. Did you persuade any one on the jury to find Mister Martin guilty just so you could start your book deal?"

"No. Absolutely not. Everybody thought he was guilty, except one other person and she decided to change her mind."

"And you didn't influence her decision in any way?"

"No, I did not. Like I said earlier, I thought he was guilty from the beginning and everyone else voted the same way," said Vicky.

"Really, because I thought someone on the jury was holding out because she believed Derek Martin didn't commit the crime and everybody else put pressure on her to expedite her decision."

"I am not aware of that, sir."

"Of course, not."

"Well, I have to make a few phone calls and I'm sure you will be hearing from me very soon. Goodbye."

Brendan hung up the phone and looked in his lawyer's diary for Judge Crawford's law clerk's phone number. He needed to get hold of him immediately to discuss this matter further.

"Landsdale Superior Court, how may I direct your call," asked the receptionist.

"Yes, I would like to speak with Kyle Davenport, Law Clerk to Judge Crawford, please," said Brendan.

"One moment as I transfer you," she replied.

Since he was unable to reach him directly, Brendan left a brief message in Kyle's voice mail. He then called Kerri to discuss what had transpired.

Heavy snow had begun to fall in the Boston area and it was the last week of school before Christmas break. There was an early dismissal at Thomas Jefferson Middle School. Buses had to park a few blocks from the entrance to the school due to the snow drifts. In spite of the fact that the school closed at 12:30, some teachers decided to finish up their work before heading out.

Lorraine Nagle was a fifth grade English teacher who always stayed after school later than three-thirty. She made sure she finished grading all of her students' tests and then posted their essays on the bulletin board. She was also involved in coaching gymnastics and was responsible for setting up the schedules for various competitions. Around three in the afternoon, she phoned her husband to tell him she was stopping off at the supermarket to pick up a few things.

By the time she placed the bags in her car, nearly a foot of snow covered the ground. As she left the parking lot at Market Basket, she turned on to the main road toward the direction of her house. The car started to shake and the steering wheel began to vibrate. Within minutes, the car stalled and rolled a few feet before stopping. Lorraine tried to start the car but nothing happened. She reached for her cell phone to call her husband but noticed it didn't work because it wasn't charged. She had left the charger at home along with the grocery list.

A man approached and asked her if she needed help. Reluctant to roll down her window, she signaled to him that she was okay. The man insisted that he take a look at the car and perhaps start it himself.

"I'm fine, thank you. My husband is coming to help me. He should be here momentarily," she stated.

"Please let me try to start it," he said as he was becoming impatient.

She thought about it for a minute and then felt sorry for the man and unlocked her front door. He climbed in and attempted to start it. After about ten minutes, he told her the battery was dead.

"Would you like me to give you a ride home?" he asked.

"That's okay, my husband is coming to pick me up," she responded.

"Look, ma'am, the weather is going to get worse as the night goes on. You need to get off the road as soon as possible," he told her trying to scare her into thinking she was absolutely stranded.

Lorraine mistakenly thought that she had no choice but to leave with him and decided to take a ride from a complete stranger instead of going back to the supermarket and calling home for assistance. They walked a few blocks and then climbed into his Ford 150 pick-up truck.

"I live about two miles from here," she stated.

He drove toward the highway but didn't get off at her exit.

"That was my exit there, we have to go back," she said becoming worried.

He ignored her and kept driving.

"Did you hear what I said? We have to turn around. Where are you going?" she asked him repeatedly.

She realized that it was a mistake to go with him. She tried to open the door but it was locked and the controls were on the driver's side.

"Open the door you fuckin weirdo!" she shouted.

He just smiled and continued driving. Lorraine then bit his hand which began to bleed.

"Ouch, you son of a bitch!" he screamed.

He punched her square in the face knocking her unconscious. He had chloroform in his glove box which he was ready to use if she regained consciousness while he was driving. He took her to his dilapidated hideout, strangled her in the basement, and disposed of the body early that morning along with three others at different locations. He drove approximately 45 minutes from his house until he arrived at a suspension bridge. He took Lorraine's body off the truck and placed five heavy bricks inside the bag. Then he dumped the body over the bridge and watched it sink. The next day, he took his truck to the local car wash to remove any evidence from the murders.

Brendan had to appear with Derek at Landsdale Superior Court to determine what Derek's sentence would be. Brendan had asked that Raymond Sciarpa be present because he had to discuss the juror misconduct situation.

"Your Honor, I have to disclose something to the court today which I believe is egregious and warrants this court to find that a new trial should be granted."

"Counselor, your client is here today to be sentenced. He has already been found guilty by a jury of his peers. Any other issues need to be addressed on appeal," said the judge.

"I understand that, Your Honor, but I feel this has caused my client a huge disservice," Brendan argued.

"Proceed," said the judge.

"I was informed by one of the jurors on the Martin trial, that at the outset of the trial, she agreed to provide information to a book publisher, which she did, and she also disclosed conversations which took place during jury deliberations."

"Your Honor, the fact that juror misconduct occurred and I'm agreeing that it had, it still does not show that the verdict would have been different absent the misconduct," Sciarpa argued.

"And how do you respond to that Mister Schneider?" asked the judge.

"I think the misconduct is severe and rises to the level of prejudice."

"How was your client prejudiced?" asked Sciarpa.

"How? Because one of the jurors had already breached her duty by signing an agreement to contribute toward a book about an ongoing trial," Brendan responded.

"What about the other eleven jurors?" Sciarpa questioned.

"Listen Raymond, you know darn well that no juror is to disclose anything until the trial is over."

"Your Honor, granting a new trial in this case will result in a financial hardship," Sciarpa said, attempting to invoke the sympathy of the judge.

"Your Honor, not granting my client a new trial would be a severe hardship. An innocent man has been wrongfully convicted, I can assure you!" Brendan yelled.

The judge looked at both of them and said, "I want to speak with this juror and obtain her side of the story before I make any ruling. I would like all of us to meet sometime next week to resolve this matter. Mister Schneider, call Vicky Cooper and find out what her availability is next week. Tell her if she fails to appear at our scheduled meeting, she will be held in contempt of court and charged with obstruction of justice."

"Yes, Judge," replied Brendan.

CHAPTER TWELVE

I T'S BEEN NEARLY forty-eight hours and there hasn't been any sign of Lorraine Nagle. Her husband had contacted the police as soon as he realized she hadn't come home from the supermarket. They discovered her car a few blocks from where she had gone shopping. Her keys weren't in the ignition. Police found two sets of footprints in the vicinity of her car. This led them to believe that foul play may have been a factor. Signs were posted with her picture and placed on telephone poles and distributed at local stores.

Debbie Meyers, the woman who was kidnaped and escaped over a month ago, saw the photo and immediately thought "Oh, God, he's gonna kill her."

She got on the phone and called the police telling them "he has her and he's going to kill her."

"Who is this?" responded the dispatcher.

"My name is Debbie Meyers. I was the woman who was kidnaped and held hostage over a month ago, but I don't remember much more than that."

"Yes, of course, but how do you know she is in trouble?"

"Well, she hasn't been found. You need to search wooded areas near cornfields," she said. Debbie could not be more helpful in describing the location because she had suffered from temporary amnesia due to the traumatic experience she encountered.

The police took her advice and searched over one hundred acres of farmland, but did not find anything. The investigation was kept open and police called in the FBI to assist them in their efforts. Sgt. Watson now began to doubt his prior conclusions about Derek. "Maybe he didn't do it," he told the other officers. "We have a woman who was kidnaped and luckily escaped without injury and now another woman in less than two months is missing," he continued.

Watson started to believe that the killer was still out there. He looked at one of the police detectives and said, "I have to call the assistant prosecutor and we need to sit down and discuss this matter in its entirety. He then rushed out of the room to make an important call on his cell phone.

It was Thursday afternoon and a call came into Brendan's office at around two-thirty.

"Hello, may I help you?" asked Bernice, the receptionist.

"Yes, this is Vicky Cooper. I was informed by Brendan Schneider to call and set up an appointment with him."

"Okay. What is your availability next week?"

"Well, can you tell me what this is in reference to?"

"He wants you to meet with Judge Crawford in his chambers to discuss the trial."

"Do you know if I am in some kind of trouble?"

"I wouldn't know anything about that, ma'am. I was just told to schedule the meeting."

"All right, then. How about next Tuesday?"

"Fine, would ten o'clock be good for you?"

"Yes, that is perfect, thank you."

"One more thing. Brendan instructed me to tell you that if you fail to show up at this meeting with him and the judge, it will be considered obstruction of justice and you could face contempt charges."

"I understand."

"Bye."

Brendan and his wife were having some financial problems and with the arrival of a new baby it would make things even more complicated. Brendan could not pay his rent, members of his staff, and have enough to make ends meet. He just didn't have the clients to run a successful office. He was brilliant when it came to criminal law and procedure. He could go up against the best prosecutors in the state and make the best arguments to convince a jury why the defendant should go free. But when it came to managing skills, he had no clue as to how to administer or organize a firm. Perhaps he should have hired an office administrator to handle his affairs, but that would have cost money.

As time went on, he contemplated sharing office space to reduce the amount of expenses incurred. He received several phone calls from accounting offices, investment brokers, and physicians, but most of them were in downtown Boston, where living expenses were twice the amount than what they were in the town of Haverford.

One day while he was in court, Bernice received a call from a family law attorney responding to his advertisement in the local paper. It sounded like a great idea and she sent him a text message immediately. *"Brendan – doctor office called looking to share office space. Phone: (978) 255-5551. Good Luck, B."*

Brendan had been busy in Judge Crawford's chambers discussing the Derek Martin trial with Vicky Cooper. The judge sat with her and decided whether any punitive action should be administered.

"Miss Cooper, please tell me the details of your conversation with the publisher."

"I was asked to disclose information about the trial. She told me that I would be paid money if a book was written. I needed the money. I didn't think anything was wrong. The media was allowed in the courtroom and they heard everything that transpired throughout the trial. Why is it a big deal if I disclosed anything that was already public record?" she asked.

"Conversations in jury deliberations are not public record, Miss Cooper, and I think you already know that. Your conduct was nothing short of reprehensible," the judge argued.

"I have a daughter who is very sick. My insurance will not cover the enormous medical costs from doctors and hospitals where she was treated. I'm sure if you were in my situation, Your Honor, you would understand," said Vicky.

"I don't think you understand. No one is telling you that you didn't have a right to discuss the case after the trial. You could have waited until then, but you decided to breach your duty and act inappropriately. Do you realize than an innocent person could have been convicted because of your failure to take your obligation as a juror seriously? This is no laughing matter. I am appalled at your behavior and your lack of compassion for the defendant. I am appalled that you stand here today showing no remorse, but rather trying to justify what you did by attempting to invoke my sympathy. I am sorry that your daughter is not in the best of health. I hope that she fully recovers. Her illness has no bearing on what you did. You need to take accountability for your own actions."

"I have done that, Your Honor. I am here today."

"That is not good enough. Miss Cooper, did you formulate an opinion about the defendant prior to trial?"

"Yes, I thought he was guilty."

"What gave you that impression?"

"I just had a hunch, that's all."

"When you were sitting in the jury box did you listen to both sides as they presented evidence?"

"Yes, I did."

"Did you avoid considering any reasonable doubt about the defendant's innocence?"

"I thought he was guilty. I didn't feel there was any doubt."

"Is it true that the jury foreman believed the defendant was not guilty and you put pressure on her to change her mind?"

"That is not how it happened."

"Why don't you tell me then how it really went down."

"She said she was voting not guilty. This went on for about ten days. Everyone was growing tired of her foolishness. She had a crush on the defendant and that's why she wanted him to get off. The other jurors wanted to go home and return to their families just like I did. I needed to be with my daughter. We persuaded her to find him guilty. We talked about the case. We removed the element of reasonable doubt. There wasn't any coercion, Your Honor. We discussed the case as we were instructed to do."

"This is what I think happened. You became so fixated on the money aspect that you ignored proper courtroom decorum. You couldn't possibly be impartial and unbiased because you had too much to gain. All the other jurors listened attentively to all of the evidence. They did not profit from their service other than what they were entitled to be paid daily. You could not have achieved the same objective when you had other interests involved. Your conduct has tainted the verdict. It doesn't matter what the other eleven jurors thought."

The judge then dismissed Ms. Cooper and decided that she would not be charged with obstruction of justice or jury tampering. He remained in his chambers to discuss the jury misconduct matter with Brendan Schneider and Raymond Sciarpa.

"I think it is obvious that the actions of Miss Cooper have significantly affected the outcome of this trial," said the judge.

"I couldn't agree more," said Brendan.

"I think what we need to consider now is whether the misconduct has tainted the verdict in such a way as to prejudice your client, Mister Schneider."

"Your Honor, if I may interrupt?" asked Sciarpa.

"By all means," responded the judge.

"The jury decided to find Derek Martin guilty beyond a reasonable doubt. Their decision was unanimous. It was not dependent upon Miss Cooper's conclusions. Yes, what she did was wrong, but she would have found him guilty anyway just like everybody else. I don't think the verdict should be questioned."

"I disagree," replied Brendan. "I believe some members of the jury would have found Martin not guilty if Miss Cooper had not pressured them into expediting a verdict."

"Who pressured anyone? The role of a jury is to deliberate. In the process of doing that, disagreements will be made and at times, it can get emotional inside the jury room. Just because Miss Cooper was firm in her decision, it should not be held against her."

"Your Honor, Mister Sciarpa is missing the point. It doesn't matter who voted guilty or not guilty. Miss Cooper did not fit the role of a juror. She did not remain unbiased. She was not to speak to anybody outside of the jury about the trial. She was not authorized to speak with publishing companies about a trial that had not yet been ruled upon."

"I agree, Mister Schneider," replied the judge. "Mister Sciarpa, you've done a fine job in prosecuting this case and your efforts do not go unnoticed. I am not here to determine the guilt or innocence of the defendant. That was the role of the trier of fact. As judge, however, I am obligated to inquire into the verdict and consider newly-discovered evidence that could substantially prejudice a defendant. I find that Miss Cooper's actions permit me to exercise my discretion and question the reasonableness of the verdict. I find that disclosing information about an ongoing trial is sufficient grounds for granting a new trial."

"Your Honor, I don't think it would be in the Commonwealth's best interest to retry this case. Think about the financial hardship and the negative publicity. I have presented the evidence and the jury voted on that evidence. It should not be second guessed."

"I have to agree, Your Honor. I don't think this city could face another guilty verdict. The African American community was outraged that Derek was found culpable to begin with. Obviously, an injustice had been served by charging an innocent man with murder. This case should never have been brought to trial in the first place. There wasn't any material evidence from the start of the trial. Everything my adversary produced was based on circumstantial evidence. It would be unfair to continue with a new trial when my client had been prejudiced from the beginning," Brendan argued.

"What do you want to do, Mister Sciarpa?" asked the judge.

"I don't know. I don't think it is worth retrying this case because there is no guarantee that the Commonwealth will be successful in attaining a guilty verdict," Sciarpa responded, becoming annoyed that his entire case which lasted nearly six months was going to result in the release of the defendant.

"Very well, I will advise that Derek Martin be released immediately if there is no objection," said the judge. After a few hours, Brendan arrived at the state prison and informed Derek of his release.

"Are you serious? I'm gonna be a free man?" Derek asked in jubilation.

"That's right, as soon as I sign some papers you can walk out of here," Brendan told him.

Derek telephoned his mother to inform her of the great news. When the car drove up to the house, Tanya was waiting at the front door. She was so excited and relieved to have her son back home. She couldn't believe that he was standing outside her house.

"It must be a dream. A wonderful dream indeed," she reckoned while glancing up toward the heavens. She latched on to her son nudging him all over in order to remove any doubt as to whether it was really him. He stepped inside into the foyer.

"Oh, thank you, God. Thank you so much, for bringing my son home," she cried while walking alongside Derek.

She embraced Brendan and thanked him for all of his assistance throughout the entire ordeal. Brendan then shook hands with Derek, and spoke of his admiration and great fortitude during the trial. Derek invited Brendan inside and offered him a glass of wine. Derek, holding up the glass, made a short speech to extol Brendan's heroic and tedious efforts.

"I want to thank you Brendan for everything you did for me. I really appreciate it. I never thought that I would see the outside world again," he said, wiping away tears from his face.

After about an hour, Brendan looked at his watch and rose from his chair. "I think I better get going," he said.

He thanked Derek and wished him well. He promised that he would keep in touch and requested the same from Derek and his mother.

Brendan then drove to the hospital to check on his wife who was due to have their third child. She had been in the hospital over twenty-four hours.

"Everything is going according to schedule," said Dr. Sahns.

"Can I have something for the pain?" she asked.

"Yes, I will give you an epidural shortly. I want to be certain that you are not going into labor. I cannot administer the drug at that point," said the doctor.

"Well, please give me something," she said, clutching her husband's hand.

"Nurse, can you give me Miss Schneider's chart please?"

"Yes, Dr. Sahns. I'll get it right away."

"Miss Schneider, I will be back at the hospital tomorrow afternoon, but if you need anything before then, you can notify Dr. Grant, the internist, who is currently assisting me at my office."

"Okay doctor, thank you."

"Here's her chart, doctor," said the nurse.

"Please make a copy of this and leave it in the file for Dr. Grant to view. Miss Schneider, I will touch base with you as soon as I arrive at the hospital tomorrow."

After the doctor administered the epidural, Brendan sat beside his wife until she grew tired and then he drove home to work on his client files.

The family room had boxes scattered along the perimeter of the wall. There were hundreds of redweld files lying on the floor that were continuously crushed every time his children entered the room.

"Kids, please stay out of here," he said, growing impatient at their refusal to listen.

"Daddy, come play with us," his older son said.

"Not now, I have a lot of work to finish and besides it's past your bedtime."

"We're not tired."

"Go to your rooms and I'll be up shortly to tuck you in and read you a story."

Brendan felt guilty that he had been spending less time with his children, but he was drowning in his own work and had no one to assist him other than Kerri.

I called Kerri on Christmas Day and she informed me that Brendan told her he was a father again. His wife, Alison delivered a baby girl named Kaitlin born Christmas Day at 5:35 a.m. She weighed nine pounds, seven ounces and was twenty-one inches in length. According to Dr. Sahns, the baby was born healthy with no birth defects or any complications, which left him concerned when Alison first entered the hospital earlier in the week with breathing problems.

CHAPTER THIRTEEN

Wª HILE FLIPPING THROUGH the pages of a magazine at the local bookstore, I happened to glance at the *Boston Globe* and saw the headlines on the front page. It read: *Woman's Corpse Found In River.* The woman described as the victim was Lorraine Nagle, a thirty-seven-year-old teacher at Thomas Jefferson Middle School.

Police found blood stains along the outer railing of a suspension bridge. Divers were called to search the immediate area and discovered her body within a few hours. The article was about three pages long and made reference to the fact that police believed a serial killer was lurking in the vicinity.

The school was notified the next day and the principal thought about how he would disclose the tragedy to the students without causing emotional trauma. He decided to have the students meet in the gymnasium where he would make the announcement.

"Good morning, students. We have some very distressing news about one of our most beloved teachers. As some of you may have been aware, Mrs. Nagle had been missing for several weeks without any sign of her whereabouts. Today, we were informed by local police that her body was discovered. I know this is a shock to all of you and I want you to know that

our school will set up counseling sessions in the guidance office for anyone who wishes to be comforted during this sorrowful time."

After his speech, the principal corresponded with several administrators and decided to dismiss the students early so that they could be at home with their families. Curfews were enforced throughout Middlesex County to protect residents and police drove through neighborhoods searching for any suspicious activity.

Streets remained vacant following sundown and those who did violate the curfew would face steep fines. The police were serious about keeping the streets off limits so they could look for clues and try to apprehend the killer. The only information they had was the description of the man provided by Debbie Meyers, who was still at home recuperating from her amnesia. She had been seeing her neurologist on a regular basis to assist with her treatment. Her physician was quite optimistic that she would eventually fully recover. Police, however, were afraid that time was running out and the killer would probably strike again.

The following Tuesday, the Thomas Jefferson Middle School held a day of remembrance for Lorraine Nagle. The memorial was held at 9:30 a.m. in the gymnasium. Students were permitted to speak about their teacher and reminisce on past experiences. Some students wanted to hold a moment of silence, but the principal was reluctant to adhere to their request.

It was the week after New Year's, and I wanted to surprise Kerri so I went to visit her at her parents' home in Huntington. It was a two-hour drive on a normal day, but with traffic and construction, it took nearly twice as long. I finally arrived at the top of the hill and located the house on my right. It was an opulent English Tudor with a stone front. There were several steps ascending from the sinuous driveway to the entrance at the top. I arrived at the front door and rang the bell. A woman of Dominican origin greeted me and let me in.

"Hi, I'm here to see Kerri," I told her.

"Come on in and I'll get her for you. I think she is upstairs," she said with a slight accent.

Her parents had to be rich to afford a home like this. In fact, every house on the block had to be close to a million. The rooms were immaculate and spacious. I sat on the sofa in the family room staring at the family pictures on top of the grand piano until she had arrived downstairs. I think it was her high school graduation picture that I was glancing at. It was amazing that she looked exactly the same. Same big bright smile. Same beautiful dark blue eyes.

"Oh my God, I can't believe you came here," she said as she exulted at my unexpected visit.

"I know, but I had nothing to do so I thought—why not drop by. The directions were perfect and it didn't take me that long," I replied kissing her.

"I'm so glad you're here. Let me show you around," Kerri said.

"So who is the woman who let me in?" I asked.

"Oh, that's Maria. She takes care of the house."

Kerri grabbed my arm and I followed her throughout the home as she gave me a tour of her parents' exquisite abode. The interior of her home was quite impressive with Victorian style ceilings and a huge solarium that added to the pleasant atmosphere. Kerri then walked into the kitchen where she prepared a few sandwiches.

"How have you been?" she asked slicing a fresh, bright red tomato and removing some cold cuts from the refrigerator.

"I'm great. Just enjoying my time off. I don't have to worry about briefing cases or studying for finals. I couldn't be better."

"I know, right? I have been so stressed from work and school – sometimes Dillon, I think I may have made the wrong choice."

"No, you didn't. Kerri, I felt the same way when law school first started. But I gotta tell ya, after meeting you, I wouldn't drop out for all the money in the world," I told her.

"You always say the nicest things," she replied. "And you're so sweet. By the way, I hope you like turkey, salami, ham, and roast beef cause that's all I have."

"Of course, that's fine, thanks. Don't go to any trouble," I told her.

"How is it outside?" she asked spreading the mayo on my sandwich which she referred to as a "*grinder.*"

"It's a little chilly, why?" I asked.

"Well, if you don't mind, let's sit on the deck and have a drink."

She poured me a glass of red wine. Based on my taste buds and her wine selections in the past, I knew it had to be Merlot. I looked out into the backyard that was about two acres long. We sat outside and talked for hours about law school and our job prospects. Kerri's parents had just arrived home while we were sitting outside breathing the fresh, invigorating, coastal air.

"We're out here," Kerri said, as she tied her hair back after the wind kept blowing it in her face.

"And who is this gentleman?" her mother asked.

"This is my good friend, Dillon from school."

"Hello, Dillon, it's so good to meet you. I've heard so much about you. I'm glad that we've finally met," she said, gracefully extending her hand. "Please, call me Carol. I hope you will be staying for dinner," she remarked after I addressed her as Mrs. Cafferty.

I really wanted to stay for dinner as soon as I learned that Carol was preparing a mean pot roast with red bliss potatoes and sweet corn on the cob. I followed that scent into the kitchen. It sure did smell darn good.

But nothing satisfied my sense of smell like her fresh homemade brownies which she removed from the oven rack with her old – fashioned oven mitts. The mitts must have been handed down from generations ago. They had a logo I didn't even recognize, but I knew it was pretty old when I saw the year in which it was manufactured. 1956 to be exact. Kerri posed her question to me again after I failed to promptly respond to her initial inquiry.

"So what do you want to do? We can go out Dillon, if you'd like?"

I loved the fact that Kerri ate just about everything. It was easy selecting a restaurant. I didn't have to worry about finding an establishment that specialized in vegetarian platters or low-carb diets.

"It's up to you, whatever you feel like doing," I told her.

"No, please stay here and have dinner with us. You have to meet my husband. He should be here any moment," Carol said.

I found her parents to be quite hospitable and generous. Of course, Kerri shared those same attributes. We decided to take the offer and remain at home. Besides, we wouldn't have found a restaurant that would have prepared a meal like the one we received that evening anywhere on Long Island.

Kerri's mother was one fine cook and I started to think that if she had passed that gene on to her daughter then I might be lucky to marry a woman who was not only great in the bedroom, but awesome in the kitchen. "Slow down, big boy," a voice uttered inside my head. "You didn't tie the knot just yet."

After dinner, we drove to the cinema to find out what was playing.

"Let's see something scary," Kerri said with excitement, as she was rummaging through her purse trying to locate her lipstick.

"How about a comedy instead?" I suggested.

She had that dismal look on her face knowing that I would give in to her desires. Once again, I conceded and purchased two tickets to watch a murder mystery. With all the local media attention in Massachusetts within the last year, you'd think that a movie about murder would be last on her list.

Kerri would never represent a criminal defendant she knew was guilty, yet, she was fascinated with trying to unravel the criminal mind of the accused. Her bookcase in her bedroom had hundreds of books about criminal defendants, serial killers, and psychopaths.

We arrived back at her house at around 11:30 in the evening. She invited me in, but I declined because it was getting late. I had at least a two-hour drive home and I was growing tired. Her mom handed me a small container filled with homemade brownies and some apple crumb pie. Then she gave me a warm heartfelt hug. Carol must have worked out at the gym like three times per week. When she embraced me, I felt my ribs snap. That was one tight squeeze. It almost knocked the wind right out of me.

Kerri was kind enough to let me stay over her parents' house, but I respectfully rejected her proposal. I felt uncomfortable about imposing on her parents, whom I had just met. I left Long Island thinking that Kerri and I were destined to be married. I also realized that I needed to buy some *Ben Gay* for my aching chest.

Brendan was in the conference room deposing his adversary's client when the receptionist received a call.

"Brendan, I'm sorry to disturb you, but I have Derek Martin on the other line."

"I'm in a deposition right now, but tell him I will call him later today."

"No problem," she said.

Brendan was busy questioning the plaintiff under oath about a personal injury she sustained while walking in a pedestrian crossing.

"Did you wait until the signal before you stepped into the street?" he asked.

"Yes, I crossed when it was my turn," she said.

Brendan was in dire need of finances and defending the owner of a trucking company was a good start. Of course, an increase in clientele wouldn't hurt either. Brendan had spent a great deal of time on this case charging $350 per hour. By two-thirty in the afternoon, he ended his questioning and escorted the plaintiff and her attorney to the elevator.

On his return, he picked up the receiver and dialed Derek's number.

"Hello?" Derek answered.

"Derek, it's Brendan. How are you?"

"I'm not doing that well," he replied.

"Why, what's wrong?"

"It's my mother. Her doctor said she's got a malignant tumor and they can't operate."

"Oh, Derek, I'm so sorry. You must be devastated."

"I don't know what to do. I mean, there ain't nobody that can help us," Derek said.

"Have you asked for a second opinion?"

"Well, the doctor referred my mother to a physician in Boston. He is one of the best but, he said her condition is very severe."

"Look, I would call as many doctors as possible until you find one that is willing to run some options," Brendan stated. "Does your mother have health insurance?" he asked.

"Yes, she has limited medical coverage, but it's not nearly enough to help her now," Derek responded.

"Where exactly is the cancer?" Brendan asked.

"It's in her pancreas and parts of her liver."

"Is she going to receive chemotherapy?"

"Yes. In fact, that is her only available option at this time," replied Derek.

Brendan hung up the phone and promised he would visit with Derek and his mother during the week.

When Brendan arrived at their house, he found Derek's mother lying down on the sofa.

"Hello, Miss Martin. How are you?" he asked.

"I'm a little tired," she said making every effort to smile at him.

"Well, you just relax. Everything will be fine," Brendan told her.

Even though Derek's mother had been diagnosed with cancer within the last month, it had already taken its toll on the rest of her body. She was quite fatigued and lethargic. She couldn't stand erect without assistance and had trouble breathing which was exacerbated by her acute asthma.

Her face was pale and she started losing weight. Her appetite had diminished significantly and Derek became concerned her condition would worsen as time went on. Some days were better than others, but she never did feel the same.

The cancer was progressing at a rapid speed and each day Tanya was not only losing the battle, she was losing her memory as well. Sometimes she would just remain motionless with a dead stare in her pus-filled eyes and somehow her family had to muster enough vitality to communicate something to her that she could understand. Just to make sure she was responsive and alert was a daily ritual.

A few years earlier, she had suffered a TIA as a result of uncontrolled high blood pressure. Tanya would ask Brendan a question and then five minutes later ask Brendan the same question as though she had requested an explanation for the very first time. They say the impact of dementia affects the family more than the patient. Derek and Janet would need the patience of Job as time went on.

Derek would contribute his part and help out with all the chores and attend to any bills that had to be paid. Her daughter would stop by in the morning and prepare breakfast. She would remain with her mother until she left for work. Brendan could see that Ms. Martin was not capable of taking care of herself and needed outside assistance. He questioned Derek about the possibility of a live-in nurse or maybe doing the unthinkable, you know, what families dread about when confronted with an ailing family member. I refer to it as the "court of last resort" or your average nursing home.

"My sister and I thought about that, but how would we be able to afford it?" Derek asked.

"I could look into it for you and make a few phone calls," Brendan said, wishing he could do more.

"Maybe we can just get somebody during the day," Derek's sister suggested, as she was opening her mother's mail.

"Well, it's a huge responsibility for either of you to undertake. I'm sure you will arrive at a compromise. I will do my part and make that phone call as promised," Brendan said.

"I appreciate you stopping over," Derek told him.

"It was my pleasure, Derek. Take care, Miss Martin. I will stop by next week to visit you," Brendan replied, before opening the front door.

She smiled and waved good-bye.

When Brendan arrived in his office early Tuesday morning, the first thing he did was call Social Services to find out information about live-in care.

"Yes, I would like to speak with someone about hiring a live-in caretaker."

"Yes, sir. How can I help you?" the woman asked.

"Well, I would appreciate any assistance you can provide. I have a friend whose mother recently was diagnosed with cancer. Right now, he is financially incapable of providing her with full-time, around the clock care. Is there anyone you can recommend to watch his mother during the day? Brendan asked optimistically.

"Well, we do have part-time workers for the early morning and afternoon shifts, but keep in mind all of our workers are off on Sundays," the woman told him.

"That's fine," Brendan said, "but can you quote me a price for six days per week?"

"Okay, that would come to seven seventy-five per week depending on the hours," she said.

"Well, we'll probably need someone from eight a.m. until five-thirty," he said.

"Yeah, that would still be around seven seventy-five," she said.

"All right, I will get back to you. Thanks for you help," Brendan said, as he hung up the phone.

It was going to be difficult finding anyone to work those hours for less money. The median charge for health care services in Middlesex County was about $750. Brendan felt expendable in not being able to make good on his promise. He wasn't conceding, just changing his available options.

"Diane, could you get me Father De Luca on the phone?"

"Sure, just a minute, Brendan," she said, as she closed one of the filing drawers behind her desk.

"Good afternoon, St. Mary's Church. How may I direct your call?" asked the receptionist.

"Hello, my name is Brendan Schneider. I would like to speak with Father DeLuca, if possible."

"Sure, just a minute, please," she told him.

"This is Father De Luca. How can I help you?"

"Father, it's Brendan."

"Oh, hi. What have you been up to? How is the law practice going?"

"It's fine, thank you."

Father DeLuca was the pastor for the last twelve years since being transferred from Jersey City, New Jersey where he was a religious instructor and member of the Consolata missionary. He was ordained in 1986 at the age of twenty-one. Some say he was called to the priesthood by God himself.

It was at the angelic age of seven when he disclosed to his parents his intent to enter the priesthood. He grew up untainted by the negative effects and immoral views of the modern world. His adherence to acts of benevolence and the sanctity of life became his primary objective. He became a pioneer for bringing people back to the church who may have drifted and fallen victim to society's overwhelming temptations.

"What can I do for you?" he asked Brendan, in his baritone voice.

"I know of someone who is in need of medical assistance and was wondering if you would ask your parishioners to pray for her and offer any other help that they can. A woman has been diagnosed with pancreatic cancer requiring around the clock care and her family is not financially capable to support her," Brendan told him.

"Oh, my, I'll tell you what. I will make a special intention at this Sunday's mass. I will also ask my parishioners to pray for her. Perhaps the school can have a few fund raisers to alleviate some of the financial burden," said Father.

"I appreciate whatever you can do, Father," Brendan said.

"Okay, Brendan. Call me if you need anything else."

"Thank you, Father. Good-bye."

Brendan felt so reassured after listening to Father's inspirational words that he decided to leave work early and stop at his church. He entered through the side door and walked down the extended center aisle until arriving at the altar. He genuflected and then knelt down in front of a statue of St. Peter. He then proceeded to walk toward the back of church where he lit a candle and placed the small donation inside the slot. Then he departed the cathedral and drove home to be with his family.

CHAPTER FOURTEEN

IT APPEARED THAT New Englanders were in for a long, drawn out, and disappointing winter season. With only the arrival of February, residents still had to endure two more months of inclement weather. Accidents ranging from minor fender benders to serious injuries were prevalent throughout the northeast. The feeling around Middlesex County encompassed exasperation and annoyance.

The weather had become an all around nuisance. Meteorologists reported that the City of Boston had seventeen days of snow since December 21st.

I was traveling on Route 495 North heading back to Ardmore when I came across a police barricade near the Lowell exit. On the opposite side of the highway, there were several ambulances and police cruisers. At first, I thought someone skidded off the road and hit the guardrail, but another driver informed me that a woman's body was discovered early that morning.

Her name was Rita Bellows, a twenty-four-year-old medical school student. Her body was found lying alongside the river. Police believed the killer wanted to dump the body into the river but may have panicked after hearing noises and decided to flee to avoid being captured. The victim's body had lacerations around her ankles resulting from being tied up for several days. She died from asphyxiation, but medical records showed she was tortured and raped prior to her death. She had burn marks over 90% of her face.

Police knew they were dealing with a professional serial killer. He made no blunders and always cleaned up his mess. He was intelligent enough to evade the scene without leaving behind a scintilla of evidence linking him to the crime.

This psychopath was quite innovative. In fact, police thought he developed his perversity as he went along. Investigators collaborated their efforts and tried to obtain a mental description of the killer. What did he look like? Was he educated? Was he abused as a child? Did he despise women? Was he rejected by them?

He had kept souvenirs from all of his victims. He was proud of his accomplishments. His desire to continue his evil quest was unending. His thrill of collecting mementos had outweighed his actual propensity to kill. Yet, he felt no physical attraction to these women. They were not viewed as people with emotions, but rather as objects, designed to be humiliated and scorned. They were his prize trophies rewarded for his gallant efforts.

The melodious chants inside his head provoked him even further. He sought glory as if what he did was valorous. He kept memoirs describing his victims and how he murdered them. He knew the most trivial details about them. It couldn't be just any woman. There had to be something about her that appeased his senses. They all had to share the same common characteristics. He admired eloquent and enthusiastic women. They had to be down to earth and not despotic. He was apprehensive of the aggressive type and felt inferior. He was the commander in charge of his iniquitous journey and he would not allow anyone to forestall his mission.

There have been a total of five bodies recovered within the last two years and law enforcement officials have not yet developed any substantial leads regarding the perpetrator. College campuses within a fifty-mile radius of Boston had tightened their security. Perhaps it was a college student on a rampage. Police were not taking any chances. Students were encouraged to walk in groups and stay indoors after nightfall.

Just a short distance into New Hampshire was Canobie Lake Park. It was a small amusement area which opened every April and closed at the end of October. It was surrounded by a miniature lake that meandered along the state's border leading to the park's entrance. In the off season, visitors stopped by to observe the unruffled setting.

Fishing and skating on the lake were strictly prohibited by the State Department of Environmental Protection. Nevertheless, many people walked their dogs or jogged along the one mile path constructed for pedestrians.

It was a Saturday afternoon, and temperatures had begun to climb to nearly fifty degrees. The heavy snow which stranded many for weeks was quickly melting. The sun's rays reflected off the lake casting a shadow on the ground. It was a perfect day for a brisk walk.

I needed to find a quiet place to relax and take my mind off studying. I drove down to the lake and sat on one of the park benches. I stared out into the water and saw a school of tiny fish. I had brought a sandwich to eat and broke off a piece of bread to feed them. As I threw small pieces into the water, I was startled by the sound of a woman screaming in the distance. I ran in the direction of the woman's voice and found her in a frantic state trying to catch her breath.

"What happened? Are you okay?" I asked.

"A man approached me and tried to masturbate in front of me," she said.

"Did you get a chance to see him?"

"Yes, he was wearing a sweatshirt and sunglasses."

"Did he touch you at all?" I petitioned.

"No, but he exposed himself right in front of me," she replied in a state of panic.

"Which direction did he run off to?"

She paused for a moment and regained her composure. Then she peered into the opposite direction. "He ran toward the parking lot."

I handed her my cell phone and she called the police who arrived within minutes as the station was only two miles up the road. Police took her statement entailing a description of the alleged suspect. Law enforcement thought that it might be the serial killer, but questioned his motive for attempting to accost a woman during the daytime.

"We have police units out in full force and if he is still on foot, we should find him," said one of the officers.

After about three hours, police found a man who fit the description of the complainant so they performed a *Terry Stop* and detained him for questioning. He was wearing a gray sweatshirt and a Boston Red Sox cap. Once they had the critical information provided by the victim, they had probable cause to arrest him. The police then performed a search incident to a lawful arrest, but didn't find anything incriminating. The man was escorted inside one of the police cruisers and driven to the station. He was placed in a line-up with five other guys none of whom were suspects. Three were police officers and the other two worked in the lab.

The complainant, a twenty-five-year-old female college student named Brianna arrived at the station to pick out the perpetrator from the fabricated list of suspects. She walked into a room with a mirror accompanied by two other men. She was afraid to walk in at first for fear of having a face to face encounter.

"Don't worry, he can't see you," one of the officers said.

"I know, but he already saw me earlier today," she told him.

"He can't hurt you. Stand here. Now get a good look at all six of these deadbeats," the officer conveyed. "Tell me which one attempted to sexually assault you," the officer expounded even though he knew who the suspected perpetrator was.

Brianna stood up against the glass peering at the men on the opposite side. She paused momentarily and then uttered the words –

"That's him. That's the guy. I know his face."

"Who?" asked the officer.

"The second one from the right," Brianna replied.

"So number Five is the one?" he asked.

"Yes. That's right."

"Are you sure?" he checked further.

"Damn sure. That's the one."

I couldn't believe it when the police identified the culprit.

"Jeffrey Guillard? – Professor Guillard?" I was shocked. My professor was being accused of exposing himself in front of a young female. A man who has earned the respect of his colleagues and students had just been taken to the police station for booking.

When it came time for a trial, Guillard pled guilty. He waived his right to a jury trial and instead placed his fate in the hands of a Superior Court Judge. Prof. Guillard appeared bewildered and morose at the time of sentencing. He was charged with third degree sexual assault which could have carried a prison sentence of up to three years. The judge was fair, however, only sentencing him to undergo psychiatric counseling and mandating that he complete one hundred hours of community service. Boy, did he luck out.

After spending twenty-one years as a full-time law professor, he was forced to resign. The law school wanted no part of this scandal. It had already had its share of publicity with the murder of Maureen Hensley. In addition to that, the law school was under attack by the media for its fiasco five years earlier. Evidently, they had a relaxed and biased admissions policy. African Americans were being admitted with lower grade point averages and LSAT scores while members of other races with higher qualifications were receiving rejection letters.

The case went all the way to the Supreme Judicial Court which held that "race" could not be the predominant factor in selecting the student body and that lowering the standards for some races but not others was a violation of Equal Protection. Some white guy from Quincy challenged the admission process on affirmative action grounds and actually won. The law school tried to argue that the underlying purpose behind its selection process was to promote diversity among its student body. The Court disagreed, holding that the policy did not advance any compelling or overriding interest on part of the school.

Guillard's marriage was on the rocks and he now had a criminal record. No other law school would hire him and with a prior conviction regarding a sexual assault, he would never be a candidate for any teaching position.

Once the news hit the local papers, he had no option but to sell the house and move out of state. His wife, who battled an addiction to alcohol had her own hurdles to overcome. The stress became unbearable, and three months after they had purchased their two-bedroom condominium, his wife filed for divorce based on an irretrievable breakdown of the marriage.

CHAPTER FIFTEEN

MID-SEMESTER BREAK WAS just a few days away and I phoned Kerri to see if she started packing for our seven day excursion to Cancun.

"Do you have everything you need for the trip?" I asked.

"Almost. I'm gonna stop at the mall tonight to get some last minute things," she said.

Our flight was scheduled for Tuesday morning out of Logan International. When we arrived two hours before our departure, we proceeded to walk through the metal detector. Kerri managed to get through without any problem. I, however, set off the beeper several times.

"Are you carrying anything with metal?" asked one of the security personnel.

"No, I already emptied all of my pockets," I replied.

"Could you please remove your shoes and socks?" requested the guard.

At this point, I was becoming frustrated and so was everyone else waiting in line behind me. Kerri, nonetheless, found it quite amusing.

"What are you laughing at?" I asked.

"Nothing, I was just thinking about something."

I had no problem with subjecting myself to being searched for security purposes but sometimes these agents went too far. One woman was stopped and frisked as though she had committed a felony. Another had all of her items dumped out of her hand bag. I guess the searches were discretionary since they didn't apply to everyone. Some walked through the detector and boarded immediately. Others were not so fortunate.

When we finally arrived on the plane, Kerri wanted the window seat. As if I had never flown before, she pointed out all the emergency exits.

I placed my items in the overhead compartment and took my seat aboard the 737.

"Here—read these emergency instructions," she said, as she handed me the manual found inside the back of the seat in front of her.

"Do you really think I'm gonna follow these instructions if there really was an unforseen occurrence with our flight?" I asked her. "Let's see. A plane travels at approximately five hundred and fifty miles per hour and reaches elevation of about thirty-three thousand feet. Now suppose the plane drops suddenly and without warning assumes a nose dive position. The ground is coming closer so I reach for the instruction booklet to explain to me how to exit the plane once we make contact with the ground because once we hit, there will be very little time to escape."

"Shut up, you idiot," she said sarcastically.

"You know I'm only kidding, honey."

Kerri didn't like to fly and thank goodness our flight was only three hours long. Every time the plane hit a little turbulence, I thought she was going to have a panic attack. I tried to calm her down by taking her hand and massaging it, but she didn't appear to be in the mood for romance at that point.

Of course, I wasn't offended because I knew we had plenty of time for fooling around once we arrived and checked in our hotel.

We touched down at approximately eleven thirty. It was a small airport with a very short runway. Our landing was pretty impressive.

I was amazed at the pilot's maneuvering of the aircraft as he had little room to execute his approach.

After we gathered our luggage, we took the shuttle to the hotel.

Our room faced the ocean and we had a splendid view of the entire island from the 12th floor.

Kerri stepped outside on the small patio and I watched her beautiful soft, fragrant hair whisk back and forth.

About an hour later, we had lunch at one of the restaurants located on the third floor. Then we went back to our rooms and changed into our bathing suits. We strolled through the hotel lobby in beach attire and carried our towels. We followed the sign for the ocean. Once our feet touched the sand, Kerri started running toward the water hoping I would pursue her in a chase.

"Come on and catch me," she said, kicking up loose sand.

I caught up with her and carried her into the water then suddenly released her into a wave. She swam out about fifty feet and then turned over and floated on her back where she remained staring into the cloudless sky above. She looked stunning when she returned from a short swim. I placed my arms around her and then we kissed. It seemed as though time stopped.

Shortly thereafter, a man approached us and asked if we would like to rent a jet ski for an hour.

"Come on let's do it," Kerri said fervently.

"Have you ever jet skied before?" I asked her.

"No, have you?" she asked.

"Of course," I responded. I paid the man $40.00 in United States currency and climbed aboard the wave runner.

Kerri had an appetite for adventure. She was always determined to try new things. I was inspired by her courage and yearning to learn more about nature. We drove out about a half mile in order to observe tropical fish that happened to be mating at the bottom of the ocean.

As nightfall approached, it became cooler but still quite comfortable. The trade winds along the Gulf coast felt so invigorating. We walked back toward the pool and lied down on the cabanas. Kerri, captivated by the stars, outstretched her hand, then dozed off momentarily. It was just long enough for me to contemplate life without her. It was a thought I would soon rather dispel.

We awoke at eight-thirty and had breakfast before boarding the daily cruise to Cozumel. The relaxing trip took approximately one and a half hours. Once we arrived, Kerri visited the local gift shops and craft stores. I hated shopping so I decided to take a walk along the beach and catch some sun. The water was just spectacular. It had to be at least ninety degrees. I walked out a quarter mile and it barely exceeded the top of my knees. The lights beaming from the ocean liners could be observed in the far distance. I started to think about maybe purchasing property in Mexico like a second home during the Winter months.

"I could live here all year round," I remember telling myself. And why not. The people were down to earth, the food was spectacular, and the ocean view was breathtaking.

After about two hours, Kerri met me on the beach carrying her flip flops and a few bags with various souvenirs and gifts. It was becoming much warmer as the day went on and I didn't want to risk getting sunburn so we walked toward a large building with outlet stores inside. I came across a jewelry store and decided to look around. I found a beautiful, exquisite 14 karat gold necklace which I thought Kerri would love. I had to get her something special since we had been dating for at least a year.

We found this tiny Mexican restaurant located on the southern part of the island. We were grateful that it didn't require a formal dress code.

By five o'clock, it was time to board and return to Cancun. Upon departure, the bar opened and I purchased a few drinks. I couldn't wait to arrive back at the hotel so I could take a shower and remove the sand from my hair.

As I stepped out of the shower and wrapped the towel around me, I had found Kerri standing in front of the bed. She was wearing only her bra and underwear. As I advanced towards the bed in response to her sexual overture, we engaged in a kiss and then she whispered, "make love to me right now."

Even though I was somewhat exhausted from sun bathing all afternoon, I wasn't about to let another intimate occasion slip away. I turned the lights down just enough to create that shadowy illusion. I laid her graceful, slender body down on the bed and removed her panties.

She began to salivate as I gently massaged her erogenous zone knowing it would excite her in the worst way.

"Take me, please!" she yelled, grabbing hold of the bed and on the verge of an orgasm.

"You're so naughty," I told her, hoping to increase her sex drive.

"You know what I want," she said in her soft, sexy voice. "Oh, yeah baby, you're so good to me," she bellowed, before becoming momentarily breathless. "Yeah, ah, ah, ah, oh God, yes!!" she cried in exultation. I tried desperately to achieve simultaneous orgasms as I applied rapid and swift maneuvers.

"Oh, yes, I'm coming! I yelled, pressing against her delicate skin. She followed with gratifying laments displaying her pleasure of my company.

I was overcome with perspiration, yet felt energized by her alluring guise. I didn't want to look away, not for a single moment. As I gazed into her wide, lustrous, eyes, I envisioned boundless ecstasy. Nothing else mattered at that point.

"I love you," she whispered.

"I love you too," I said, caressing her hair.

She placed her head on my chest and I held her soft, gentle hand.

We lied on top of one another feeling each other's heartbeat until it slowed. Then we fell asleep for the entire evening.

After we touched down in Boston, I drove Kerri home. I helped her carry her luggage and a few other belongings inside. She checked her messages and learned that Brendan had called needing assistance on a new matter. Even though Brendan was handling criminal defense cases, he still took those involving plaintiff litigation.

Evidently, a woman came into his office looking for representation for her young daughter, Heather Riley, who was diagnosed with leukemia. Apparently, her daughter went to the hospital complaining of chest pain. The emergency room physician ordered blood tests. The results of the blood tests came back negative and she was treated for gastroenteritis. Two months later, while undergoing a routine physical examination, it was discovered she had leukemia. The hospital defended on grounds that the laboratory that drew the blood work mislabeled the blood.

"I need you to get all the medical records from the hospital where she was treated," Brendan told Kerri.

This was Kerri's first experience with personal injury and she hadn't taken any courses in law school, except Torts which was in her first year.

"I'll get the information from the file right away," she said.

Brendan, occupied in his office with his feet on top of his desk, pondered which parties he should be suing for malpractice.

"I think we can hold the hospital liable under the doctrine of respondeat superior, even if it turns out the laboratory was a separate entity," he stated to Kerri, as she left his office carrying the file.

"Find out who exactly drew the blood from the hospital emergency room because this person could have been responsible for mislabeling the patient's name," he told her.

Brendan was determined to win this case and recover a large sum of money for the plaintiff and her daughter. He diligently spent the majority of his time on this medical malpractice claim. In fact, he told his receptionist not to take any new cases, nor set up appointments with prospective clients.

"If anyone calls for legal advice or representation, just tell them we cannot handle any cases at this time," he told Bernice.

"I just got off the phone with someone at the hospital in the records section, who informed me that the lab technician working in the emergency room that evening no longer is employed there," said Kerri.

"That's okay. Here's what we'll do. We will file suit against Bedford Care Medical Center naming the emergency room doctor and the lab as defendants. We can always amend the Complaint to include any new parties later, Brendan said," eager to get the ball rolling. Brendan expected Kerri to draft up the Complaint which he would revise prior to filing it with the court.

Kerri printed out a copy of a Complaint that Brendan filed with Landsdale Superior Court three years ago to use as a sample legal document.

Brendan's primary objective was to get the hospital to admit liability and pay for Stephanie's outstanding medical bills and future costs for treatment, which she is currently undergoing at another hospital.

"So far to date the family has incurred medical expenses of $75,000. I want to have the Complaint drawn up by the end of today so the hospital can be served with process no later than this week," Brendan told Kerri.

"I will have it ready for your review by this afternoon," she added.

By three-thirty, she was just about finished and handed it to Brendan to examine.

"This is really good," he answered. "You named the proper defendants and listed all the counts of the Complaint. I think it's ready to be filed.

"Brendan drove down to the Middlesex County Courthouse and filed the Complaint which officially began the lawsuit. The defendants were served via subpoena service in downtown Haverford.

By the beginning of the following week, Brendan received his first letter of correspondence from a law firm defending the hospital. It stated that the hospital was not the proper defendant to be sued because it had no knowledge of the mistake by the lab. The hospital had twenty days to provide a responsive pleading to the counts in the Complaint.

A few weeks had passed, and Brendan finally received a copy of his Complaint from the court along with a docket number. The trial was scheduled for April 10th at 9:00 in the morning. David Abrahamson, an associate attorney from the law firm of Lynch and Weinberg met with Brendan in his office to discuss the case.

"At this time, I see no reason to hold the hospital liable since the plaintiff has failed to establish the causation factor," said Abrahamson.

"I disagree," said Brendan. "But for the hospital's failure to label the patient's blood properly, she would not have waited an additional two or three months to be diagnosed with the disease. Her blood was determined to be negative when in fact, it was returned from the lab containing a high white blood cell count. Now there's some healthy person out there who received horrible news that he or she has been diagnosed with leukemia due to the negligence of hospital staff."

"Have you considered the chain of custody? Do you know exactly what procedure or technique was used from the outset of drawing blood to labeling it and examining it? How do you know the blood wasn't mislabeled after it left the hospital?" asked David.

"First of all, the lab is on the hospital premises. Blood is not transferred anywhere. The lab technician is an employee of the hospital and because he was negligent while acting in the course of employment, his liability imputes to the hospital. He was not acting as an independent contractor because the hospital employed him and had control over his actions," responded Brendan.

"What about the plaintiff being contributorily negligent?" asked David.

"What the hell are you talking about?" Brendan responded, becoming irritated at his attitude.

"I'm talking about your client waiting two months before obtaining a second opinion or seeking a follow-up with her own physician."

"My client was told by hospital staff that her blood results were negative. Who gets a second opinion on blood work that turns out to be negative? The hospital treated her for gastroenteritis and specifically stated that is what she had been diagnosed with."

"You wouldn't seek another opinion if your condition didn't improve?"

"Her condition didn't get any worse in those two or three months. In fact, a routine examination by another doctor revealed her illness," Brendan told him. "Otherwise, she wouldn't have learned about her leukemia until much later and then it may have been too late."

"Have you received all of the records you requested from our office?" asked his adversary.

"Not yet. I'm still waiting on the charts from the doctor who treated her for gastroenteritis," said Brendan.

"Well, I already sent you everything that was given to us," David said.

"Fine. If I need anything else, I can call other treating physicians who were working in the emergency room that night."

"Yes, but understand that there isn't a doctor anywhere in sight who's going to testify against another physician; so if you think you're going to get an expert at trial–think again," David said, trying to intimidate him.

"Right now, my only concern is expediting this trial. I am not concerned about the reluctance of a few physicians to provide evidence of a testimonial nature. When the time comes, I will rely solely on medical reports and the personal knowledge of my client."

"Very well, but you will still need an expert to prove negligence regarding the blood samples," said David.

I'm sure there will be no conflict in finding someone who can provide such information."

David then told Brendan "if there's nothing else, I have a meeting to attend."

"Great. I think we pretty much covered everything," said Brendan.

David gathered his documents and quickly placed them inside his briefcase then advanced toward the door and departed the office.

"What an asshole," Brendan stated to his receptionist. "That guy is the reason why lawyers get a bad reputation."

I felt bad for Brendan who really cared about his clients. He wasn't out to make a name for himself. He didn't come form money so he had nothing to prove. He wanted to make a difference in the world and be a voice for others who were economically disadvantaged or faced with hardship. It was just frustrating for him to have to deal with lawyers who had their eyes focused on one thing; the almighty dollar.

I was in my last year of law school and excited about graduation. I didn't have any jobs lined up and hardly knew anyone with connections. My goal at the time was to pass all of my classes and then prepare for the most grueling examination ever; the Multistate Bar.

CHAPTER SIXTEEN

I T WAS THAT time of year again when the Merrimack School of Law would hold its annual softball game at Brooks Field in downtown Ardmore. The faculty had dominated the series within the last ten years and were victorious eight consecutive times. Rumors spread quickly that this game would be different. The 1Ls' (referred to as first year students) were more athletic. And if that wasn't enough they had two men who were part-time weight trainers.

One of them was named Bruce, who went by the name "Bubba." Bubba was built like an ox. His biceps were so extraordinarily large they looked awkward bulging from his closely fastened Gold's Gym tee shirt. His hands were twice the size of average men. Bubba spent a half-hour before the game trying to find a bat that didn't have the weight of a feather. You didn't want to meet up with him in some dark alley even though Bubba was harmless and probably one of the nicest guys in the school. His brawny, muscular physique would have intimidated just about anybody.

It was early afternoon on a Saturday in the middle of April and dark clouds started rolling in. The forecast called for sporadic showers throughout the day. There were few spectators who had attended due to the inclement weather. Nevertheless, that didn't stop the game.

This was a tradition and they probably would have continued to play even if a tornado was expected to touch down.

"Okay, everybody line up and get in some type of batting order," said Professor Kinney, who was in charge of running the game each year.

The rules were simple. Everybody had to be given an opportunity to bat at least once. The game would be a full seven innings unlike a real major league baseball contest. The students picked heads and won the coin toss which meant they had the choice to bat first or take the field. They chose the latter.

Mickey Donovan walked toward the mound as the rest of the team took their assigned positions. Mickey managed to retire the first two batters with ease, but struggled with a new member of the adjunct faculty, Daryl Stone, who kept fouling off the ball. He was a new comber at our school. Last year, he graduated Harvard Law School and then applied for a part-time position at Merrimack. He was young, good-looking and single. The women who attended probably came out just to watch him run around the bases in his *Nike* shorts. You could tell that he worked out in his spare time. After the ninth pitch, he hit a towering fly ball toward the fence in right field, but it was caught to end the inning.

It was time for the students to demonstrate their expertise and show off their talent. They were the underdog and until they defeated the faculty, talk was cheap and ownership of bragging rights would continue to vest in the law school staff. After two ground outs and one pop fly to center, they were retired in order. So much for the new breed of talent on campus. The faculty couldn't really pass judgment as they had difficulty getting men on base as well. It wasn't until the top of the sixth when the game's first threat of a big inning ensued.

The pitcher walked two consecutive batters and gave up a double to left field which was mishandled by the outfielder. Poor defense contributed to two runs and gave the faculty its first lead with only one out. But that's all they would manage to score as a double play ended the inning.

It was the student's last chance to stand up to a group of pompous, washed up wannabe players who should have stuck to their day jobs.

They were trailing 2-0 with the meat of the order coming up. It was so quiet in the stands you could hear Bubba's name being chanted. "Let's go, Bubba" – Let's go, Bubba – .

Bubba took the first pitch which was high and inside. The next one couldn't have been placed more perfectly around the front of the plate.

Bubba utilized all of his strength and athleticism and swung into the pitch. The crack of the bat said it all. It was hit high and deep and you knew it was gone once it left the infield. The sign in right showed 240 feet and the ball soared at least fifty feet beyond that. It was now just 2-1 and the students had begun to smell victory. The faculty was not accustomed to close games. Their smallest margin of victory was four runs in 1996. Now they were on the edge of their seats wondering if their dynasty was on the brink of destruction. Two batters would come to the plate and both would reach base safely.

It was now first and second with nobody out. Time was called to make a pitching rotation. The infield moved in and hugged the baseline to prevent anything but a single. The pitcher released the ball and the batter swung popping it up toward second. One out. The next batter took two pitches that were called strikes and swung on the third. He grounded toward first for the second out. The players advanced making it second and third, but they were down to their final at bat.

It was up to Scott to bring home at least one run to tie. He wasn't adroit and looked uncomfortable standing there. The pressure was on. A base hit could inevitably seal the victory. He barely made contact with the second pitch but it was hit hard enough to get past the first baseman. Tie game. Two outs. Runner on third. Now the best player on the team came to bat. He wasn't in a hurry. He let the pitcher throw him a few before making his selection.

The count was 2 and 1 and the fourth pitch was thrown shoulder high. He got the bat under the ball and swung evenly through with his arms fully extended. It was a line drive that soared over the second baseman and dropped into center field. The students had done it. The streak had come to an end. They were champions for a day on the field, but they knew who was boss in the classroom. Following the game, everyone was invited to Professor Kinney's home for a barbeque.

As time went on, Kerri and I would see each other less frequently. She was preoccupied with accommodating Brendan at the office. Her job became paramount and even surpassed our relationship. I felt isolated and solitary. I had become accustomed to sharing my life with this extravagant woman only to discover the inevitable truth that we might not be together someday.

I could see how she enjoyed her position at work. She was gaining considerable experience and had the opportunity to obtain hands-on training from a young, astute, attorney, who graduated number one in his class. I couldn't compete with those numbers. I was just an average student with ordinary legal skills who was about to graduate law school. I could sense her attraction to him, although it was surreptitious.

Even though he had a family of his own, Kerri didn't seem to mind spending all of her free time with him. If there was a Bar Association Dinner or seminar, she wouldn't hesitate to attend it with Brendan. My plans seemed to take a back seat.

The thought of becoming insignificant left me demoralized. I now had to accept the fact that I was no longer her main course. Perhaps I was overreacting. Had I lost my mind? Maybe I was just envious of their relationship. Kerri deserved better. I should have been happy for her. She needed her space and I was smothering her with ideas of cohabitation and starting a family. Maybe I scared her off. I do admit, there were times when I rambled on about the possibility of Kerri having children. I was just too damn excited about life. I couldn't keep my hands off her. Her love was infectious. I felt it the moment we laid eyes on each other at the top of the stairs.

I wanted to surprise her one evening so I dropped by her apartment only to find Brendan's car in the parking lot. She had invited him over for dinner. I stood from a distance in order to remain secluded. The curtains in her living room were wide open which provided me with a transparent view of the interior. I could see her smiling as she gestured something to him. They looked as though they were enjoying each other's company. I could see her pouring him another cup of coffee. That gave me the impression that he wasn't leaving anytime soon. After fifteen minutes of scouting the premises, I left and drove to the Winston Tavern.

"I'll have a scotch," I told the bartender.

"Coming right up," he said. "Hey, you've been in here before haven't you?" he asked.

"Yeah, why?"

"Well, Debbie's been asking about you. You're a lawyer right?"

"Not officially. I haven't graduated from law school yet," I told him. "When did Debbie come back to work?" I asked.

"Oh, last week she started. She worked a couple days," he said.

"Is she feeling better? Did her memory come back?"

"I heard she started to remember more details. Nobody thought she would remember much after that whole ordeal so anything new is an improvement," the bartender said, as he brought me my drink.

He was absolutely correct in his portrayal of Debbie's condition. Her physician remained confident that her memory was not placed in further jeopardy. This obviously animated the police who now had something more to add to their scanty list of clues.

She was a victim and therefore, her statements to police had to be taken seriously. She was the only person present at the scene who could provide first hand knowledge. Her allegations would prove to be reliable and trustworthy. Police, however, were unable to obtain any substantial evidence to link them to the murderer.

Debbie arrived at the police station on a Friday morning accompanied by her parents. They were escorted into a large conference room located in the back of the building. One of the officers entered along with an investigator.

"Good morning, everyone. My name is Stanley Hooverman and I'm one of the leading investigators authorized to handle this case."

After everyone introduced themselves, Stanley asked if he could be alone with Debbie to ask her a few questions.

"If you don't mind, I think it would be more beneficial to question your daughter in private," he said.

"That's fine. We'll wait outside for you, Dear," her father said, kissing her on her forehead before leaving the room.

Even though Debbie was glad to have her memory back she still had horrible nightmares and suffered from severe anxiety. Her family was concerned that having Debbie describe those dreadful events again to police might be intolerable. Police assured them if at anytime she became upset they would cease questioning her entirely. Stanley grabbed one of the pens in the tray on the table and grabbed his note pad.

"Now can you recall the events on the evening you were kidnaped?" Stanley asked as he pressed down on the record button of his dictaphone machine.

"Yes. I remember going to a gas station and picking up cigarettes. I returned to my car and he jumped up holding a knife to my throat."

"Did you get a look at him at that moment?"

"No. He was wearing a mask. It was also dark because I had just driven on to the main road."

"What happened after that?" he asked.

"He blindfolded me."

"How long were you in the car?"

"Oh, about twenty minutes," she said.

"Tell me about what you saw inside the house and I want you to be as specific to detail as possible," Stanley told her, hoping to find the missing piece that solved the puzzle.

"I remember him taking me downstairs. He threw me on the bed and then removed my blindfold. But I wasn't able to get a clear view of his face. I'm sure he had a mask on anyway. I was still tied up."

"How did you untie yourself?"

"I used a sharp piece of glass and cut the rope that was tied around my wrists. I was scared because it was dark and I couldn't see where I was cutting."

"Did you end up cutting yourself?"

"Yes. I cut my finger," Debbie said, as she paused momentarily to gather her thoughts.

"Did it bleed a lot?" he probed.

"It wasn't a deep cut but it bled for a few minutes," Debbie said.

"Where did you go next?" he asked.

"I tried to escape and came across a room."

"What did you find inside the room?"

"I opened the door and went inside where I saw a freezer. I lifted up the top door slowly and then – I'm sorry – It's just still so depressing to talk about," Debbie replied catching her breath and trying not to become emotional.

"I understand completely. If you want, we can take a break," Stanley said, handing her a box of Kleenex.

"No, that's okay, I want to do this. I have to do this. I want this guy caught," said Debbie pausing to blow her nose.

"Okay. Did you see anything inside the room besides the bodies? Were there photos lying around or anything that stood out?"

"I don't recall seeing anything other than what was in the freezer. I remember being so scared I just ran out crying."

"How did you come across the other rooms?" asked Stanley.

"I guess by accident. Once I turned the lights on I could see more easily."

"What about once you arrived outside? Could you describe the exterior of the house?" Stanley asked optimistically.

"Not really. I couldn't tell you what the house looked like because it was so dark and wooded. I just remember running away from him," she said, as she took a sip of water to clear her throat.

"Didn't you tell police that night that you caught a glimpse of the perpetrator?"

"Yes, from a distance of about one hundred feet, but I never said I saw his face."

"What about the truck? Could you describe it?"

"It was a pick up truck."

"How about the make or model?"

"I'm not sure. It could have been a Ford. I don't know."

"You didn't see the color?"

"Not really. I mean it could have been black or blue, but it's hard to say."

"Is there anybody out there that might have a personal vendetta against you? Do you have any enemies? Anyone at work who might be jealous of you?"

"No."

"Have you broken up with any boy friends recently?" he asked.

"No. I haven't been in a relationship in over three years."

"And where is that guy now?"

"Three thousand miles away in California."

"L.A.?"

"San Quentin."

"I see. What was he in for . . . if you don't mind me asking."

"Armed robbery and felony murder."

Stanley just stared at her in disbelief before deciding to wrap things up for the afternoon.

"Well, as you know, it's going to be difficult to grab this guy without more evidence or factual information," Stanley said. "We need something substantial. If you could just remember the area where he had driven you, that would really help narrow this investigation."

"I'm sorry. I wish I could do more, but I just can't jog my memory," said Debbie leaving the conference room feeling dejected.

"Thank you for coming in. I will call you if anything else comes up. And if you thing of anything, anything at all, don't hesitate to call my office," Stanley advised her.

"I won't," Debbie said.

I was becoming more and more discouraged with Kerri's lack of affability. I had sent her numerous text messages and left voice mails at her office, yet she failed to correspond. I couldn't comprehend why she was ignoring me.

Did I do something to offend her? From the moment we had met, I had been a complete gentleman who showed her nothing but respect, placing her in the highest regard. This was how she showed her appreciation? No way. I wasn't deserving of that.

I needed her to know that I had invested too much into our relationship to watch it all fall to pieces. Why would she spend all of her time with someone who already has a family? Even if I were jealous, it would be justified under the circumstances. If she wasn't responding to my calls, then there was only one thing to do. I decided to stop by her office to discuss the situation.

"Hi, can I help you?" asked the receptionist who was perusing a romance novel.

"Yeah, I'm here to see Kerri," I informed her.

"Do you have an appointment?" she asked.

"No, I'm her boyfriend."

"Oh, you must be Dillon. So nice to have finally met you. I'll buzz her to see if she's at her desk. She's not picking up, I'll have her paged."

"Sure, no problem."

"Oh, this is Kerri calling," she said watching her extension light up. "Hi, Dillon is here to see you. Okay, I will. Dillon, just go through this door and make a left. Her office is three doors down on your right."

"Thank you very much."

"Dillon, what brings you here?" she asked.

"Well, I couldn't reach you on my cell and you didn't call me back," I told her.

"I've been so busy with researching cases and filing motions, I just haven't had any time."

"I know but we haven't been out in a long time. I miss you and it's just not the same. Things are not the way they used to be."

"Dillon, what do you mean? How have things changed?"

"Well, for starters you could spend less time with your boss and more time hanging out with me."

"I have a job. I need experience. You think I want to do this all day? I would love to relax at home but that isn't gonna pay back my student loans," she said, becoming slightly annoyed.

"Okay, you work eight hours a day. Great. What about after you get home?"

"I'm tired. Sometimes I just want to curl up in bed and read a good book, Dillon."

"Were you too tired to cook your boss dinner the other night?"

"What are you talking about?" she asked with an astonished look on her face. Her jaw dropped and I should have realized at that moment that I may have crossed the line. Instead, I continued the conversation which resulted in a somewhat heated argument.

"I know exactly what I'm talking about," I said in disgust.

"I think this conversation is over!" she yelled.

"You're not being fair," I shouted back.

"I'm not being fair, Dillon? This is crazy. You don't own me. I have a life outside of you. I can come and go as I please. I didn't think I had to check with you first before I made plans. Besides, who gave you permission to follow me around?"

"I didn't follow you around."

"Really? Then how would you know who I had invited to my home?" she asked.

"Look, I stopped by one evening to visit you and I saw Brendan's car parked in the lot. I didn't want to come in so I walked near your apartment and stood outside. I saw you from a distance. You were having dinner."

"You fucking spied on me, Dillon?" she scoured while raising her voice so that anyone sitting in the next office could hear.

"No, I didn't spy on you. I could see you with the naked eye," I replied, trying to tone the conversation down to avoid being heard by a potential eavesdropper.

"All right. This is just crazy," she said. "Just leave, please."

"You don't understand, I came by to see you that night because I missed you. How would you feel if I were spending time with another woman?" I remarked.

"What do you think is happening here, Dillon? Do you think I'm having an affair with Brendan? Huh? – Well? – Oh, my God, you do! You know what, just forget it. I thought we trusted each other. You really think that I would jeopardize our relationship by having an affair with a married man who has three children? You truly have disappointed me. I thought you were better than that."

"I didn't think that, Kerri."

"Oh, no. I think your conduct pretty much said everything I needed to know. Look, I have a lot of shit I need to do so if you don't mind –

"Will you call me?" I pleaded.

"I don't know, Dillon. I need some time alone right now."

The last thing I wanted to do was destroy the one good thing in my life. I guess I just overreacted. The stress from law school finals and preparing for the Bar Exam had changed my personality. I thought I was easy going and composed, but Kerri made me feel like she saw a different side of me. That was not my intention at all. I just needed her around more often. If only I could get her to see that. I left the office feeling embarrassed that someone might have overheard our argument. I knew if I lost her, things would never be the same. At all costs, I had to maintain my serenity.

Don't panic, I told myself.

We had been together for over a year and we never had a fight, not even a disagreement. We saw eye to eye on just about everything. Then I found myself presumably at rock bottom, trying to search for answers to salvage what was left of our relationship. How could I not see this coming? I'm such an idiot for not giving Kerri her space. Why did I have to drive over to her apartment that night? She probably thinks I'm some creep who enjoys stalking women.

I had to get back my respect. I would do whatever it took to succeed in obtaining her trust. I wasn't giving up that easily. She was definitely worth fighting for and I refused to throw in the towel. After a few restless hours, I latched on to my discomfort, took some sleeping pills and found myself drifting into another world.

CHAPTER SEVENTEEN

IT WAS A moderately sunny day and Brendan was sitting earnestly behind his desk, gathering all the necessary documents from Heather Riley's file, the young thirteen-year-old girl, who was recently diagnosed with leukemia. Even though Bedford Care Medical Center treated Heather in the emergency room, they didn't have many reports to send Brendan. In fact, Brendan thought hospital staff may have been advised to destroy any records to avoid liability. It would be almost impossible to prove such spoliation.

Brendan did request authorization to disclose Heather's medical file from the other facilities where she had undergone treatment. There were over two hundred pages that contained information on blood test results, charts, dietary supplements, therapy, and medications.

Through his investigation, he discovered that Bedford Care was involved in litigation several years ago when a family brought suit on behalf of their deceased son who was mis-diagnosed, then subsequently died from a ruptured appendix. Brendan understood that mistakes could be made. He also knew there was a vast difference between standard negligence and gross and wilful misconduct. He based his trial on the latter. Clearly, there can be no excuse for mislabeling a patient's blood and then attempting to conceal the mistake when it was discovered after the fact.

The hospital knew they were wrong, but they weren't going to admit anything, at least not until they were sure there was going to be a trial. The lawyers representing the hospital called Brendan several times trying to make offers of settlement but Brendan rejected their proposal after notifying Heather's family. He wasn't intimidated by the hospital or their administrators. He was anticipating going to court and having the matter adjudicated in a swift and timely fashion.

"Kerri, I need the defendant's supplemental answers to interrogatories," he said.

"Okay, I will get them for you. I have all the discovery in the yellow coded folders," she told him.

"I have to be in court at ten this morning. Could you make copies of those rogs and bring them to me when you arrive at the court house?"

"Sure. Do you know what room you will be in?"

"Yes. It's going to be room 308 with Judge Eliott," he said, before grabbing his keys and leaving through the back door. He climbed in his Acura and raced to the court house. The jury had already been selected a few weeks earlier and Judge Eliot was ready to begin the proceedings.

It was Brendan's purpose to have Heather present at the trial and available to testify when the opportunity arose. It would be more palpable if the jury could see the plaintiff rather than perceive her injuries through her parent's testimony. Brendan was skilled at persuading juries to find in his favor and his eloquence was quite influential. Juries in Massachusetts have been known to award large judgments in personal injury litigation. In the past, corporations and other entities were successful in camouflaging accountability due to their status as a business enterprise. Under modern statutes, however, corporations can no longer mask their own liability.

America has become fed up with big companies making exorbitant sums of money and escaping culpability because they have the money to hire widely acclaimed in-house counsel. Plaintiffs no longer have to settle for the minimum. They can go after the defendant with the deepest pockets. Companies know this and fear jury verdicts. Their best option would be to settle the matter as quickly and efficiently as possible.

Judge Eliot walked out of his chambers and entered the courtroom precisely at 10:00. If you were an attorney appearing before him you made it your business to arrive early. He was reluctant to endure anyone who arrived later than scheduled. In fact, as a penalty for being tardy, an attorney could find his case dismissed from the docket.

"Is the plaintiff's counsel ready to address the jury?" he asked.

"Yes, Your Honor," said Brendan. "Good morning, ladies and gentlemen. This case involves the negligence of the defendant, Bedford Medical Center, and its staff in failing to exercise reasonable care in the handling and labeling of blood specimens. Bedford Hospital had a duty of care which it owed to the plaintiff. That duty involved handling blood samples in a manner that is representative of any ordinary hospital in the community. Bedford breached that standard of care owed the plaintiff. But for the defendant's failure to properly handle the plaintiff's blood samples, the plaintiff and her family would not have found themselves in this dreadful situation. Bedford Hospital should be liable for damages arising from such breach. This is not going to be a long trial. In fact, this should be an open and shut case. Liability is obvious. The defendant is the responsible party and after hearing all of the evidence presented, you will find Bedford Hospital liable. Thank you."

"Thank you, Mister Schneider, said the judge. If defense counsel is ready we will proceed."

"Good morning, ladies and gentlemen of the jury," said George Harvey, one of Bedford's numerous counsel. "This is an interesting case. The plaintiff has filed suit against Bedford because she had been diagnosed with leukemia. Bedford only treated her on one occasion.

At the time she entered the emergency room, she had chief complaints of chest pain accompanied by fever. The physician on duty ran some blood tests and took x-rays. Her x-rays revealed nothing. The blood work came back negative. She was discharged from the emergency room within two hours. Evidently, her symptoms did not improve. The plaintiff, however did not seek the advice of another doctor until two months later when her pain intensified. It was only at that moment when she discovered the horrible news.

It would be foolish to think that the hospital should be responsible for the plaintiff's future diagnosis. There is no proof that the plaintiff had leukemia at the time she entered Bedford Medical Center. If she had, it would have been discovered that night by competent members of the staff.

Ladies and gentlemen, there has been too great a lapse of time to attribute the plaintiff's illness to that of the defendant. There is no causation element present. Plaintiff's counsel cannot demonstrate that "but for" the mislabeling of blood, the plaintiff would not have been diagnosed with leukemia at some future time. Her condition never improved. Her family was put on notice of this and took no affirmative steps to alleviate their daughter's misery. Instead, they waited until she visited with her family doctor to mention her symptoms.

The parents contributed to their daughter's suffering by not being responsible and seeking immediate medical assistance once they knew her condition did not improve. After listening to the testimony of doctors from Bedford Hospital and other expert physicians, you will find the defendant is not liable for the plaintiff's illness. Thank you."

The hospital administrators present at the trial had to become slightly concerned when the jury didn't appear to be sympathetic of defense counsel's opening argument. The majority of them didn't even make eye contact with George Harvey. Their lack of interest was sending an explicit message to the defense table which was "You're going down!" Sometimes juries are difficult to read. Just when you think the verdict will be in favor of the plaintiff they surprise you with a shocking result. This jury was different.

Because it was a civil case, there were only six jurors with two alternates. Five of the six jurors were females ranging in age from twenty-five to sixty. Their demeanor displayed an immediate desire to resolve this controversy as soon as possible. Some became jittery in their seats; others kept staring at the clock on the wall.

That all changed when Brendan called his first witness. All twelve eyes converged on the young girl as she gradually walked up to the witness chair. If she weighed ninety pounds that was a lot. You could hear the brittle bones in her knees crack when she sat down. She spoke not a word and already some jurors became emotional at her physical appearance.

Brendan didn't waste time calling experts to the stand to substantiate his claim. He went right to the source. He didn't hesitate and give the defense time to discredit testimony from other physicians. He knew the defense attorney wouldn't dare cross-examine Heather in her condition. He could ask his witness anything and not have to worry about his adversary objecting. If he did, the jury would make him pay. What better way to describe facts to a jury then to have the plaintiff testify as to her own personal knowledge and experience?

Brendan approached the witness chair and smiled, then asked Heather to state her name for the record.

"How old are you?" he asked.

"Thirteen," she said in a soft, feeble voice which was practically inaudible.

"Could you describe the events that took place on the night your family brought you to the emergency room at Bedford Medical Center?"

"Yes. I complained about having chest pains right after dinner. At first, my parents thought it was just indigestion or something but it got worse."

"How long would you say you remained at home before going to the hospital?"

"Maybe two hours or so."

"What happened when you arrived at the emergency room?"

"Well, my parents had to fill out some information while I was brought into another room and checked by a nurse. I think she took my temperature and blood pressure."

"Then what happened?" he asked.

"Um – I went back to sit with my parents in the waiting room until I was called."

"How long did you wait in the emergency room before you were seen by a physician?"

"Maybe forty-five minutes, I'm not sure," Heather said.

"Okay, what did the emergency room physician do when you were called into the room?"

"He asked me some questions and then examined me. I think he called someone in to give me a test for my heart."

"Do you mean an EKG?" asked Brendan.

"Yes, that's what it was."

"Do you remember what happened after that?"

"Yes. They took blood tests and then brought me downstairs to the radiology lab."

"Did they give you a chest x-ray?"

"Yes."

"What were the results of the x-ray?"

"The doctor told me that the x-ray was clear," Heather informed him.

"What does that mean?" he asked.

"He said there wasn't any problem."

"What about the blood tests?"

"Well, about an hour later the doctor came into my room and told me the blood work came back negative."

"What did he say was wrong with you?" asked Brendan.

"Well, he never diagnosed me with anything but said you probably have gastro something."

"Gastroenteritis?"

"Yes, I think so."

"Were you discharged soon after?"

"Yes, I was."

"Did the chest pain go away once you arrived home?" Brendan questioned while looking over at the jury box.

"Not really. It didn't become worse but it still bothered me."

"Did you tell your parents?"

"Yes."

"What did they say?" Brendan scoured.

"They told me to continue taking the medication that was prescribed to me by the doctor," Heather responded, becoming upset.

"How long did you take the medicine?"

"I had enough pills for about two weeks," Heather said, as she glanced over at her parents sitting in the back.

"Did the pain go away once you finished taking all of the medicine?"

"No. I still had discomfort."

"Did you seek additional medical advice?" Brendan asked with great interest.

"Not right away because my doctor couldn't see me until a month later. He was completely booked with appointments."

"How long did you wait until someone could see you?"

"About six weeks."

"Describe what happened when you went to your doctor six weeks later."

"He took some more blood tests, a few x-rays and the results came back positive," Heather replied.

"Positive meaning?"

"I had leukemia," she said.

"How did you feel at that moment?" Brendan asked.

"I was shocked. I just sat there and cried. I was devastated. My mother was with me and she cried too."

"What did the doctor tell you about treatment?"

"He said that I may need a bone marrow transplant and blood transfusions."

"Did you have the transplant?" asked Brendan.

"Yes."

"How do you think this happened?" Brendan petitioned.

"What do you mean?" she inquired.

"How did the hospital make this mistake?"

"Objection. Counsel's statement is assuming facts not in evidence."

"Sustained."

"How do you think your doctor could diagnose you with leukemia but the hospital wasn't able to?"

"From what I understand, the blood tests that I took at the emergency room were somehow misplaced or mislabeled."

"Do you think it's possible to have blood tests come back negative the first time and six weeks later show evidence of leukemia?" he asked intending to demonstrate the hospital's liability.

"Objection."

"Overruled."

"No."

"I didn't think so."

"Could you describe your overall health today?"

"Well, I'm in remission right now," Heather stated.

"Oh, that's wonderful, good for you."

The jurors were also delighted after hearing the news.

"Do your parents have health insurance?"

"Yes," Heather said.

"Are you covered under your parent's policy?" Brendan asked in order to arouse the jury and play on their sympathy.

"Yes, but the company told us they can't pay for any more future costs."

"Why not?"

"They said the policy only covers 60% of the medical bills."

"How much do your parents owe in medical bills?"

"About $90,000."

"Did your parents try to get in touch with the hospital after your diagnosis?"

"Yes."

"What happened?" Brendan urged.

"Nothing. No one called us back. They didn't answer my mom's letter. It's like they didn't care."

"Is there anything you want to say today to the defendants sitting at that table?" Brendan asked pointing in the direction of his adversary.

"Because of you, I had to have lots of surgery, blood transfusions and I missed school. Now my family has no money to pay for anything. We may have to sell our house," Heather remarked shedding a few tears.

"Thank you, Heather. Nothing further, Your Honor."

The defense would be half-witted to attempt a cross-examination. Instead, defense counsel requested a recess to discuss an offer of compromise with the plaintiff. Brendan rejected their first proposal that was only $500,000.

"I'm not wasting my time talking to you unless you give my client something to compensate her for her injuries," Brendan said.

"What do you think is fair?" asked one of the other attorneys representing the hospital.

"You tell me. If it was your daughter and the hospital fucked up, how much would you want? I'm not afraid to walk back in there and continue this trial."

"Wait a minute. Let me talk to a few people first," said George.

He left the room and went outside to discuss the matter with the Chief Executive of Bedford Medical Center. After twenty minutes, he returned with his offer of settlement.

"He has offered your client two million dollars."

Brendan then went to share the information with Heather and her parents who implored him to accept the offer.

"My client is happy with your offer and wishes to acquiesce to the terms."

"Very well. Should we go inside and tell the judge?"

"Your Honor, the defense has made an offer to the plaintiff which the plaintiff finds fair and equitable," Brendan told him.

"Is this true?" asked the judge, who directed his question at Heather.

She nodded affirmatively. The judge then thanked the jury for its service and dismissed them immediately. Brendan breathed a sigh of relief once the ordeal was over. He felt fortunate that his adversary was cooperative with the plaintiff's demands. He had to be ecstatic knowing that he would be entitled to at least $660,000 (approx. 33% of the settlement). He couldn't wait to arrive home and share the news with his family.

CHAPTER EIGHTEEN

LOCAL TELEVISION STATIONS interrupted their daily scheduled programs to notify residents of yet another mysterious killing in Haverford. The body of a young female was discovered lying face down and trapped against tree branches that extended out into the shallow area of the river.

Law enforcement officials who originally thought they were tracking the serial killer's path had once again been outwitted by his vicious sabotage. The killer had changed his pattern. He must have known that police were increasing their level of security and he altered his course. He was no longer compelled to dispose of the body in a clandestine fashion. It's as though he took delight in having the body discovered in plain view. This made his job a lot easier since he could now discard the body in an instance.

It was a game between him and the police. The river was his home field and he had every advantage. He had become so confident that he convinced even himself of never being captured. His methodical approach in examining the river was alien. Lying in wait for his next unfortunate soul was foremost. He was anything but a novice. Experience was his good luck charm. He had killed so many that he lost count. What would drive a man to take the lives of so many innocent women? How could he not feel remorseful for his actions? He had to be someone with multiple personalities; one who could easily adapt and turn off his evil mind at any moment, as if it were a light switch. His cleverness failed to arouse a scintilla of suspicion. He fit in as any ordinary citizen.

Every zealous effort was made to be friendly and congenial. He was admired by his co-workers who would never suspect him of anything like this. He lived a double life and he was proud of it.

The wilted house in which he lived was his sanctuary. He saw value in each corpse as if it were preserved in an art museum. His handling of the corpus delicti was done so conscientiously that one could not fathom his reasoning for disrespecting them while they were alive.

He knew exactly when to strike again. In fact, he selected his prize in advance. Stalking his victims was a prelude to his annihilation. He followed them into department stores, banks, the post office, even church. He had memorized their schedule. Unbeknownst to them, their expectation of privacy had been violated.

The only clues about this cowardly monster were that he drove a truck and was fascinated with the river. All the other intricate details could not be deciphered. He was affable when circumstances called for it. Otherwise, he kept his distance to avoid discerning his true identity. He lied about his age, his family, and his residence. He lived alone but had two dwellings. He rarely visited the small cottage outside Manchester, New Hampshire which he used primarily for mailing address and business purposes.

The broken-down house which he purchased a few years ago was utilized solely to fulfill his compulsive desires.

Aside from all the killings, he enjoyed watching classical films. He had seen *Gone with the Wind* over a dozen times. He loved to cook but ate all of his meals alone. Practically his whole life was spent in isolation. He didn't have any siblings. When he was four, his mother became pregnant, but her husband forced her to have an abortion. His father was abusive and a compulsive gambler.

The killer became manic depressive and emotionally disturbed. Having to accept his father's quandary commanded his inner most thoughts. He loved his father and wanted to reconcile by compensating for all the time they hadn't spent together. Once his father was sent to prison, that all changed. He knew he would never have a normal relationship with him again. He vowed never to speak with him. He hated what his father did to his family.

As time went on, he found it difficult to maintain a relationship with women. He was reticent and inexperienced. He had been hurt so many times before. He suffered from anxiety and panic disorders. At times, thoughts of suicide entered his mind. Eventually, those horrible thoughts would manifest into a severe nervous breakdown. He had lost all intellectual faculties. Any perception of reality vanished and was replaced by delusional impressions. He suffered from hallucinations that chastised him day and night and prevented him from falling asleep. The voices in his head told him what he had to do. He tried desperately to expel them but was overpowered by his stronger, assertive, personality.

"*I have to make them pay,*" he told himself, before setting out for his ensuing pursuit. He wrote everything out in his diary that he kept in his chest drawer located in the bedroom. He would check it daily as if he were performing an inventory. The meticulous details described in the book were quite graphic.

Ironically, he loved the thrill of subduing innocent women, yet had a strong repulsion toward himself. He had compunctions about not having a normal childhood. He blamed himself for his father's behavior and didn't want to imitate his evil ways. His childhood was anything but ordinary. His father was physically and verbally abusive toward his mother. The beatings occurred on a weekly basis. Of course, the alcohol intensified the violence. His father was inebriated more than he was sober. The smell of alcohol permeated the home. The stench was so bad at times, his mother would sleep outside.

She wanted desperately to flee, but he had always threatened her with serious bodily harm if she ever tried to take her son and leave. All his mother could think about was finding a way to end her misery. Her only mistake in life was marrying the wrong man. She knew if she asked him for a divorce he would kill her. Her only option was to remain in the home and subject herself to continuous punishment, even though she did nothing to deserve it.

Luckily, her husband was sent to prison after engaging in a fight at a bar where he cracked a beer bottle on top of someone's head. The man remained in a coma for three weeks as a result of massive head trauma. He died from the injuries. Her husband was found guilty of manslaughter and sentenced to fifteen years in the penitentiary. She prayed that her son would never follow in his father's footsteps. Unfortunately, that prayer would go unanswered. Her son would become far more sinister than she could ever have imagined. He made his father look like a conciliator. He redefined the word evil and replaced it with perversity and vileness.

It was the first Saturday in May, and Brendan had just opened his front door to pick up his morning newspaper. He sat down at the kitchen table and glanced at the "local community" section while sipping his freshly-brewed hazelnut coffee. He happened to come across an article printed about his client's lawsuit against Bedford Hospital. The article described Brendan as a prominent attorney who wasn't disinclined to zealously represent his client's interest. His wife Alison was walking down the stairs when he called her into the kitchen.

"Honey, you have to look at this," he said, pouring himself another bowl of cereal.

"What is it?" she asked.

"The newspaper printed the article about the Riley family and mentioned me."

"See, you're a popular lawyer around here," she responded.

They were accustomed to budgeting their money and barely could pay their mortgage when it became due. Now their lives were about to make a transformation. Brendan had anticipated the arrival of a settlement check which he was entitled to more than one half million dollars. They weren't going to live in their tiny home any longer. It was time to say goodbye to the precipitous decline in the backyard which posed a risk of injury to others.

As they sat at the table, they discussed the possibility of moving now that they had a third child and would obviously need more space.

"Why don't we consider purchasing a home in Ardmore?" Alison recommended.

"Well, I thought about that," Brendan said, "but what about the property taxes?"

"Oh, we can afford the taxes. Besides, the school system is phenomenal and it would be perfect for our children," she said, glancing at the real estate section of the paper.

"I don't know. I mean Ardmore is really expensive. The average home is probably worth $700,000," he said, hoping his wife would consider other alternative neighborhoods.

"Shall I make breakfast?" Alison inquired.

"I already had cereal," Brendan told her.

"That's not breakfast. I'll make some eggs," she said, wiping down the table and counter top.

"Why don't you take the children to the park for a few hours. I have to run and get my hair done and I also want to make an appointment for a manicure."

"Well, I thought I was going to work on my files today," Brendan said, becoming discouraged at being overburdened with his caseload.

"Honey, the children want to spend time with you. You've been working a lot lately and it's the weekend."

"Okay. I'll take them to the park for a few hours and maybe we can catch a matinee. Did you see the movie section?"

"No. It should be there."

"Well, it doesn't matter. I'll let them decide what they want to see when we get there."

"Thanks, dear. I owe you. Kids, in a little while, Daddy is going to take you to the park and then you're going to the movies," Alison told them.

"Yippy!" the children yelled.

"I'll drop the baby off at my mother's," she said.

Brendan grabbed the keys from the basket that hung from the wall and went outside to start his car. He happened to see the postman walking up the street toward him. Brendan decided to wait for his mail before he set out for the park.

"Good morning," said the postman.

"How are you?" Brendan asked.

"Fine, thank you," the man responded, as he handed Brendan the check he had been anxiously awaiting.

Brendan ran back inside to tell Alison that the check arrived. "Honey, it's here."

"What is it?" she yelled down to him, as she was getting dressed in the bedroom upstairs.

"The money is here."

"I'll be right there."

Alison ran down the stairs taking two at a time as she had normally done.

"Hurry up. Open it," she said.

Brendan ran his finger across the top of the envelope and slid out the check.

"Wow, six hundred thousand dollars. I can't believe it."

"Oh my God, Brendan. What are we going to do with all of this money?

"For starters, I think we should put a substantial part of it away for the children's education."

"I agree," Alison said. Brendan requested that they should invest some of the money.

"I don't know. We have to be careful where we put our money. I think it's too risky," she said.

"Well, for now we can put it in the bank," he told his wife.

"I think that would be the best option, Dear."

He gave his wife a kiss and then left with the children.

When he returned that afternoon, Alison could tell something was troubling Brendan.

"Honey, what's wrong?" she asked him.

"I met Miss Martin's daughter downtown coming out of the hair salon. She informed me that her mother was starting to take a turn for the worse."

"Oh, no, that's terrible," she replied with enormous pity.

"Is there anything we can do Brendan?" she inquired.

"I don't know. The family has been taking care of her so far, but they may not have enough money to cover the funeral costs."

"Why don't you visit with the family and tell them you would like to help with the expenses?"

"I don't want to make them uncomfortable."

"Don't be silly, Brendan, they would appreciate it. Besides, Derek looks up to you. You saved his life, remember?"

"Yeah, I guess."

"Good. Why don't you stop by some time this week and tell them of your intentions?" she asked with enthusiasm.

On his way back from Portsmouth, New Hampshire, Brendan paid a visit to Derek and his family. He rang the doorbell feeling somewhat awkward and was greeted by Janet at the front door.

"Hey, Brendan, what brings you here?" she asked with a grateful smile.

"I need to talk to you and Derek if you don't mind," he responded.

"Derek isn't home now, but come on in and have a seat on the sofa. Can I get you anything to drink?"

"Oh, no thank you, I'm fine. I just had lunch before I left the court house."

"So what's up?"

"Well, I know it is none of my business, but I would like to help out with your mother's funeral arrangements. I guess what I'm saying is my family and I would like to provide you with financial assistance when the time comes."

"Oh, Brendan, thank you, but you don't have to do that. You have done so much for our family already," Janet said.

"I want to do this. Please accept my offer to pay for your mother's funeral expenses."

"Oh, how sweet, Brendan. Thank you for the lovely gesture, but I can't let you do that."

"Please, it's just a little something," he added, handing her a check in the amount of $25,000.

"Oh, my God. I don't know what to say. I can't believe it. I know Derek will be so happy to hear of your great generosity," Janet replied staring at the amount on the negotiable instrument she had just been given.

"I'm glad that I could help. Call me if you need anything," Brendan said, giving her a warm and genuine hug.

"I will, Brendan. Thanks for stopping by."

A few days later, I ran into Kerri at the law school library. I was hoping to reconcile our relationship. It's been nearly four months and we haven't gotten back together.

"So what are you working on?" I asked.

"Oh, I'm just researching some statutes for a paper that's due in a few weeks," she replied.

I felt at a loss for words. I couldn't tell her how miserable I was without her in my life. This was my chance and I blew it. The one opportunity to liberate myself from guilt and I cracked under pressure. And I want to be a public defender? How the hell can I get up in front of a jury and persuade twelve jurors if I don't even have the audacity to confront Kerri?

Regardless of the situation, time was running out. Graduation was right around the corner and if I didn't act quickly, I would lose her forever. Luckily, I found her inside the auditorium. I approached and sat in the seat adjacent to her.

"Would you mind if I took just a few minutes of your time?" I asked.

"Sure. What's up?" she responded.

"I know I wasn't being fair when I misjudged you and I probably came off as being controlling or jealous. I don't want to be thought of as that person. Kerri, I really care about you and I want this to work.

I don't want to lose you. I'm really sorry for acting so infantile by driving over to your place. I just wanted to spend time with you and I feel like we're drifting apart here."

"Dillon, I care about you too. If I didn't, why would I let you make love to me like that? When you thought I was having an affair you hurt me deeply. What do you think that did to our level of trust?"

"I know. And I'm regretting that every day. It's monopolizing my thoughts. I just can't get you out of my mind. I think about you everywhere. I want to spend the rest of my life with you, Kerri. You're so different than any other woman I had ever been with. I'm not afraid to be myself with you."

"Dillon – what scares me is that you were being yourself. I don't want someone who is going to control my life. I have been on my own for many years and I like my independence. I want a man to love me and respect me enough to allow me my space and trust me enough to let me have friends outside of our relationship."

"I couldn't agree more. But I'm not that person. It was wrong for me to act that way. It was an isolated incident. I don't want to be judged based on that particular occurrence. Can't you see how much I really care about you?"

"Honestly, Dillon, I know you care about me. For a while, everything seemed to be going smoothly. We were connecting. We understood each other. There was a certain chemistry between us and everybody could sense it. At some point, our relationship moved too quickly. I felt rushed and constrained. I know you didn't do it intentionally, but I was starting to feel trapped," she said, glancing through her purse in search of a piece of candy to suck on.

I pleaded with her that afternoon to reconsider, but she needed time and I understood that. We were still friends and that was most important. I was glad that she got to hear my side of the story, my version, straight from the heart. I said all I had to say. The ultimate decision was in her hands. If we were destined to be together, then time would surely tell.

I drove back to my apartment where I poured myself a drink, then sat on the couch surfing the channels on the television. I was drowning in my own sorrow and watching romance movies didn't help.

Kerri was a constant reminder of how great my life used to be. I missed those quiet evenings cuddling near the fireplace. Her body against mine rolling around on the floor. Everything made sense back then. I felt comfortable approaching her with any problem I may have had. I was confident that she would never turn me away. When I was in her presence, I felt safe and at ease. She had a way about making people feel better about themselves. She was decisive, never argumentative. She thought things through logically and systematically. Her outlook on life was always positive. She didn't have time to waste dwelling on what could never be. I won the jackpot when I found her, but I gambled her away.

CHAPTER NINETEEN

THE TEMPERATURE ON this particular day didn't rise above fifty degrees, even though it was approaching the third week of May. It was a bleak, damp and dreary afternoon. Tanya Martin took her last breath less than forty-eight hours ago. She passed away in her home just the way she wanted with her son and daughter present. She knew it was her time and her fate was inevitable.

She departed this life peacefully leaving behind her legacy; a life filled with sacrifice and devotion to God. Her only wish would be for her children to continue in that noble tradition. Tanya had come full circle. As a child, she witnessed firsthand the negative impact of racism and its consequences upon her entire family. Her parents, both mill workers, found it difficult to find adequate living conditions.

As they soon discovered, finding a home would not be as conventional as they originally thought. It was customary at that time, although discriminatory by modern standards, to refuse to sell property to African Americans. This form of anti-racial behavior continued until around 1940. Even though slavery had been abolished over a century ago, it didn't eradicate the prejudicial views embraced by those ambushed by their own ignorance.

Her family migrated from the South in 1942 following years of abuse and threats from local townsmen. Her parents didn't retreat at first, but stayed their ground, protecting their property and upholding the principle that they too were equal in the eyes of the law. At first, they were not intimidated by words alone. But words were soon replaced by selfish and odious crimes against humanity. These crimes removed a man's dignity and character.

One evening, while asleep, a radical group of young men approached Tanya's property setting fire to her house and burning crosses on her front lawn. Her parents had to weigh the cost of fighting for independence against the risk of harm to their only daughter. If people weren't going to change then her parents would have to transform their own lives. And so they did just that. They took what little money they had and headed north hoping that they would be treated with dignity and respected as human beings, not pieces of chattel.

As Tanya grew older, she too faced typical prejudices associated with her job. She interviewed for her first job as a secretary at the age of sixteen. She was rejected based on the color of her skin. After graduating from high school, her parents advised her to enroll in college. She applied to three schools, but was rejected by all of them even though she attained top grades and scored in the 90th percentile on the entrance examination. Education was everything to her and she vowed to herself that someday she would receive her college degree.

At the age of 40, she attained a bachelor's degree in sociology and became a social worker in Landsdale. She raised two children teaching them the importance of values and self identity. Her children remember some of her mother's best advice. "Your word is all that you truly own," Tanya told them, when they were old enough to understand the meaning of character. Prior to her death at age seventy, Tanya had to grapple with one more bout of racism. This time it didn't come in the form of cross burning or the inciting of violence, but rather a closed minded jury.

She witnessed the wrongful conviction of her son for first degree murder and once again, bigotry and indifference were resurrected.

Was her son convicted solely on account of his race? Did the jury do exactly what has been done to blacks throughout time? Did they see race as a predisposition to commit crime? This jury based its decision on circumstantial evidence, but maybe they would have evaluated the evidence in a distinct fashion had the defendant been white. Fortunately, she was alive to see her son released from prison.

Hundreds of family members and friends entered through the massive, bronze, church doors and walked toward the pews. Everyone who attended was handed a tiny booklet containing a list of psalms and passages from Scripture.

The organist began playing as the casket was gradually rolled down the center aisle. Janet and Derek walked directly behind their mother and took their seats in the first row closest to the altar. The Rev. Charles Holloway began with an opening prayer and then addressed the large crowd with a short, mollified eulogy.

"We are gathered here today to celebrate the life of Tanya Martin. She was many things to all of us including, a mother, a wife, and a friend. She will be remembered most for her generosity toward others. Her promise to live life to the fullest had been effected. God is pleased with her and now is ready to reward her with an eternal covenant of his own. That covenant states Tanya will be saved and each of us can be assured of that same promise when we meet our creator someday. Now, Tanya has been brought to a sanctified and righteous place.

A place where she will suffer no longer and any transgressions or iniquities manufactured on this earth, will be removed by the grace of God. Her home is now in the heavens above the skies and beyond all existence. She now looks down on us from above, healthy and pure, an angel to guard us along on our journey much the same way that God sends his spirit to renew our lives when we find ourselves troubled and despaired.

There will be moments when we think about her and become emotional. We will feel this way because life will no longer be the same without her. The best thing we can do to remember her is to honor her today. Let us reflect upon those events where Tanya was a participant and constituent in our lives.

Let us pray now that our sister Tanya will be carried through the gates of heaven sharing in eternal happiness with her Father in paradise. Amen."

Reverend Holloway was well known for giving succinct eulogies. His use of reverent phrases to enlighten the congregation was his main ambition and it worked on this precise day. Many who entered the medieval church in an emotional state departed with a deeper understanding and acceptance of Tanya's journey. They were deeply moved by the Reverend's speech and made it known to him as they descended the stairs.

"Your speech was quite emphatic, Reverend," said a member of the church assembly.

"May God bless you today," he responded, clutching the woman's hand. The funeral procession concluded once everyone arrived at the cemetery. Each person present placed a carnation on top of the casket and returned to their cars. Janet and Derek remained behind to spend their last few moments with their mother. It was difficult for Janet as reality began to set in. Her mother would no longer be around to visit. The home she was raised in was now vacant and lifeless. She hugged her brother and cried in his arms. "Goodbye, mama," she whispered. "I will always love you."

Janet opened her umbrella and proceeded to walk toward the car. She turned around once to get a final glimpse of the casket, then she climbed in the limousine and drove off.

It was Friday afternoon when I parked my car at the Ardmore train station. I walked up the escalator that was not in working order and approached the ticket window.

"I'd like a round trip to Boston," I said.

"That will be ten seventy-five," the agent responded.

"Do you know what time the next train arrives?" I inquired.

"About fifteen minutes."

I walked outside and stood on the wooden platform hoping the train would arrive on time. I had a two-thirty interview with a prestigious law firm in downtown Boston adjacent to the government district.

Within minutes, a train approached on Track Four, but I wasn't sure of its destination.

"Does this train go to Boston?" I asked the conductor, who was just about to signal the engineer to leave the station. He nodded affirmatively and I boarded carrying a small briefcase containing my portfolio. After traveling about three miles, the train momentarily came to a screeching halt and remained idle while everyone on board waited patiently.

I hope this doesn't take too long, I muttered. I wanted to make a good first impression at my interview and arriving late would surely result in my résumé being thrown in the waste basket. About a half-hour later, I arrived at the law firm. I was fifteen minutes early and I signed in at the reception area.

"Someone will be with you shortly," said one of the assistants.

I walked over to the magazine rack that contained mostly legal journals and periodicals about auto insurance. I was hoping to read the newest edition of *Sports Illustrated* or *Rolling Stone* but had to settle for *The Boston Lawyer.*

I really wanted this job. I felt I belonged here. The starting salary for a first year lawyer at this firm was $80,000, not to mention full health benefits, bonuses and an unbelievable vacation plan. I knew even if I interviewed well and came across as highly qualified for this position, I would lose out against any candidate from Harvard. In fact, ninety percent of the associates, and partners at this office graduated from Harvard Law School. Could I really compete with these statistics?

When I walked inside and showed the hiring partner my résumé, I felt like I was wasting his time. I was just as good as any other first year associate who, like myself, knew nothing about the practice of law other than what was taught to them by law professors.

But I lacked the most important factor. My diploma didn't come from Cambridge. I attended an average school and attained above average grades. I was also a member of law review and published three articles during my career at Merrimack. He didn't ask me about any of those publications. I could see he had very little interest in continuing the interview and tried to wrap up the conversation as quickly as possible. He shook my hand and gave the same speech every other employer gives – *We have your résumé on file and we'll call you.* I interpreted that to mean, *Get lost pal, you don't have a chance in hell of being hired.*

I left the office around noon and then took a stroll along Beacon Street. It was a spectacular day to be outside. There was plenty of sunshine accompanied by a scanty breeze. Some pedestrians were walking their dogs along the three mile strip toward University Place. Students were completing their last week of college exams. Those that finished early took to the streets and filled every bar along Yawkee Way.

The trolleys were running on schedule, but you'd be lucky to find a seat. I headed back toward the Commons and sat down on a park bench under a maple tree while glancing at the magnificent view. I loved coming to this city. I considered it my second home. It was peaceful and liberating.

A few days later, I went to the law school to pick up my cap and gown for graduation. It was going to be held in downtown Ardmore at the Civic Center. I had been there only once before to view a holiday concert sponsored by the Knights of Columbus. While standing in line, I saw Kerri coming out of the room carrying a bag and fixing her hair.

"Hey, Kerri, how's it going?" I asked, affectionately placing my hand on her shoulder.

"Good. I just dropped by to pick up my items for graduation," she replied.

"Do you have any plans later?" I inquired, anticipating her participation in my endeavors.

"I have to study for my Entertainment Law final that I have this week," she answered.

"I was hoping we could spend some time together, you know—maybe catch a movie or go to dinner."

"I'm just too busy right now, Dillon. Maybe when exams are over we can go out and celebrate," she told me.

It's ironic in a way. When law school first began I couldn't wait for graduation to arrive. Three years of studying and reading thousands of pages of cases made me question why I attended in the first place. But after meeting Kerri, I didn't want those three years to end. I wish there was some way I could slow time down and buy back a few months. If I could press rewind and hit play all over again, I would make everything right.

The reason I had left my home in New Jersey was to launch a new endeavor. The timing felt right. Although spontaneous at first, I had a gut feeling that life in New England would be so much better.

Kerri and I had a certain chemistry. All of our friends said we made a perfect couple. They thought we would be married someday. I wanted that to be true. I was committed to this relationship. I was in it for the long haul. There wasn't any exit door for me to open because I wasn't going anywhere.

I envisioned a home with a family maybe two or three children and a dog or a cat. We would throw parties for our friends and have cookouts on the patio during the summer months. I knew Kerri would make a wonderful mother. She loved being around children. If she couldn't be an attorney, her other choice would have been a teacher. She had great maternal instincts. I watched her with her four year old niece.

"Come give Aunt Kerri a big hug and kiss," she would say, when her sister would visit with her daughter from out of town.

"Can you braid my hair, Aunt Kerri?" asked the little girl.

"Of course, sweetie. Come sit next to me."

Kerri did more than satisfy my ultimate desires. She defined my world and completed me as a human being. I wanted to grow old with her and experience every emotion throughout our journey. Each day together was like turning the page of a striking romance novel.

I portrayed her in an ivory, satin wedding dress walking down the aisle with her gleaming smile. We would meet at the altar and exchange vows while grasping each other's hand. Our marriage would then be consecrated and sealed with a kiss symbolizing the love and devotion which we felt for each other. As time went on, I was just hoping to eventually wake up from a bad dream.

CHAPTER TWENTY

B RENDAN PICKED UP his files and gave his wife a kiss before leaving through the front door. He stopped off at a bagel shop on his way into work and purchased a fresh cup of coffee and an egg sandwich on white toast. It wasn't like Brendan to eat breakfast so early in the morning. In fact, he rarely ate breakfast at all, except for cereal or pop tarts. His stomach had been bothering him for several months. The discomfort became worse when he learned of the passing of Ms. Martin. Of course, the stress from clients didn't help either.

Alison had contacted a real estate agent in Eastern Massachusetts and listed their house on the market. The asking price was $340,000. They decided that they would move toward the beach near Portsmouth, New Hampshire or Kittery, Maine.

It was just passed seven when Alison decided to go upstairs and take a shower.

"Kids, get ready for school," she said, as she walked by their rooms and found them playing on the floor. She grabbed a towel and wash cloth from the bathroom closet. She shut the door, removed her clothes, and climbed into the shower. After fifteen minutes, she opened the glass door and stepped down. She toweled herself off and applied skin cream to her face and other parts of her body.

"Mommy's almost ready," she told her children. She put on her sweat pants and sneakers and was ready to take them to school.

"Kids, where are you? It's time to go."

When she heard no response, she went downstairs thinking they were watching television. She was startled to find they were not there.

"Come on, quit fooling around. You're going to be late," she said. She went into the living room and found her furniture turned upside down. She ran into the kitchen to look outside, but did not see her kids anywhere. She stepped outside on the patio and called them by name.

"Trevor? – Brian?" When she came back inside, she grabbed the phone and was going to call the police. As she started to dial, her arm was seized by a man wearing a mask. He had a tattoo on his wrist. He threw her down to the floor and pommeled her repeatedly until she was knocked unconscious. He then carried Alison to his truck and drove off.

When she awoke, she found her clothes full of blood and she was in excruciating pain. She could barely move on her side after sustaining multiple bruises. Her face was swollen and her nose was fractured. Her hands and feet were chained to the bed.

"Somebody, please help me!" she cried.

After a few moments, the squeaky door on top of the stairs opened and she could hear someone descending.

"I made you something to eat," he said.

"Who the fuck are you?" Alison asked.

"No, no, no. That's not the way to start off a friendship," he told her. "I want you to introduce yourself to me in a pleasant manner."

"Go to hell you sick bitch!" she shouted at him.

"I don't like women who talk down to me. Now show me some respect or I will make you pay. Believe me, I can have my way with you," he threatened.

"What did you do to my children?"

"Children, what children?" he asked sarcastically.

"Don't play games with me. Where are my two sons?" Alison demanded.

"Oh, yes, your boys. Sweet kids. You did a fine job raising them. They are very respectful. You know—they let me right in the house. I didn't even have to force my way in. Did you always teach your children to invite strangers into their home?"

"Tell me what you did to my kids, please," she pleaded.

"Well, since you are begging me, I will confess. I tied them up and put them in the closet. Don't worry, your husband will be home from the office tonight and he will find them when he puts his clothes away."

Alison began to worry and asked, "How do you know my husband?"

"I know everything about you Alison," he replied with confidence.

"What do you want from me?" she insisted.

"Isn't it obvious? I want you. I think you are perfect for me."

"What are you talking about? I'm married, you can't have me. Just let me go before they find you."

"You listen to me, bitch. No one is going to find me because nobody knows where I am. The police have no clue. I made sure not to leave behind any traces of evidence. So you see, you and I are going to spend a great deal of time together. Brendan will have to purchase that brand new house all by himself."

"Why are you doing this? What has my husband done to you?"

"Your husband has nothing to do with this," he said.

"Then why do you want to hurt me?"

"I don't want to hurt you. I am seeking revenge against those deserving of punishment. An eye for an eye. That is what the Bible says, doesn't it?"

"I don't understand what you mean."

"Oh – she doesn't understand what I mean? The poor little woman needs an explanation. Well, let me fucking explain. I decide who lives and dies."

"Who gave you the right to play God?"

"Don't you lecture me about God. Where was God when my father left? Where was God when I was ridiculed by people like you?"

"I understand, but what does this have to do with me?"

"Look, you don't understand shit. You don't know what I've been through. Don't act like you care."

"Let me help."

"Shut up. You think I'm stupid. I see what you're trying to do. You wanna get inside my head and play doctor or psychiatrist with me? I'm not falling for your tricks," he replied with indignation.

He grabbed some duct tape and was about to place it over Alison's mouth.

"What are you doing? Please, I'll be quiet. You don't need to put that on," Alison remarked, turning her head away from him.

"I told you to shut up. Now I won't have to listen to you."

She lied there in the dark worried about what he would do next. She thought about her children and Brendan. Her entire life flashed before her eyes. She began to cry thinking that this was how her life was going to end. All the dreams she had growing up were now shattered. Her fate was now in the hands of a brutal killer who showed no mercy.

He was nothing short of a coward. He couldn't confront his victim unless his face was shielded from view. He wasn't assertive enough to look at them directly in the eyes. Ironically, he couldn't muster sufficient temerity to converse with women, in general. He feared them as though they were demonic. Killing them would acquit himself of torment. It would liberate him as far as he was concerned. He grew more confident after each murder, but never could vanquish his revulsion toward the opposite sex.

It was around four-thirty in the afternoon, and Brendan had just logged off his computer for the day. He had finished typing a thirty page brief for the 1st Circuit Court of Appeals which he was going to file the next morning. He picked up his umbrella and briefcase then progressed toward the elevator.

Once he stepped outside, Brendan took out his cell phone and tried to call Alison, but couldn't get a signal. He noticed his phone needed to be charged. He climbed into his car and drove right on Claremont Street to avoid the long traffic lights. As he merged on to 495, traffic was at a standstill. If he traveled a mile in twenty minutes, that was gaining momentum. Brendan was looking forward to having a hot meal with his family after another rough and stressful day at work. He finally arrived at home around five-fifteen and pulled into the garage. He entered through the side door and announced his presence.

"Hi everyone, Daddy's home."

He walked inside, but didn't see anyone, so he thought maybe they had gone for a walk and left a note. He checked the kitchen table, but didn't find one. Brendan was surprised that Alison hadn't started cooking dinner. He opened the refrigerator and poured himself a glass of sweetened iced tea. The air conditioner wasn't on inside the house and Brendan was anxious to remove his clothes and take a quick shower to cool off. He walked upstairs and went into the bathroom. Just as he was about to turn on the sprinkler, he heard a blaring sound converging from the bedroom.

"Hello? Is anyone there?" he asked, while positioning himself outside of harm's way.

The sounds grew more intense and Brendan picked up a rod from where the bathroom towel hung and carried it with him into the bedroom. He gradually opened the door and found his children with their hands tied and their mouths masked with tape.

"Oh God, what happened? What are you doing in here?" he asked them, as he pulled off the tape from their mouths.

"He took Mommy," said Brian.

"Who? Who took Mommy?" he demanded.

"The man who came inside the house," replied Trevor.

"How did he get in?"

"We let him in," Brian told him.

"Didn't I tell you to never invite strangers into the house?"

"Yes, Daddy. We're sorry," they cried.

"It's okay. Are you hurt?" Brendan asked.

"No, Daddy we're not hurt."

He ran into the bathroom to retrieve a pair of scissors to cut the rope around their hands.

"I'm going to call the police. Wait here and don't move until I get back."

Brendan dialed 9-1-1 and gave the dispatcher his address as he was shaking nervously. She informed him that the police would be arriving on the scene within minutes.

When the police entered the house, they ransacked the entire area including the upstairs searching for fingerprints.

"When did this happen?" asked one of the officers.

"I don't know," Brendan responded. "I was at work."

"Do you have any idea who might want to kidnap your wife?"

"I can't really think of anybody at this moment," he told them.

"How is your marriage?"

"I beg your pardon?"

"Look, it's just standard procedure for us to probe into your personal life if we're gonna try and find your wife. Would you say that you've had marital problems recently?"

"My marriage is fine. We're in the process of selling our home. What does my marriage have to do with my wife being missing?"

It was somewhat ironic that Brendan who was accustomed to interrogating witnesses for a living would be subject to such inquiry within the confines of his own home.

"Could you tell us if you noticed that your wife had been acting differently within the last few weeks?"

"No. My wife hasn't acted any different. She is the same woman I married on our wedding day.

"Well, maybe she wasn't kidnaped."

"I don't understand," replied Brendan, who paused momentarily. "You think my wife staged the whole thing? You think she would run off and leave her two children alone inside a closet without food or water? What is wrong with you people? I called you on the phone because my wife was taken hostage. Ask my kids. They saw everything."

"Would you mind if we question your children?" one of the officers requested.

"Please, do," Brendan said, as he went into the kitchen to get a glass of water. His hands were quivering so much from all the excitement that he dropped his drink. A thunderous echo permeated the outside wall.

"Everything okay in there?"

"Yes. I'm fine. I just broke something. Not a big deal."

As Brendan was sweeping up the glass that fell to the floor, the children, accompanied by the officers, went inside the den to answer some questions regarding their mother's despondent vanishing.

"Let's start from the beginning. You remember getting up. What did you do after that?" asked one of the veteran officers.

"We waited for Mommy to make us breakfast," said Brian.

"Where were you when the door bell rang?"

"We were upstairs in our rooms playing?"

"Where was your mother?"

"She was taking a shower," Trevor answered.

"How long was she in there?"

"I don't know about fifteen minutes," said Trevor.

"Do you remember what the man looked like?"

"He had a mask on and black gloves," Brian stated.

"How did he come in?"

"I let him in," Trevor replied.

"You just opened the door?"

"I opened the door and he forced his way inside and then took us upstairs."

"Did you try to call the police at that point?"

"No, because he told me to follow him upstairs or he would hurt our Mommy," Trevor informed the officer.

"Then what did he do?"

"He took us and put us in the closet. Then he tied us up and covered our mouths with tape," Brian said.

"Did you boys eat anything today?"

"No!" they both shouted in unison.

"Well, we'll fix that. What do you like? Do you like pizza?"

"Sure. Pizza is fine," the boys answered striving to maintain a positive outlook.

"Hey, Larry, order a large pizza and get some soda, will ya?"

"Sure thing. Right away, Sarge."

Based on the description provided by the children, the police knew that Alison was most likely abducted by the serial killer, but they didn't want to disclose that fact to Brendan since the outcome was quite obvious. Instead, they tried to convince him that it was a ransom situation originated by a disgruntled client.

When the pizza arrived, Brendan was too upset to eat. He paced back and forth trying to figure out who could have committed such a horrible act. He spent the night weeping and calling members of his family to inform them of Alison's unfortunate disappearance.

As midnight approached, it was time to turn in. Brendan knew there was nothing more he could do but wait for the police to call him. He prayed aloud for about an hour for the safe return of his wife. He found it difficult to fall asleep. The room was empty and he began to realize just how abandoned Alison must have felt. He had never been apart from his wife since they were married eight years ago.

Alison felt isolated and horrified. She knew Brendan and the children must have discovered her missing by now and she could no longer maintain her composure. She sobbed for hours and prayed that she would be reunited with her family.

After she got hold of herself and accepted the fact that she was a hostage, she thought of ways to buy herself more time. Alison had to somehow get inside the mind of the killer, but that would become her greatest challenge. She had an incentive not to relinquish weathering the storm. Her children were in her mind at all times. She told herself she was going to make it. She wasn't going to die at the hands of a selfish and abominable predator.

CHAPTER TWENTY-ONE

I T WAS A splendid afternoon and the smell of Spring filled the air. The moment we had anticipated for three years had finally arrived. It was Graduation Day for the Class of 2002. Students assembled outside the Civic Center dressed in cap and gown embracing their friends and becoming emotional.

Administrators began calling out the names of students in order to line everyone up so that commencement exercises could be carried out in a timely fashion. After an hour, the students made their way inside the large auditorium. As the traditional music of pomp and circumstance was played, the students marched down the side aisles and took their designated seats in the first five rows.

Dean Marshall then addressed the crowd with a message for the graduating class. He stated that he hoped students would take their legal experience seriously and remember why they attended law school.

"The client is most important in your role as legal counsel. If you entered this profession to make an exorbitant amount of money, you need not pursue your endeavor. Remember your moral and ethical obligation. Do not turn away from your personal views. Be sure to weigh your decisions accordingly. You are a reflection of the entire legal community. Continue to be an example

as you lead your lives and develop professional relationships in your careers. Your actions will speak highly of your character. You have entered a respected and prestigious occupation.

Over the years, the practice of law has been the subject of great debate. Attorneys have been disbarred, suspended, and reprimanded for engaging in immoral conduct that constitutes a violation of the rules of professional responsibility. These are isolated occurrences. They are not indicative of the entire legal community who strive to promote justice and fairness for the disadvantaged, the poor, or even the accused. Remember your obligation to your clients, your community and yourself."

After his short speech, he then introduced the guest speaker who spoke for about a half hour. It was getting humid inside the auditorium and there wasn't any ventilation. Students were becoming restless sitting there wondering when their diplomas would be distributed. I couldn't wait to get mine. Three years of hell and it finally paid off. We had earned our Juris Doctorate degrees. Now the hard part would be studying for the Bar Examination and then trying to find a job so we could begin to pay off our student loans.

I tried to get Kerri's attention as she was leaving the building. I didn't want this to be the last time that we saw each other. When she didn't see me waving my hand, I called out for her as she grabbed the handle on the door.

"Kerri, wait."

"Hey, Dillon, Congratulations! We did it."

"Yes. The same to you," I said.

"Are you going back to the law school for refreshments?" she asked.

"Probably not. My family is here and we're going to celebrate by going out for dinner."

"That's great, Dillon."

"Listen, Kerri – "

"Dillon, I know what you're going to say. What we had was great. You're a really nice guy and I'm glad that I met you. I think we just need to find ourselves. I know that I need to reexamine my life and I can't do that with a relationship."

"But I thought we loved each other?"

"Dillon, I do love you. Maybe you loved me more. I don't know. I'm sorry if I misled you. Those were not my intentions. You need to move on also. I'm not sure what it is you want to hear. If it's closure, then I'm telling you now that this relationship is over. I'm sorry, Dillon, but it's better this way."

That would become one of the worst days of my life. And it had to occur on my graduation. I would never forget it. Three years of being in love with a beautiful, sophisticated woman and I watched our relationship crumble to the ground. What was I going to do now? Kerri was the air I breathed. Without her, I couldn't possibly survive. Reality had finally set in, but I was still in denial. I was so optimistic that I was out of touch, period. Weeks had passed and I found it difficult getting out of bed. I cried a lot and kept looking at her picture. I wasn't ready to take it down from the wall in my bedroom.

I remained indoors refusing to communicate with the outside world. Anxiety and depression would begin to take its toll. Anti-depressants became my new breakfast cereal. I would refill my prescription more often than I would refill the coffee liners from the automatic machine located on the kitchen counter. I didn't even like coffee. But I needed something to drink that was going to energize me. I was up to five cups per day and so wired I couldn't think straight. My thoughts wandered through my head so quickly I was unable to make any sense of them. The pain was so strong at times it felt like my body crashed into a brick wall. Sure I knew there were plenty of fish in the ocean, but I wanted Kerri. It was too hard to let go, yet chasing her and convincing myself that we would be together someday wasn't doing me an ounce of good.

Brendan dropped his children off at his in-laws and took the baby to his parents' home in Derry. He had barely slept an hour tossing and turning all evening wondering if his wife's disappearance was some kind of horrible dream. Miraculously, he didn't let his personal life interfere with his job. Any other person would surely have had an emotional breakdown by now. But Brendan persevered. He kept his mind busy and focused on the one thing he was good at – Practicing law. He went to work because he had an obligation to his clients.

It wasn't a secret once the newspapers got wind of what happened. Everyone at work rushed him as he came off the elevator.

"Oh, my God, Brendan. You poor dear. Everything is going to be all right," said his receptionist.

Brendan, feeling uneasy about the situation, made an effort to smile and acknowledged the good nature of his employees. Then he made a statement to everyone present: "I'm sure everyone is familiar with the fact that my wife was abducted from our home early last week. My family hasn't received any updated information about her disappearance. I appreciate all of your prayers and concerns, but I think it would be best if we focus on the task before us which is the practice of law."

The police were tired of being on the losing end. Each time the killer succeeded it was a total mockery to law enforcement. They were beginning to take this personally. The unfortunate aspect to this whole situation was that police weren't any closer to the killer than when the first victim was tortured and killed over two years ago.

It was going on four days and Alison breathed a sigh of relief after awakening unharmed. She remained curious, however, wondering why the killer had kept her alive all of this time. What was his underlying motive? What did he see in Alison that he didn't observe in other women? This occupied her thoughts and instilled in her feelings of apprehension. She called out for him in the dark. She wanted to confront this faint-hearted creature face to face, but such an encounter was implausible due to the fact that he had disguised himself before making such an appearance.

"Hello? I need to speak with you. Can you come down here?" she asked.

A few moments later, the killer came downstairs to see what she wanted. He stood on the opposite side of the wall dressed in his usual attire with his face camouflaged.

"This better be important," he told her.

"What is it that you're doing if you don't mind me asking?"

"It's really none of your business."

"Fine. Don't tell me. It just doesn't seem logical for you to bring me here and not share your information. I guess my interest doesn't phase you. I could have helped you achieve your goal."

"Nonsense. This was all my idea and I will take the credit. Haven't you read the papers? I am a celebrity, highly renowned and acclaimed. Everyone is interested in what I have accomplished."

"I don't want to take any credit. Besides, you were the mastermind behind all of this. Only a genius could have contrived such a perfect plan," she said not having a clue as to what the killer's motives were.

"So you think I'm a genius?"

"Absolutely. You must be highly intelligent to evade the police every time," Alison replied, hoping to pacify the killer and get on his good side. "I think you're clever and the police – well, they're just plain jealous."

"Jealous?"

"Of course. I mean think about it. You get all of these beautiful women inside your home and the police can't do a damn thing about it. They are probably looking for you right now. If you ask me, I think they are full of envy," she said.

"I guess you're right."

"What are you going to do with me?" she asked in a sedate manner.

"I haven't decided yet," he replied, before walking back upstairs.

It was going to take a lot of effort on Alison's part to earn the killer's trust. But the only way to be certain her life would be spared was to discover the killer's whereabouts. His coup de maître was forthcoming. Time was of the essence if authorities were going to bring this executioner to justice.

Brendan called Kerri in the afternoon to inform her of what happened. She didn't know about his wife's disappearance. She took off from work that week to prepare for graduation and to be ready to move out of her apartment at the end of the leasehold. You could see the look of astonishment in her eyes once she heard the news.

"What? Oh, my God! When the hell did this happen?"

"Earlier in the week," Brendan responded.

"Have the police found anything?"

"Not really."

"Were there any witnesses? Somebody had to see something," Kerri said forcefully.

"The person came to our house. He was let in by my younger son."

"How did he know where you lived?" she asked.

"I don't know. That's what is so strange. This person obviously knows a lot about our family. He knew exactly when I left for work because he waited for me to leave the house before he entered. I think it's someone who wants money. They must have found out that I won a big settlement. He took Alison as ransom."

"Did your children see him?" Kerri asked.

"No. His face was covered," Brendan replied.

"What did the police do?"

"They searched for prints. You know, the usual," he said.

"Did they tap your phone?" she asked inquisitively.

"Yes."

"Do you have any idea of who it could be?" she asked.

"No. I can't think of anyone who would want to do this," Brendan replied.

"Well, you can't just rely on the police to find this guy. You have to do a little investigating of your own. You can't afford to waste any time."

"Kerri, I appreciate your concern, but I'm an attorney remember? I represent criminals. I don't hunt them down. That's the job of law enforcement."

"Fine. Let the police handle everything and you know what the consequences will be? Alison will become another statistic. Another woman who mysteriously vanished and was never found. You owe it to your wife to make every effort to find her. You owe it to your children. Do you want them growing up without a mother?"

"Of course not. I'm just saying we should let the police do their job. That's what they're paid to do," he told her.

"Brendan, have you thought that maybe your wife was abducted by the serial killer? It's been over two years since Maureen Hensley died. This killer is still out there. How many more victims do we have to read about? Yes, the police are doing everything they can, but it's not enough. They have their hands full. You know as well as I that they are understaffed around here."

"Wait a minute. I never said Alison was abducted by the same perpetrator who murdered Maureen Hensley."

"No, Brendan, but I am. It doesn't take a genius to figure this out. Think about it. All of his victims were young, pretty, vibrant women – just like Alison. Why would a complete stranger walk into your home and risk getting caught? He was stalking your wife. This guy is not killing at random. I don't care what the police think. I think he already knows who his victims are going to be. There must be similarities between all the women that just haven't been exposed yet," said Kerri.

"Look, I can't fucking think straight right now. My heart is pounding. I feel like my head is five times its normal size. How am I supposed to find out what these women had in common?" Brendan asked with little tenacity. "Our relationship was fine. We were excited about going on a vacation with the kids and we were selling our home. Alison wanted to move toward the beach closer to Maine, possibly."

"Okay, for starters you need to speak in the present tense when talking about your wife," she added.

"I'm sorry. You're right."

"Do you have some recent photos of your wife that I can copy and distribute?"

"Yes, I can get them for you."

"Good. Someone out there will recognize your wife and hopefully provide the missing link to this whole thing."

"Where are you going to place her picture?" he asked.

"Everywhere, Brendan."

"Do you think she is still alive?"

"Yes, I do."

"What are you going to do?" he asked with anxiety.

"Don't worry, I'll handle this. You stay at home with the children and wait by the phone in case the police hear anything."

"You can't do this alone," Brendan told her.

"I'm not. I'm going to call my friends to help."

Kerri hung up the phone and called a few of her friends from law school to see if they wanted to help her distribute flyers in the area. She spent the next day posting Alison's picture on the windshield of cars and handing them to customers at supermarkets. Kerri was quite optimistic about finding any clues to help bring Alison home. She drove to the local library and looked up articles on microfilm about the latest victims in order to establish some foundation for tracking the killer's path.

After approaching the reference desk for assistance, she was pointed in the right direction. Placing her pocketbook on the table, she glanced at the list of periodicals on the shelf.

Let's see, I need to look at articles within the last two years, she thought. There were at least one hundred articles and Kerri didn't have any information to facilitate her search. Requiring material on missing women and unable to narrow her research due to unfamiliarity with the hardware, Kerri found the task much more difficult than anticipated.

"What the hell am I looking at?" she said, becoming frustrated at her inability to make progress.

After clicking on various icons within the library's internal computer system and coming to the realization that she had no clue whatsoever in operating the program, she called a reference assistant who recommended that Kerri sit through the fifteen minute tutorial before beginning her assignment. By the time the library closed for the evening, Kerri had printed out over one hundred pages on articles written about dead bodies discovered along the Merrimack River. She walked over to the front desk and paid the librarian the fee for copying the material.

Brendan, although afflicted with great sorrow still found time to play video games with his children. It was around seven-thirty when he heard a knock at the front door. After turning on the porch light and opening the door, a police officer introduced himself.

"Good evening, Mister Schneider, I presume?"

"Yes. Is everything all right?" Brendan asked.

"I'm afraid I have some terrible news. About an hour ago, a body was found outside Newton and we would like you to come down to the hospital and identify it."

"What am I supposed to do with my children?" he wondered, while starring in disbelief.

"Officer Flanagan will remain here with your children while we escort you to the medical examiner's office," said one of the deputies. Brendan retrieved his jacket and told his children he would return shortly. His hands had begun to shake uncontrollably as he sat in the back of the police cruiser. He was overcome with nausea and on the verge of an anxiety attack.

"Are you okay?" asked one of the men.

"Yes. I'll be fine. I just feel a little queasy," he told them.

"We can pull over if you like."

"No. Keep going. I'll be okay."

They arrived at the examiner's office and went upstairs to view the body. It was a two-story building made of old-fashioned brick. The musty smell in the hallway was strong enough to make you vomit. Brendan had to hold his nose while working his way up the steps. Once inside, Brendan took off his jacket and placed it on the floor that was filled with dust and cobwebs. The officer then escorted him through the door leading to the room where the cadavers were kept.

"Okay, you may want to put some smelling salt under your nose to prevent fainting or headache," said the medical examiner. Brendan adhered to his recommendation and placed a small amount of salt as directed.

"All right, I'm going to pull the sheet down now," the examiner told Brendan, who was beginning to become emotional. He took down the sheet and Brendan afraid to look at first, gradually turned his face and opened his eyes. Tears flowed down his face and gasping for air he said in a faint voice, "That is not my wife."

"Excuse me?" said the examiner.

"I said – this woman is not Alison."

The police thought the deceased woman matched Alison's description and were appalled at learning they had discovered another unidentified body. Brendan, although grief stricken, was relieved once he realized his wife may still be alive. He arrived back home an hour later and found Kerri's BMW in his driveway. She immediately opened the front door and just stared at him thinking he had just been given the most unpleasant news.

"Hey, Kerri."

"Hello, Brendan."

"I went down to the medical examiner's office because I had to identify a body," he said.

"I know. Officer Flanagan told me when I first got here. I'm so sorry, Brendan. I thought we had enough time to catch this guy before he hurt your wife. I really wanted to help find Alison. I wanted to believe she was still alive."

"Wait a minute. Let me finish. I didn't say the woman I looked at was Alison."

"What are you saying, Brendan?"

"I went down to identify the victim. It turns out that the woman on the table wasn't Alison after all."

"Oh, Brendan, I'm so relieved. This is marvelous. Alison is alive. I know she is. We're gonna find her and bring her home," Kerri declared with exhilaration.

CHAPTER TWENTY-TWO

A WEEK HAD PASSED, and still no sign of Alison. Brendan's facial expression had said it all. He was at his darkest moment. The love of his life, his eternal flame, his other half, was missing. Traumatic times such as these can make the strong vulnerable and predisposed to engage in conduct that ordinarily, they would reject without thought.

He started to question whether he would ever see Alison again. He craved love and companionship, but couldn't get either one from his significant other.

Kerri fell asleep on the couch one evening after putting the kids to bed while Brendan was busy representing someone with a traffic violation in Municipal Court. He returned home around nine-thirty and found her lying on the sofa. He gently touched her arm and she awoke.

"Kerri, why don't you go inside and sleep in my bed. It's more comfortable. I'll sleep on the couch."

"Oh, Brendan, it's getting late. I better go home."

"Please, I would really like you to stay tonight. I don't want to be alone if you don't mind."

Feeling sorry for him, she decided to take him up on his offer. She kicked off her size nine and a half Steve Madden's and wandered past the foyer leading to the stair case. She arrived at the top of the stairs and walked into the master bedroom. She washed her face in the bathroom and brushed her teeth. Then she returned with her hair tied back and climbed into the newly furnished, queen sized bed.

"Would you like an extra blanket?" he asked.

"No. I'm fine. Thank you, Brendan," she replied.

Brendan closed the door and turned down the lights in the hallway. He walked downstairs into the kitchen and grabbed a bottle of Heineken from the refrigerator that happened to be the last one. He sat at the table reminiscing about his life for over an hour. After he grew tired, he walked outside and tossed the empty bottle of beer into the recycling bin in the backyard. Upon his return, he lied down on the sofa and dozed off within minutes of his face hitting the pillow.

Brendan slept for about three hours, but it wasn't tranquil. He quivered in his sleep and had a horrible nightmare. He shouted out Alison's name several times. Brendan awoke distressed and was sweating profusely. Kerri was startled by his yelling and ran downstairs to comfort him.

"Brendan, are you okay? I think you were dreaming. Oh, honey, you're sweating and shaking."

Kerri went to get a towel with ice and a glass of water for him to drink.

"Here, put this towel around your face and drink this," she told him.

"Thanks. I'm okay," he reassured her.

"Do you want to talk about it? It might help you feel better?" Kerri suggested.

"No, I'll be all right, Kerri. I'm just a little stressed right now."

Kerri then removed the towel from Brendan's face. She pulled up his blanket and gave him a kiss on the cheek. Then they stared into each other's eyes. She smiled at him and he grabbed her hand. Brendan pulled her close to him. For a moment, he convinced himself that Alison was gone for good. He had a deep feeling of sexual desire and attraction toward Kerri.

"Brendan, we can't do this," she said.

"Please, Kerri, just tonight. I need you."

"It's wrong. You're a married man with kids. We can't. It's not fair to your wife. I won't be a party to this."

"My wife isn't coming back and you know it."

"No, I don't know anything and neither do you. You have to remain strong and have faith. Now you can drown in your sorrows or you can help me try and put all of this together. But regardless of your choice, Brendan, I'm going to find your wife alive."

"The police have done everything they can. I'm trying to be strong, but I also need to be realistic here. There is a strong possibility I may never see Alison again."

"I need you to stay positive. Look at me, your kids need you to stay positive."

Brendan paused a moment while thinking about Kerri's words.

"You're right. I've been a little selfish, I'm sorry. I just can't make any sense of this. I want this horrible nightmare to be over."

"I know, but for now we need to take it day by day," Kerri replied while observing the time on the VCR clock.

"Well, I guess I'll get back to bed," he said.

"Good night, Brendan. See you in the morning."

"Good night, Kerri and thanks for everything."

The Fourth of July was right around the corner and wholesalers were advertising Class C fireworks that were legal in New Hampshire. So many cars jammed these outlet stores it looked like South of the Border. The biggest purchases were roman candles and sky rockets. This store had everything from cherry bombs to M-80s'. There was something for every age group including children, who became overwhelmed at the sight of sparklers. These were dirt cheap and a box of twelve cost one dollar. This place made out like a bandit and they were open only two months out of the year.

Kerri drove down to Portsmouth which was an hour from Ardmore and watched the fireworks display that evening. She had met up with a friend from law school who was helping her track down the person responsible for Alison's disappearance.

"Hi, Kerri. How are you?" Meg asked before embracing her.

"Great. I'm hanging in there. I have the Bar Exam to think about," Kerri replied.

"Please, don't remind me. I haven't even looked at any of my notes yet. I can't believe the exam is in three weeks."

"Are you taking it in Boston or Springfield?" asked Kerri.

"I'm going to Springfield. There are fewer people and I think it will be less stressful. I know people who take it in Boston say it's a real nightmare," Meg said frantically. "So how did everything work out with Dillon, if you don't mind me asking?"

"Oh, no – it's okay. I don't mind. I told him we needed to go our separate ways. He was reluctant at first, but I think he's over it now. I wished him well. He is really a good guy. I hope he finds somebody to make him happy. It just wasn't meant to be."

"It's a shame. Everybody in school thought you guys were gonna be married and everything. You were always together."

"Yeah, but Dillon wanted to move too quickly. I wanted to take things slow. He wanted a marriage and a family. I wasn't ready for that. I think he expected too much out of the relationship and I just couldn't offer him what he desired."

"How is Brendan handling everything?"

"Not good. He's not the same person. You can see it in his work. His concentration just isn't there. I told him to take a leave of absence, but he refused. I feel so bad for him and the kids."

"That's so good that you are there for him. He is really lucky to have you for a friend."

"Thanks. He is a great friend too. That's why I need to help him. And I need your help too, Meg."

"Well, I found some stuff that you might find interesting. I'm not sure if it will help though."

"No, by all means—please share your information with me."

"Okay. I found that all of the female victims were college graduates."

"Yeah, what else?"

"They lived within one hundred miles of each other."

"Okay, but I need something to link this to the murderer."

"I also found that all of these women, except Alison were pregnant at one time, but decided to have an abortion. They belonged to the same pro choice organization."

"What? Stop right there. You mean these women knew each other?"

"Yes."

"Meg, you may be on to something. Oh, my God. That's it."

"Tell me what the hell you are talking about," Meg said, becoming flustered at her inability to comprehend the situation.

"Don't you see Meg? The killer pursues women who terminated their pregnancies. He hates these women for some reason."

"Maybe he didn't know they had abortions," Meg told her.

"Impossible. There were too many killings. It's more than coincidental. This guy knew these women," Kerri responded. "He may have been a doctor for all we know."

"Why would he want to hurt innocent women?" Meg asked.

"I don't know. This is a psychotic serial killer. Don't ask me to explain what's inside his mind."

"How do you know he's not killing for another reason?"

"I'm not sure, but we need to call every hospital in the state and find out who has access to medical records," Kerri instructed.

"What makes you think the killer had access to medical records?" Meg asked. "Kerri, you're assuming the killer is an employee of a hospital. Besides, there are hundreds of medical centers in this state not to mention thousands of employees. How would we find this guy anyway?"

"Look, do you want to help me or not?"

"Yes, I just think we're going about it all wrong."

"How would you like to handle this?" Kerri asked, while becoming annoyed at Meg's lack of interest.

"I think we should find the doctors who treated these women first and then visit those individual hospitals. Otherwise, we are working backwards," Meg advised.

"Fine. Let's obtain the phone numbers of the victims' families and see if we can piece this together."

"I think that would be our best option, Kerri."

"I hope you're right."

"The part that doesn't make sense is why he would want to hurt Alison. Alison never had an abortion," Kerri said.

"I don't know, Kerri. Maybe he is seeking revenge against Brendan."

"What did Brendan do?"

"Maybe it's what he didn't do."

"What are you talking about?" Kerri retorted.

"Brendan handles a lot of criminal matters. Isn't it possible that Brendan couldn't get some guy off and now that he's out of prison, he's seeking vengeance."

"Meg, Brendan only represented one defendant on trial for murder and he was released after being wrongfully convicted."

"Well, somebody has it in for him."

"I don't think so. I think this guy is after women who had abortions, period."

"Then why Alison? Why a woman who had a family?"

"Because he wants her."

"What?"

"That's right. All of these other women he killed because they did something evil in his eyes. They were sinners. They needed to be punished. He administered their execution. Now he found someone who he actually respects and he can't kill her because he would recognize his own wrongdoing. The other murders in his mind were justified. Killing Alison wouldn't be. Perhaps he has finally found what he perceives as the perfect woman."

"If he doesn't kill her what will he do with her?" Meg asked with curiosity.

"He will keep her for his own unless we find him," Kerri told her.

"Should we split up and go to different hospitals?" asked Meg.

"Not right now. Remember, we only want to obtain medical records. We're not investigators. I don't want them to know what we're doing."

"Wait a second. Didn't you tell me that Alison recently had a baby?" Meg inquired.

"Yes, a few months ago. Why?"

"Shouldn't we check the physicians and medical staff at the hospital where she delivered?"

"Meg, that is an excellent idea. I think you and I are going to find this creep and when we do he's gonna pay."

Kerri and Meg drove to Salem Medical Center where Alison had been treated during her pregnancy. When they arrived, they asked a gentleman employed by the hospital to direct them to the medical records department.

"Walk down this hallway until you see the elevators and take it to the fourth floor," he told them. Once they arrived at the window, they asked the woman if they could obtain Alison's paperwork.

"Are you picking up records for Miss Schneider because we didn't receive any authorization release form," the woman responded.

"This is an emergency situation," Kerri replied. "Miss Schneider is not able to retrieve her records and her husband Brendan has given us permission to obtain them."

"I understand, but you have to request them. We can't just stop what we're doing and copy them. They're in archives and we have to pull them from storage. It will take a few days."

"We don't have that much time."

"I'm sorry, but that is our procedure. If you like, I can have you fill out this form and when the records come in we can call you."

"Fine," Kerri said, growing angry at wasting valuable time.

They exited the hospital parking lot and paid the fee which was only $3.00 for the first two hours.

"Now what do we do?" asked Meg.

"We sit and wait. There's nothing to do now," Kerri said. "I think somebody at Salem is responsible for all of these killings. Only the doctor and members of staff could obtain personal information about these patients. If Alison was treated at Salem and later abducted isn't it safe to assume the killer works there?"

"I guess," Meg replied.

"I'm telling you I have this gut feeling that this guy works at Salem Medical. It makes sense. You'll see. When we get those records we'll find out who worked on the day Alison was kidnaped and who was off," Kerri stated with all the confidence in the world.

Kerri called Brendan at his office to give him a progress report on any possible leads, but the receptionist told her he was in court all morning. She decided to meet up with Brendan at the Middlesex County Superior Court Administration Building. She searched the library on the first floor and then the civil assignment office, but came up empty. She thought maybe he might turn up in the cafeteria, but that was closed until lunch. After walking up three flights of stairs, she had finally found him speaking with another attorney in Judge Crawford's court room.

"Kerri, what are you doing here?"

"Hi, Brendan. I called your office and they said you were here."

"Kerri, I have to appear before the judge in about fifteen minutes."

"I just wanted you to know that Meg and I visited the records department at Salem Hospital and they said it would take a few days to get all of the necessary paperwork."

"That's fine. I'll have to wait until then. You really think somebody at the hospital is responsible?"

"That's the feeling that I'm getting, Brendan. Nothing else really makes any sense."

"Well, I will trust your instincts."

"You know I won't let you down."

"Kerri, this is the Honorable Timothy Crawford. Judge Crawford, I would like you to meet my good friend and assistant, Kerri Cafferty. Kerri recently graduated law school and has helped me with many of my cases. Now she is committing herself to an even greater task in trying to help me find my wife."

"It is a pleasure to meet you, Kerri," said the judge. "I hope you are successful in capturing the individual who did this."

"Thank you, Your Honor. It was nice meeting you as well," she said.

"Kerri, if you're not busy tonight and you want to stop by, I'll be home all evening."

"I have to see, Brendan. I'll call you later."

When she left the court house, she took out her cell phone and hit speed dial to call me at my apartment. I was shocked when I picked up the receiver and heard her voice on the other end.

"Hello?" I answered.

"Dillon, it's Kerri."

"Hey, how are you? I'm so glad you called me."

"Look, Dillon, it's not what you think. I'm not calling to ask you out or anything like that. I need your help."

"What do you want?" I replied with much discouragement.

"I need you to help me find the killer?"

"Kerri, what are you talking about?" I echoed with confusion.

"The person who kidnaped Alison," she replied, as though I should have already known that.

"How can I help? I'm not a police officer."

"You can help by making some phone calls and visiting hospitals where the killer might be working."

"How do you know he works in a hospital?" I asked.

"Because the only way he could have found their addresses was to obtain the information while they were undergoing treatment at the hospital."

"Why must the killer be from the hospital?" I insisted.

"Damn it, Dillon, don't argue with me. I need you to trust me on this."

"Fine. If you think this guy did it – what was his motive?"

"He hates women who had abortions. All of the victims have terminated their pregnancies."

"Doesn't Alison have children?"

"Yes, but this guy won't kill her."

"How are you so sure?"

"Because he likes her. In his mind she is what a woman should be. Are you going to help me, Dillon?"

"Do I have a choice?" I asked with banter.

"What does that mean?"

"I don't know. It just seems like the only time you call me now is when you need help with something or you're trying to be a hero for Brendan."

"A hero? I respect Brendan. He gave me a job when I needed experience. I owe him. He has a family. I'm not doing this for the glory, Dillon, I can promise you."

"Do you love this guy?" I asked.

"Dillon, why are you doing this to yourself?"

"I just need to know," I said.

"No, Dillon. I told you before, Brendan and I are friends. Is that what you needed to hear?"

"No. What I need to hear is that you still care about me, but I can see that isn't going to happen."

"I don't know why I bothered calling you. I thought maybe you might come to your senses. Boy, was I wrong."

"See, there you go again. Put all the blame on me. It's not my fault that you ended this relationship. All the while I'm blaming myself as if I've been some horrible person. You're the one who gave up on me."

"Whatever you think, Dillon. I'm sorry I upset you."

"Kerri, in spite of what you think I care for you and I'm still upset about what happened. Yeah, I know you're over this but I'm not. I'm sorry. It's gonna take some time. I mean I have feelings. When someone breaks up with me, I kind of take it personally."

"Look, I know how you feel, Dillon. I told you I want to maintain a friendship, but we wouldn't be intimate any longer. The choice is yours. You know where to find me if you're interested in cooperating with us."

I pondered a moment about what she had said and then replied, "Okay. What would you like me to do?"

"I want you to find out where these women had their abortions. Was it in a hospital, a medical facility, wherever. Find out who the doctors were and any staff members who assisted them. Also look at the dates. The dates are most important. I want you to check the date each woman was abducted and see if any physicians or employees having access to records were off from work that day."

"How many women are we talking about?" I asked.

"Right now, there are four, but who knows. There are probably some who are unaccounted for. Just focus on the names I give you. Here, write these down: "Maureen Hensley, Rita Bellows, Lorraine Nagle, and don't forget to question Debbie Meyers, the bartender. I need you to do this as soon as possible."

CHAPTER
TWENTY-THREE

I PROMISED KERRI I would look into those names that she had given me. When the alarm sounded, I awoke still feeling exhausted from lack of sleep the night before. I was so tired, I put the milk back in the kitchen cabinet after pouring myself a bowl of cereal. My face had that shaggy and ruffled look from not shaving in a few days.

Once I took a cold shower, I felt energized and started making headway. I put on my Levi's and tennis shoes and departed for Salem State Medical Center. After traveling a few miles, I noticed a light turned on inside the dashboard of the car. I was low on gas. I pulled into the nearest Exxon and rolled down my window.

"Hi, can I have twenty dollars of the regular please." I couldn't believe that twenty bucks would barely fill half of the tank. If prices continued to soar I was contemplating selling my car. And that's nothing. I felt sorry for owners of trucks and SUVs' who were shelling out $75.00 each time they filled up. Driving became a nuisance. Of course, everybody could have switched to mass transit but how long would that last? People in New Hampshire couldn't welcome that opportunity because no train ran through their state. Car pooling was another option, but I didn't want to impose on someone nor did I want to rely on that person to get me to my destination. These gas companies sure had us over a barrel. *No pun intended.*

I arrived at the hospital and parked in the back lot designated for visitors and over-night guests. I took the elevator to the fourth floor and followed the sign for the records department. When I approached the desk, a woman assisted me.

"Can I help you?"

"Yes. I'm here to pick up medical records for an Alison Schneider that have been requested a few days ago," I told her.

"Sure. Let me check."

A few moments later, she returned holding a packet of papers about an inch in length. This looked like it was going to cost me a fortune.

"How much is it per page?" I asked.

"Seventy-five cents," she replied.

"Oh, crap. How many pages are we talking about?"

"One hundred and twelve."

"Okay, so that's like what – I don't know – maybe twenty bucks," I responded without a clue. Now I know why I went to law school.

"Try eighty-four dollars," she said, smiling at my inaccurate estimation.

"Do you accept checks?"

"Yes. Make it payable to Salem State Medical. Sir, I will also need two forms of identification."

"Sure, I have my driver's license and my law school ID."

"All right, you're all set. Have a nice day."

"Thank you for your help."

I took the papers Kerri requested and drove to her apartment. When I arrived, the door was already partially opened. I knocked first, then stepped inside. I found her sitting on the living room floor clutching a diet soda.

"Hi, Dillon. Can I get you something to drink?" she asked.

"No. I'm good thanks," I told her.

I handed her the package of papers that she had requested. She inspected each page looking for names of physicians and significant dates.

"Here. Okay. She was treated on December 5th. Her physician was Dr. Sahns, but he didn't return to see her until three days later. Why? Hand me those papers that show the date Maureen Hensley was last seen. Look, the police reports show Maureen was probably abducted sometime after December 7th. She went to dinner with her mom and aunt the night before and they never saw her alive after that."

"Kerri, you're jumping to conclusions. That's definitely a big jump. I mean the guy took off work a few days. You need more than that."

"Dillon, I think he should still be treated as a suspect. It's more than just a coincidence."

"The police wouldn't even detain him for questioning."

"Please, Dillon. I don't need you to be disagreeable right now."

"I'm not trying to argue with you. I'm stating the facts. The fact that this guy happened to be out of work the same time a woman was abducted is a far cry from probable cause. You would have half the male population brought into the station house."

"Really? What if I told you Dr. Sahns also treated Rita Bellows for a urinary tract infection?"

"That means nothing, Kerri. It shows he's a popular doctor."

"Come on, Dillon. Give me some credit here. You don't think this sounds suspicious?"

"Let's assume you're right. Where do we begin to look? Where is the murder weapon? We can't just go to the police and say arrest that man."

"No, I didn't say that. I think we should follow him home and see if he leads us to anything."

"Kerri, I know you want to find Alison. But you have to be realistic here. We can't harass this guy. We'll end up being sued and we can kiss our careers good-bye."

"Dillon, just go with me to his house and if nothing turns up, I'll drop it."

"Fine."

"He always does his rounds later in the afternoon. He has office hours in the morning. I know what he looks like. I've seen him before. Just meet me there around four in the afternoon."

As usual, Kerri met me right on schedule. I don't think she was late for anything her entire life.

"Dillon, I called his office and the nurse practitioner told me he was still here. Let's find him," she said.

We started with the first floor and split up. Kerri checked the oncology wing and the pediatrics section of the hospital. I walked leisurely toward cardiology and the telemetry unit. Both of us were unsuccessful at finding him. The second floor had only the cafeteria and kitchen so we didn't bother inspecting it. As we stepped off the elevator on the third floor, we heard his name being paged over the intercom.

"Dr. Sahns – two . . . two . . . five, stat. Dr. Sahns – two . . . two . . . five, stat."

We knew he had to be on the floor somewhere so we waited by the nurses' station. Within minutes, he arrived carrying his chart and stethoscope.

"Yes, you can start her on the morphine drip." he told one of the nurses.

He signed some paperwork and authorization forms and then told everyone to have a good night. He was going home to his wife and kids.

"I think we're wasting our time here, Kerri. He doesn't look like a serial killer to me."

"What does a serial killer look like Dillon?"

"Damn it, this guy has a family for Christ's sake."

"We only have to follow him."

"But what good will that do? If he's going home he's not going to kill anybody tonight."

"I just want to see where he lives. Debbie Meyers said the killer lived near a wooded area surrounded by cornfields and farm land."

We followed him to the parking lot and watched from a distance as he climbed into his brand new Porsche with glossy rims and a dual sun roof. Then Kerri and I traveled behind without making it obvious that he was being pursued. I was growing angry at having to drive for over forty-five minutes. I knew we weren't getting anywhere, but I drove to pacify her. I had to show her I still cared. I was just glad to have her sit next to me. It was like old times again. His car exited the ramp and turned into a development of similar homes. He pulled into the driveway. The garage door lifted, he drove in and then he was gone.

"See, I told you nothing would turn up. He's not the guy."

"Okay, Okay. I guess you're happy you told me so."

"Come on, Kerri, I'm trying to be nice here. We know it isn't him because of the area. I don't see any farms and his house is next to ten other houses. I don't see any dark road or cornfields."

"Now what do we do?" she asked.

"I'm going to bed."

"Tomorrow, Meg and I are going to Bedford to obtain more information."

"Well, I hope you find what you're looking for."

I drove Kerri back to the hospital so she could pick up her car. It was after nine, and I hadn't eaten any dinner. I was too tired to cook and settled for pizza and a soft drink. By ten – thirty, I was out like a light.

Two weeks later, the killer displayed his frustration when he brought Alison her dinner. He entered the basement that resembled a dungeon and approached her wearing a dark outfit. He was infuriated that her husband had begun to search and detect clues that might lead to his incrimination. Now Alison had to worry that the killer may seek revenge of another kind.

"Your husband has disappointed me," he told her. "If he was wise, he would refrain from doing something he might soon regret."

"What are you talking about?" Alison inquired.

"Your pretty boy, Brendan. It seems he has given up the practice of law and now wants to play police officer. He thinks he is coming to save you. But we both know that will never happen."

"Look, why don't you let me go? They are going to find you eventually."

"Shut up. Do you realize I have the power to keep you alive or kill you in an instance?"

"I know you won't hurt me."

"Oh, really? What makes you so sure. I have killed before I can kill again."

"Because you want me. Tell me, why are you avoiding me? Why do you hide your face and remain a coward?"

"I told you to shut up. You better pray that lover boy stops playing investigator or your children will become orphans."

"My husband doesn't even know who you are."

"Your husband has been requesting your medical records and asking a lot of questions. I would hate to have to silence him for good."

"Leave my husband out of this. If it's me you want fine – then finish me off like you did those other women."

"You are very courageous to say that."

"No, I'm tired. I'm tired of being trapped and treated like a prisoner. I have done nothing wrong."

"A prisoner? I'll tell you what it's like to be a prisoner. Try having a father who was never around and a mother who stayed in the relationship even though he beat her repeatedly because she convinced herself that she loved him. If that's not bad enough, tell me how it feels to be born by accident. My mother didn't want me. She decided to have an abortion because my father told her to. The only reason I'm here today is because the abortion was botched and my mother's health was at risk. I was never expected to be born. My own mother abandoned me. Do you see now why I hate women who decide to terminate their pregnancies? You all remind me of her. And you think I don't have a right to play God? What right did they have to play God? None. And now I've made sure no innocent child would ever be deprived of life again. I am setting the record straight. I am punishing those who kill by injecting them with their own venom."

The killer intended to justify his actions through the process of analogy. Terminating the lives of women were equated with torturing embryos during an abortion procedure.

"You can't be judge, jury, and executioner. You don't have the right to take life no matter how justified you think you are."

"Bullshit! Every time I kill, I save another life," he said, with rage.

"You're sick. You don't know what reality is."

"You're a hypocrite."

"No, I live my life and don't judge others," Alison replied.

"Would you have an abortion?"

"No, I wouldn't."

"Yet, you think it's all right for women to terminate their pregnancies because it's their choice? Are you sure I'm the real executioner?" he asked scornfully.

"I don't know who you are. And I don't know why you have taken me as your hostage. I have not done anything to offend you."

"I have watched you over the years. You have delighted me in the worst way. Your husband is a lucky man. But you are with me now."

"Don't you understand I have a family? I am not yours. You can never have me. You will never belong to me. When the police find you, you're going to rot in prison."

"Like hell I am. There are people out there who support what I do. They would say keep up the good work. They understand the mission and my struggle. Apparently, you don't, which is a shame. You aren't any different than all the other pro choice killers. Those are your murderers. Lock them up."

"Why are you so upset? You're alive. Your mother didn't kill you."

"No, but she wanted to and that's why when I found out over twenty years later, I poisoned her."

"You took your mother's life?"

"Yes. I had to – she hated me. Funny thing is everybody thought she died from heart failure. I must leave you now for I have a very important project ahead of me. I will return later this evening," he told her.

Alison tried desperately to think of who the killer might be, but couldn't conjure up any suspects. She thought of Brendan's friends and those he had met in law school. Maybe it was somebody who was jealous about their relationship. Perhaps it was a disgruntled client who was seeking revenge. Defense lawyers always have to be circumspect when it comes to those individuals seeking the advice of professionals. I think about that quite often and wonder if I should have chosen another profession.

Kerri and Meg had just left Bedford Medical Center to retrieve patients' records and were driving home on a dark, winding road with a steep decline. The weather was unpleasantly cold and wet as it had just begun to rain which made the roadways quite slippery. This was a hazardous thoroughfare to be traveling, even on an ordinary day due to the outlandish dimensions of the street.

Many drivers had lost their lives in this area because they took the obvious danger for granted. You could see exactly where these tragic accidents took place as you drove by and observed crosses made of palms planted in the ground. As Kerri looked in her rear view mirror, she noticed an unmarked car behind her starting to accelerate and pursue her, leaving very little space between the front of the car and her bumper.

"Why is this guy right on my tail?" Kerri asked.

Meg turned around to get a glimpse of the car and told Kerri to speed up.

"I can't go any faster, Meg. This road has curves."

"Well, do something because I think we're being followed."

As soon as she said that, the rear of Kerri's car was struck with a high degree of force.

"Son of a bitch, I can't believe he hit me."

"Just step on it and let's get outta here!" Meg shouted frantically.

"Get his license plate number, Meg."

"I can't see. He keeps moving from side to side. I can't see it."

"He's trying to pass you, he's coming up on your side!" Kerri roared."

"What do I do?" Meg asked in horror.

"I'll try to run him off the road."

Kerri must have felt like she was driving on the Indy 500 preventing the other driver from gaining any momentum, but she lost control of the car which allowed the driver to get through.

"He's gonna run into us, damn it."

"Hold on, Meg," Kerri uttered loudly, as the driver intentionally whacked the right side of the car and drove off.

Kerri was left with substantial damage to her car after landing in a ditch. She also had a flat tire. After replacing it with the donut, the girls were able to drive the three miles they needed to get home.

"Kerri, I told you we should have stayed out of this," Meg cried.

"Don't worry, he was just trying to scare us."

"Well, I think he accomplished his goal."

"Meg, if we stop now, we'll never find Alison."

"I'm done, Kerri. Please, just drop me off at the house," Meg replied trying to catch her breath. "I'm not getting any more involved. Our lives are at risk. I don't wanna end up dead with my body parts spread out all over the river."

"Fine. I will hunt this guy myself."

Kerri dropped Meg off and returned to her apartment. When she arrived inside, the first thing she did was hit the play button on her answering machine to retrieve her two messages. She listened attentively while opening her mail. The first message was from Brendan telling her he would be out of the office tomorrow because he had to attend a pre-trial settlement conference in New Haven. The second message was from a male with a deep voice who threatened Kerri with imminent bodily harm if she didn't abandon her pursuit of the killer. The message read:

"You seem to be quite the confident one. I can assure you if you continue in your quest, they will be looking for you as well. I will not warn you again. Stay out of this or you will pay the ultimate price."

Kerri began to shiver wondering how he managed to procure her phone number that was unlisted. She bolted down the front door and sealed off all the windows. Paranoid that she might be subject to immediate danger, she obtained the metal bat in her closet and carefully examined all of her rooms. Her search revealed nothing. Then, she phoned the police in order to trace the call. They reached their destination within ten minutes and were led into the kitchen. Kerri played the message again and they advised her to take his intent to inflict harm, seriously. The police also placed a tap on her phone in case the alleged killer called her again.

"We can find out where the call was placed by tomorrow. I don't want you to leave your apartment for any reason. If he calls again, do not hesitate to dial 9-1-1. Have a good evening, ma'am," said one of the enforcement officers. Kerri locked the door behind them and kept the baseball bat beside her at all times. I'm sure she was wondering if perhaps she had taken her agenda too far. But Kerri was a strong woman. She wouldn't back down from anything, even violent threats.

She had begun the role of prosecutor. It was now up to her to prove her case. Find the person responsible for abducting Alison and killing those other innocent women. It started out as a favor to Brendan. Now it has become her only mission in life. She would do whatever it took to capture this horrifying and atrocious demon even if it meant sacrificing her own life.

———

Of course, I knew that if I became involved in the hunt for the serial killer, my life would be placed in peril as well. I was hoping Kerri would come to her senses and let New York's Finest handle everything. It's not like the search was abandoned. The Massachusetts State Police Troopers were communicating their efforts with the FBI and other law enforcement agencies. Kerri was wasting her time trying to find the killer by applying the process of elimination. She had too many potential suspects as choices. If not this doctor then that doctor. Before you knew it, Kerri would be questioning every physician who performed an abortion. Okay, she had managed to obtain the killer's interest, possibly, even intimidate him enough to alter his course, but he was too clever to back off. I loved Kerri and I would have done anything to assist her, but I also realized nobody is worth dying for. Her outlook was quite different.

Brendan gave her the first position she ever had in the legal profession. He taught her the ropes. He helped her financially when funds were unavailable. He wrote her letters of reference and made some phone calls to judges for possible openings in judicial clerkships. Brendan basically spoon fed her. In her mind, she owed him big time. But I didn't have a stake in this. I went to law school, period. I never signed up to be a volunteer investigator. My whole take on this was quite simplistic. Don't bite off more than you can chew. Whoever this guy was, he made it known of his intentions to carry out any threats. Although his warnings may have constituted mere words, they shouldn't have been taken with a grain of salt. Kerri was in too deep. She knew too much. Her interest became an obsession. If she wasn't careful, she would be another statistic.

The police department phoned Kerri the next morning and told her that the harassing phone call she received was placed from a public telephone outside the city limits of Landsdale. They weren't able to obtain any other information including fingerprints or voice exemplars.

It was July 21st, the day before the dreaded Bar Exam and I started packing for my two night stay in Boston. My apartment was only twenty-five miles from the site of the exam, but I didn't want to risk arriving late because of traffic congestion or road construction. Besides, it was just easier to stay in the hotel where the test was actually going to be administered. The downside was that it cost $350 per night. Okay, I know it's Boston, but I expected a suite for that kind of money. Instead, I stayed in a single room with absolutely no view of the city. Seven hundred dollars thrown away and I didn't even take the exam yet. Forget about sleep. I was lucky if I was in REM mode for an hour.

I tossed and turned all night wondering about this test. Three years of studying my ass off in law school and it finally came down to this. If the price of the hotel wasn't steep enough how about forking over an additional $800 to take the Bar. Now factor in review courses, materials, study guides, practice questions, and you're talking a thousand and some change. But I loved this city and I was glad to visit it again; no matter what it cost.

It was approaching noon, and I took the elevator down to the lobby. I proceeded through the revolving glass doors and was now outside. It had to be at least ninety degrees and temperatures were expected to climb for the next four hours. My goal was to forget about the exam and do whatever I could to clear my head.

I walked a few blocks to the Commons and found a pleasant, cool spot in the shade directly under a beautifully, landscaped maple tree. It was a perfect day to be outdoors. Mothers were pushing their newborns in strollers. Pedestrians were walking their dogs. Joggers sprinted along the path leading toward Beacon Street and the Charles River. Crowds started to gather along the Commons and prepared to board the famous duck tour. This trolley made visits to Boston's historical district, the theater, Faneuil Hall and Fenway Park.

The sidewalks were overflowing with employees who had just clocked out for lunch. Many congregated on the corner near the hot dog stand. You couldn't beat the price of a wiener. The owner had a special that day: One hot dog with chili, sauerkraut, and a small drink for only $2.00. What a bargain if you were budgeting your money. Of course, I didn't have to conserve anything. I was living off student loans. My philosophy was spend it until it's gone. And so I did.

I went to Cheers and selected a rib eye steak with three sides. Since I was in Beantown, I knew it wouldn't be prudish if I ordered anything but Samuel Adams. I wasn't really a big fan of ale, but I tried it anyway. There were a lot of tourists who came in just to get a view of the interior and to see what it was like compared to the television show that ran for thirteen years. Nearby college students assembled around the tables looking at the daily lunch specials on the board directly overhead and made their selections. I could feel the melodrama in the room. Trying to interpret what was being said was another story. All I heard was a cacophony of screams and utterances.

As I glanced over in the corner, I noticed a beautiful, middle-aged woman standing by the jukebox. I thought about approaching her but what would I say? I didn't have any pick-up line. Hey, I was in the city voted "most likely to find romance." This was it. If it was going to happen it would be here. You snooze . . . . you lose. I was tired of coming up short. I got up from the bar stool and headed in her direction. Before I could ask her if she would like me to buy her a drink, I was tapped on the shoulder. I turned around and saw a tall man standing in front of me with a vicious look in his eye and a tattoo on his right arm.

I peered into his eyes in an attempt at manipulation, but soon discovered he did not lose an ounce of courage. I stood my ground and amid onlookers, addressed the man with oversized hands.

"Can I help you?" I asked.

"Get the fuck out of my face!" he yelled.

"You came in my face," I told him.

"You want to settle this somewhere else?" he threatened.

"No, sir. I haven't had my lunch yet. I'll just to go back to my seat."

"You touch my girl and I'll knock your block off." It would have been nice if someone told me that was his girlfriend. It was just my luck. Had I gotten into a fight with that loser, I would have ended up staying overnight in jail or the emergency room across the street. I finished my meal and took a stroll down toward Fenway. Even though it was a weekday, the Red Sox were playing an afternoon double header against the Yankees. Good luck finding a ticket. This meeting was sold out over a month ago. If you were desperate, you could have taken a chance and purchased your ticket from a scalper, but I wasn't risking buying from an under cover cop, who was feverishly awaiting to make an arrest.

CHAPTER TWENTY-FOUR

I TRIED TO get to bed by nine o'clock so when I woke up I would have plenty of time to take a shower and eat breakfast. I ordered off the room service menu and selected three eggs over easy, fresh fruit, home fries and a tall glass of orange juice. Then I placed the tag on the outside of the door. That was the best twenty bucks I'd ever spent; not to mention the service charge which was half the bill. Like everything else, I just added it to my tab. Some of my friends recommended that I visit the salon downstairs and have a therapeutic massage before walking into the exam room, but I wasn't forking over anymore dough.

"I'll take my chances and hope to avoid a panic attack," I told them. By 7:45, I started heading downstairs before the lines extended toward the outside of the hotel. I wanted to get to my assigned seat as soon as possible. I was nervous enough and having to listen to students review their mnemonics was contributing to my anxiety. I loved those students who brought their BARBRI books with them to the testing center. I felt like telling them, if you don't know it by now, you won't know it on the exam either. Why would they even think about reviewing that day when they had over two months to prepare? Determining who the first-time takers were was easy. They were the ones carrying plastic bags filled with prescription drugs and other medications. The repeaters knew what to expect and sauntered through the door carrying only their number 2 pencils and a box of ear plugs. The test began right on schedule.

Exactly at 9:00 and not a minute later. Three hours of agonizing questions before a short lunch break only to return and do it all over again. When the first half of the exam was completed, I turned in my materials and headed for the cafeteria. I surveyed the entire lunch room hoping to recognize Kerri, but after looking fixedly into a crowd of over fifteen hundred students, everybody looked the same.

She's gotta be here somewhere, I surmised. I approached some of her friends to ask if they had seen her.

"Hey, Sue-Ellen. Did you happen to see Kerri?"

"No, Dillon, I haven't, but I think she's in Room 1 since her last name begins with "C.""

"Didn't that group finish the test yet?" I asked.

"Yes. Everybody came out already," Sue-Ellen replied.

I walked down a few rows until I found one of her study partners standing in line at the register.

"Excuse me, Meredith. Did you happen to see Kerri today?"

"Hey, Dillon. No, I didn't see her today at all. But I know she's here. She told me she was taking the test in Boston," she replied, as she handed the cashier money for her sandwich.

"This is really weird," I told her.

"Don't worry, she'll turn up. I would get in line before it gets too long. You only have forty minutes before we have to report back."

"Okay. I'll talk to you later. If I don't see you, good luck on the second half."

"Thanks, Dillon. You too," she said.

I walked outside the cafeteria momentarily and approached one of the proctors standing outside the room where Kerri was supposed to be sitting for the exam.

"Could you tell me if Kerri Cafferty is on your list?"

"Sure let me grab my roster," she said, as she put on her glasses. "Now, let's see – Kerri – what was the last name again?"

"Cafferty."

"Oh, yes. Here she is . . . Examinee Number five-six-two. She should be in Room One."

"Great. Thanks for your help."

"Is something wrong?" she asked.

"No. I was just trying to find her. I was hoping to join her for lunch."

"Well, don't worry about her. Go get yourself something to eat before the lunch room closes for the day. You don't want to go another three hours without eating," she despaired.

I was starting to feel a little unsteady and went back inside to purchase a sandwich.

"Great, all the sandwiches are gone," I groaned.

"We have tuna, roast beef or ham and cheese left," said the cashier.

"I'll take tuna fish with a bag of chips and a medium soda."

"That will be five twenty-five," she said.

At least these prices were reasonable. Now all I had to do was find a seat and eat my lunch within fifteen minutes. I walked back and forth until someone finally got up to throw their refuse in the recycling bin.

"Is this table taken?" I asked.

"No, go ahead. We're finished here."

"Thank you."

Just as I sat down to eat lunch, my friend Sue-Ellen advanced toward the table.

"Good, you're still here."

"What's up?" I asked, wiping away a piece of lettuce stuck to my lip.

"I heard that Kerri didn't make it here today."

"What? I just found out she's in Room 1."

"Are you sure?" Sue-Ellen inquired.

"Yeah, the proctor pointed her out on the list."

"Well, someone who knows her from school said she wasn't here so maybe she became ill over the weekend."

"I just verified her attendance less than fifteen minutes ago."

"But did you actually see her?"

"No, but you can come with me and see for yourself. Her name is on the list. She'd obviously signed in. She is somewhere around. Maybe she's just avoiding me."

"Don't be silly. Why would she do that."

"You mean you haven't heard?"

"Heard what?"

"Kerri and I have split up."

"Oh, no. I'm so sorry, Dillon. I had no idea," said Sue-Ellen.

"Well, don't feel bad. It came as a shock to me too."

"I hope everything works out for you both."

"Thanks, but it appears that it's over for good."

"Oh, maybe it was for the best, Dillon. I'm sure you'll find somebody else and forget all about Kerri."

"So what did you think of those first one hundred questions?" I asked. "I'm lucky if I answered half of them correctly."

"They were definitely tough," she replied.

"I didn't notice any future interests, but I'm willing to bet they'll appear this afternoon."

"You're probably right, Dillon. Hey, I don't mean to cut you off, but it's getting close to one o'clock so I'm gonna head back upstairs."

"Okay, Sue-Ellen, I'll talk to you later."

By four-thirty, the exams were collected and everyone departed the building and went outside for some fresh air. I went back to my hotel room and sat on the bed. Something just didn't feel right. I became worried; not because I thought I did horribly on the exam, but for another reason. Kerri wasn't the type of person to back out of anything. I'm almost certain she attended every class in law school for the entire three years. Even if she was feeling under the weather on this particular day, she would have made every effort to be present. I just couldn't see her throwing away eight hundred bucks. I approached the hotel lobby and spoke with a woman in charge of reservations.

"Could you do me a quick favor?"

"I'll try," she said, making every effort to accommodate my request.

"I was hoping I could check to see if a friend of mine had checked into the hotel this past Tuesday."

"Okay, but I cannot give out the room number."

"That's fine."

"What's your friend's name?" she asked.

"Kerri Cafferty."

"It'll be just a few minutes. Bear with me cause our computers have been slow all afternoon."

"Take your time. I don't have anywhere to be."

"Well, we have a Kerri Cafferty who reserved a room for Tuesday and Wednesday night, but she never checked in."

"Really?" I responded with consternation. I stared at the floor while thinking for a moment until the woman posed her question to me a second time.

"Anything else I can do for you?"

"No, that's all I needed to know. Thank you."

"Have a good day, sir."

Something just wasn't right. I felt as though Kerri was in some kind of danger, but I wasn't absolutely certain. If my instincts proved correct, then I would do whatever it took to rescue her.

CHAPTER TWENTY-FIVE

AFTER CHECKING OUT of the hotel the next day, I drove back to the apartment in Ardmore and immediately checked my messages. No light was flashing so I knew no one had called. I became paranoid. I didn't want to drive to Kerri's place without being invited. I felt awkward now.

Before, I could just show up at her doorstep and be welcomed with open arms. Now I felt like a stranger. Even if she happened to be home, what would I say to her when she answered the door? "Oh, *Hey, Kerri, I was just wondering why you didn't show up for the most important exam of your life?*" I could see it now. Her argument would be that I'm keeping tabs on her and I should get a life. But what if she really was in danger and I sat back and did nothing? I couldn't live with myself. I phoned Meg to see if she heard from Kerri within the last twenty-four hours.

"Meg, it's Dillon."

"Hey, what did you think of the exam?" she asked humorously. "I thought it was pretty hard."

"Me too. But we'll find out our results soon enough. The reason I'm calling is to see if you spoke with Kerri recently?"

"No, not yet. I wonder how she did on the test."

"Funny that you mention that but I didn't see her both days."

"What do you mean?" she asked curiously.

"I don't think she was there."

"Of course she was there, Dillon. She registered to take it in Boston."

"I know. I asked the proctor and her name was on the list, but I don't think she actually showed up."

"Why would she pay all that money and not show up?"

"Meg, everyone I asked didn't see her."

"Dillon, there are over a thousand students who take the Bar in Boston. You're not going to find everybody you know."

"Okay, but why didn't she check into her hotel?"

"How do you know that?"

"Yesterday, I went downstairs to the hotel lobby and spoke with one of the agents in reservations. Kerri was booked both days, but never checked in."

"Maybe she canceled that room and made other arrangements."

"Where? This hotel was in an ideal location. Why would she stay further away than necessary?"

"Dillon, you're worrying about nothing. I'm sure she took the test and she'll call me eventually."

"I don't know, Meg. I think I should drive over there and check on her," I said, becoming filled with doubt.

"Listen, tomorrow I have a doctor's appointment in the morning. I shouldn't be there long. Why don't I stop by her place after I get out?"

"Can I meet you there?"

"Let's do this – I'll call you when I'm leaving the office. Kerri is only ten minutes away."

"Sounds good. I'll be waiting for your call."

"All right, Dillon. I'll see you there. Bye."

Meg hung up the receiver feeling disconcerted over what I had just told her. She dialed Kerri's number, but got her answering machine. She tried again a few hours later, but reached the same result. Her inclination was to drive over there herself, but it was getting late and she needed to give the dog a bath.

"Come on Scooter, jump in the tub."

Scooter barked and obeyed her command. He looked exuberant as he leaped into the water. When Meg was finished bathing him, she gave the miniature pug his usual grooming and then offered him a late snack. She climbed into bed and watched a movie while Scooter snuggled next to her.

The next morning, I parked my car in the visitor lot outside Kerri's apartment and waited patiently for Meg to pull up. After fifteen minutes, a black Lexus drove into the complex and I could see Meg through the side window.

"Sorry I'm late," she said, grabbing her purse in the back seat. "Somebody didn't show up for their appointment and it screwed up the schedule."

"That's okay, I haven't been waiting long."

"Do you want me to go inside myself, Dillon or do you want to come with me?"

"What do you think I should do?"

"Kerri won't be mad if you come upstairs. It's not like she said she never wanted to see you again. You're still friends. She'll appreciate the fact that you cared enough about her to drive over here and check on her."

"I hope so."

Meg and I walked toward the back door and buzzed her room on the intercom. We waited a few minutes and heard no response. "Maybe she went out," Meg said.

"Let's look for her car. She drives a BMW," I told her.

"What color?"

"Light Blue, with New York license plates."

Meg searched the first three rows and I walked toward the rear of the lot where Kerri usually parked because she wanted her high-priced vehicle out of harm's way.

"Any luck?" Meg shouted.

"Not yet, I don't see it."

Before I could respond, I heard Meg blurt out, "Found it!"

I ran in her direction and stood in front of the car. My heart started to pound rapidly. "Let's see if the door is open," Meg stated.

"Nope. It's locked," I said.

"I'll look inside the car."

"I don't think you'll see anything, Meg. The windows are tinted."

"You're right. I have to see through her windshield. Dillon, look."

"What is it?"

"Doesn't that look like the green packet used for admission?"

"I think you're right, Meg. I knew I should have done something earlier. This is all my fault. I should have helped Kerri."

"Dillon, you didn't know this was going to happen."

"But I should have done something more."

"First of all, we don't even know if she's in any kind of trouble. She could have gone out with someone."

"Meg, are you that naive? Don't you see her car parked here? She didn't show up for the test, no one saw her in over forty-eight hours, and she hasn't called you or anyone else. Kerri is in a vulnerable situation whether or not you want to admit it."

"Okay, calm down. It's not helping to get all worked up."

"If something happens to her, I'll never forgive myself," I said.

"Drive me over to the police station and we can file a missing person's report."

We jumped in my car and cruised to the station house that was about two miles away. We walked to the front of the door and saw a sign that read "*Main Entrance Around Corner.*"

"That's just great. We have to go back around," Meg said.

We finally arrived at the reception area and called out for a police officer since no one was seated at the desk.

"Excuse me, is anyone here?" Meg inquired.

"I'll be right with you," a gentleman replied. "Sorry for the delay, but there was an accident on the interstate and I had to obtain the information. What can I do for you folks?" he asked enthusiastically.

"We would like to fill out a missing person's report?"

"How long has the person been missing?"

"We're not sure. All we know is we haven't seen her in over three days."

"How do you she's missing?" he asked.

"Because she didn't show up for a very important exam and her car is parked outside her apartment, but she hasn't answered the door when we stopped over," Meg told him.

"I need more of a factual basis than that. She could be visiting relatives. Maybe she decided at the last minute not to take the test and instead took a vacation."

"No, Kerri wouldn't do that. She wanted to get this test over with. She had been preparing for it over two months. She had to take the test in order to obtain her license to practice law."

"Oh, I see – you kids went to law school."

"Yes."

"Funny, I always wanted to go to law school but never followed through with it. I still regret it to this day. Is it really as hard as they say it is?"

"It was the worst three years of my life," I told him.

"Well, maybe it's better that I didn't go," he joked. "Look, I'd like to help you, but the police won't put out an APB unless the person filing the report demonstrates an immediate threat of danger. Right now, you're looking at somebody who isn't at her apartment or who hasn't taken an examination. If it was a child, of course, we would be concerned because a child normally doesn't go missing. But this woman, Kerri, I think you said – doesn't require any supervision. She's an adult and as such she is entitled to come and go as she pleases. She wasn't under any duty to notify you of her whereabouts."

"But what if she is in trouble?" I asked him.

"Have you spoken with members of her family?"

"No."

"Well, why don't you start there. Make some calls and see if she had been in contact with anyone else within the last forty-eight hours. Then come back and maybe we can help."

"So you're not going to do anything about this?"

"I can't ma'am," he responded, raising his hands in the air.

"I don't believe this. A woman is missing for three days and it's not serious enough to take appropriate steps to notify the public?" I asked.

"Again, I apologize, but without more my hands are tied."

Meg and I vacated the police station feeling betrayed by the officer's disservice. Our friend was missing and no one took our urgent plea to find her seriously. I should have tried harder to deter Kerri from involving herself in this whole matter. Maybe if I didn't screw up the relationship she would have spent all of her time with me instead of making an effort to stumble upon the killer.

The thought of losing her to someone else was bad enough, but having to accept her demise was too much to endure. And the guilt would have devoured me like a flesh eating bacteria. I put her in this horrible situation. I doubted her intuition. I didn't support her in her quest for justice. Now I found myself having to search for the only woman I had ever loved. I would do whatever it took to bring Kerri home alive.

CHAPTER TWENTY-SIX

MEG AND I drove back to Kerri's apartment and waited for someone to exit the building, so we could get inside the door, since we didn't have a key. I had called numerous tenants, but no one buzzed us in. Finally, after hanging around about fifteen minutes a woman left the newly renovated complex carrying her child. We managed to sneak in behind her.

"Excuse me, do you live here?" she asked.

"No. We're just visiting our friend, Kerri."

"Oh, yes, of course. She is upstairs on the right."

We took the stairs and walked to the end of the hall. I had been in her apartment a few times, but always seemed to forget her apartment number.

"Here it is," Meg said.

"Go ahead and knock," I told her.

Meg banged on the door and called out for Kerri, but didn't get any reply.

She turned the door knob and found it unlocked. We both tip-toed through the kitchen afraid of what we might find once inside.

"Maybe we shouldn't be here," Meg said.

"No, we're here now. We have to search the place," I replied.

"Everything seems to be in order," she said.

"That's just the kitchen. We need to look all over down here and upstairs," I said.

"You want to search upstairs?" she asked.

"Yes. You stay down here. If you see or hear anything, yell up to me."

"Okay, Dillon."

I ran up the steps and examined the bathroom and bedroom.

"No sign of her," I shouted. "You find anything?"

"Not yet. Everything is neatly arranged in her closets and it doesn't look like there's been any foul play here."

"Then where the hell is she?" I asked.

"Maybe she had a call from her family. You know there could have been some emergency back home."

"Wouldn't she have called one of us by now?"

"Dillon, look!" Meg screamed, pointing at the night table.

"What is it?" I asked, running down the stairs taking two at a time.

"Her answering machine is flashing. It proves she hasn't been in her apartment recently."

"You're right. Let's listen to her messages."

Meg hit the play button on top of the machine and we listened attentively to her three calls.

Message 1: Wednesday 2:25 p.m. "Hi, Kerri, it's Sue-Ellen. Just calling to see how you did on the exam. Call me when you get in. Bye."

Message 2: Wednesday 6:32 p.m. "Hey, Kerri, it's Mom. Give me a call when you get this. Dad's car broke down so we're going to pick up a rental. I guess that's what happens when you buy an American vehicle. Talk to you later."

Message 3: Thursday 5:40 p.m. "Kerri, it's Brendan. Call me on my cell. I'll be at the court house all afternoon."

"Dillon, this means Kerri hasn't been here since early Wednesday."

"Meg, we need to do something. We're going to have to notify her parents. This is so uncharacteristic of her not to return phone calls.

I'm afraid Kerri's life is at risk. The police are going to have to get involved and I mean right away."

"Does Kerri have caller ID on this phone?"

"Let me check. No. I don't see anything like that."

"Don't you know their number?"

"I don't have their number," I told her.

"Well, we need to look for it here before we leave," Meg replied. She searched a desk located in the bedroom adjacent to the window. After opening the left drawers, she pulled out all of the contents and stumbled upon a message book with a list of phone numbers arranged in alphabetical order.

"Here, Dillon, look through these papers while I scan this book for numbers."

"There's nothing in these papers, Meg, except receipts for paid bills."

"Are you sure?"

"Yes. I'm looking right at them."

"Fine. Where do Kerri's parents live?"

"Huntington."

"Is that Massachusetts or New Hampshire?"

"Neither. They live in Long Island."

"As in New York?" she asked with a look of wonder on her face.

"Right."

"Maybe we can call information to obtain their number," Meg advised.

"I wouldn't bother. I don't think their number is listed."

"How would you know?" she asked.

"Because I visited Kerri over Christmas break last year at her home in New York and she gave me the number, but I misplaced it. When I called 411, the operator told me it wasn't available."

"Great, so we can't even tell her parents."

"Maybe we can get the information from law school. They have to have all of her personal information in their records," I surmised.

"Should we take a ride to the law school now?" asked Meg.

"It can't hurt. Somebody in the registrar's office should be there to help us."

"Let's go then."

We took my car and arrived at the school within fifteen minutes. I was optimistic to see that the parking lot wasn't vacant, but once we reached our destination, we encountered a sign on the office door which read "*Registrar closed until August 5th.*"

Once again, we both felt defenseless and departed the campus overcome with bewilderment at not obtaining the pertinent information we so desperately needed.

After six consecutive days of 90 degree weather, Bostonians were hoping for a change in the forecast. High temperatures, became an impediment and deterred many residents from attempting the outdoors. Television stations warned viewers about heading outside for relatively long periods of time. The UV index had to be a ten and the humidity was off the charts. Luckily, I had central air in my apartment. It was definitely the hottest August I had ever recalled. It was so torrid that many towns permitted fire hydrants to be turned on for cooling off purposes.

The municipal pool was an alternative to the scorching temperatures, but it soon became overcrowded as the cars kept rolling into the parking lot, even though there weren't any vacant spaces available. The rescue squad was excessively busy on this particular day transporting elderly patients to the hospital who were suffering from heat exhaustion. You had to be crazy to venture out unless the beach was your final destination.

I was surprised to learn that protesters didn't cancel their march in Budd Lake Park located three blocks from where I lived. It was a pro choice movement involving over two hundred activists whose leader was quite rebellious. She was popular in the community, but for the wrong reasons. She had been arrested twice for violating an ordinance that required the approval of a permit before engaging in conduct not within the confines of a public forum. She was very outspoken about free choice and didn't mind sharing her views with members of the opposition.

Three days following the protest, her bruised and swollen body was discovered lying face down in a wooded area adjacent to the New Hampshire border. Once again, the killer could not contain himself. His irresistible impulse to terminate human life was without subjugation. Another day to judge another sinner. Another day to bring salvation to her tarnished soul. In his mind, it was an attempt at deliverance from evil. He was a hypocrite blinded by his own iniquities. Yet, he attended church regularly and adhered to the traditions of religious dogma.

Abortion was the greatest evil in his mind. It was murder without justification, one that could not provide for any reasonable defense. Police haven't discovered a motive. But Kerri was right. The killer's main purpose was to hunt women down who terminated their pregnancies through medical procedures. I was on my own. It was now up to me to convince an entire community about the unidentified perpetrator. Everyone had their own personal sentiments. But I knew I was right. I didn't care what they said. I had a mission to accomplish and a friendship to rekindle. Thank God, I had Meg to assist me. She was the only one besides me, who believed in Kerri's disappearance.

If the police didn't want to squander valuable time hunting for clues, then I guess I would do it myself. For starters, I tried to get in touch with Brendan, but it felt like tracking him down was more difficult than searching for the murderer.

Every day he traveled to a different county. Even his secretary had trouble keeping tabs on him. I needed to get in touch with him for several reasons. He may have seen Kerri the day she disappeared. I finally caught up with him at the Landsdale Superior Court House where he was standing outside the Assignment Office.

"Excuse me, Mister Schneider?"

"Yes, how can I help you?"

"You don't know me, but my name is Dillon Fletcher. I was Kerri Cafferty's boy friend."

"Oh, yes, of course. I heard a lot about you. What brings you here?" he asked with a surprised look.

"I was hoping you could tell me if Kerri had been in contact with you recently."

"To tell you the truth, I haven't spoken with her in about a week."

"I'm having trouble getting in touch with her as well."

"Have you tried her apartment?"

"Yes. Funny thing, Brendan – when I arrived, I found her door unlocked, but no one inside. She didn't check her messages either. I think she is in trouble."

"What do you mean?"

"I think she was kidnaped."

"Oh, come on now, that's ridiculous."

"I'm serious. She was spending a lot of time visiting hospitals looking for leads in your wife's disappearance."

"My wife has been missing for months. You think the person responsible for her abduction has Kerri too?"

"Yes."

"This is crazy. Why would this guy want your ex-girlfriend? My wife was taken from our home against her will by someone who has a personal vendetta against me."

"I disagree, sir. I think Kerri and your wife have been held hostage by the serial killer and I need your help to bring them home safely."

"Not this again. Look, Kerri tried to convince me that this serial killer had something to do with my wife's kidnaping. I don't want to keep rehashing this inside my head. My kids and I have struggled with this and are trying to move on. I'm not giving up on Alison. I pray every night that she is alive and will return home safely. But I have to be strong for my children now. If you don't mind, I have to be in court this afternoon. If you don't hear from Kerri in a few days, call my office."

He stepped onto the elevator and took it up to the third floor. I sat down momentarily to fix my shoelace that became untied. When I stood up, I noticed a manila folder on the chair belonging to Brendan.

"Oh crap, I bet he needs this for trial," I muttered.

I took the elevator upstairs and searched the entire third floor. I asked one of the court officers if he knew which room he was in.

"Brendan? Yeah . . . . try room three oh six," he said.

"Thank you."

When I arrived, I found a vacant room with the lights on. Even the court reporter wasn't there. I glanced at my watch and noticed it was close to 12:30 in the afternoon, and surmised that everyone had gone to lunch. I decided to wait for him rather than just leave the folder on the table.

I had some time to kill, so I walked around the court room observing pictures on the wall and the Proclamation of the Commonwealth that was framed in the corner near the American flag. Suddenly, I got this urge to climb up the steps and sit in the judge's chair. I must have been crazy. If someone came in and saw me, I would have been arrested for trespassing.

I grabbed hold of the gavel and inspected it. It was located next to a few books entitled "Mass General Laws" that were statutory regulations. I banged the gavel against the desk several times and noticed I had loosened the handle.

I became frightened after hearing the sound of a female voice approaching. My hand shook and I knocked the gavel to the ground. The handle flew off and the top landed in the far corner of the room. I was shaking uncontrollably. Luckily, the woman didn't hear the commotion and turned down another corridor on the opposite side of the hallway. I couldn't just leave the gavel in a state of disrepair. I damaged it, so I had to restore it as quickly as possible.

When I retrieved the handle, I heard a rattling sound inside. I held the handle up towards the light and could observe something visible inside. Because the handle was rather narrow, I wasn't able to slide my finger inside to extract the item. I then found a pencil in one of the drawers and stuck it through in order to grab the contents at the bottom. Whatever it was, it was stuck and I couldn't get it to budge at first.

I applied too much force and broke the pencil in half. Now the pencil was jammed inside as well. I needed something else to use, so I searched all the drawers and came upon a long, thin piece of metal. I carefully inserted the metal inside and loosened the pencil enough to slide it up and pull it out. I tugged at the bottom of the handle to remove the other small part until it wasn't firmly attached.

Then, I shook the handle and suddenly the piece that was dislodged landed in my hand. As I gazed closer, I was astounded at what my eyes had seen. It was part of a bracelet, and there was a name engraved on the back. It read: "Maureen."

CHAPTER TWENTY-SEVEN

MY HEART WAS pounding and my face went numb. My hands were trembling so wingedly, it appeared as though I was having a seizure. I took the bracelet and put the gavel back where I found it. When I departed the room, I looked at the sign on the door. I was shocked when I read it. *"Hon. Timothy Crawford."*

I can't believe it. The judge is a killer, I concluded.

Who would ever believe me? Who could I tell? The police didn't believe me when I told them Kerri was missing. If I returned to the station making allegations that a judge was a serial killer, they might consider I undergo a psychiatric examination. There was only one person that trusted me and that was Meg. When I awoke the next morning, the first thing I did was call her. She could detect the fear in my voice and knew immediately that something, wasn't right. She decided to come over after stopping for her morning coffee.

"I'm so glad you could come here," I said.

"Dillon, what's up? You look like you've seen a ghost. Are you feeling okay?"

"I need your help and advice about something Meg."

"Shoot."

"Yesterday, I went to the court house to find Brendan and I was sent to one of the judge's chambers. When I got there, nobody was inside because they had adjourned for lunch. I waited for them to come back. Meg, you won't believe this, but while I was there – I found part of a bracelet that was hidden inside the judge's gavel. It had the name Maureen on it. I found the killer, Meg. It all makes sense now. The judge has Kerri and killed all those women. But how do I prove it?"

"Dillon, calm down."

That was easy for her to say. Meg always maintained her composure and never got rattled about anything.

"Dillon, there are lots of people with the name Maureen. Maybe the bracelet belonged to one of his children."

"No. This bracelet was broken and the name isn't very legible. And I found it inside a gavel as though someone surreptitiously placed it there. Here, look at it."

"You took this bracelet from the court room?" she asked with intense and profound fear.

"I had no choice. I found it when it fell on the floor."

"Dillon, who is the judge?"

"Timothy Crawford."

"Tomorrow, we'll go back and return the bracelet."

"Meg, are you out of your mind? I'm telling you this guy is a murderer."

"Dillon, you have no proof."

"Meg, remember Maureen Hensley? They found her bracelet near the river. I bet you all the money in the world that the bracelet in my hand fits the other piece the police have in their possession."

"Why would someone hide a bracelet where it was that easy to be found?"

"Because he never thought someone would look inside the gavel, but he was wrong."

"Dillon, here's what we do. We go down to the Landsdale Police Department and show them the bracelet. If it turns out to be the missing link to all of this, then I will stand by you one hundred percent. But right now, you're just speculating."

"When do you want to drive there?" I asked.

"We can go now if you want," she replied.

She grabbed her purse and we headed out in my car.

"I hope this bracelet matches. If it does, we'll find Alison and Kerri," I said optimistically.

We arrived at the Landsdale Police precinct around ten in the morning. The police were definitely going to be glad to see us if the instrumentalities discovered less than twenty-four hours ago contained evidence of criminal activity. Meg and I were greeted at the door by one of the commanding officers.

"Good morning, folks."

"Hello, sir. We need to speak with somebody who has handled the recent serial killer case."

"What do you need to know?" he inquired.

"Well, I think my friend and I have stumbled upon something very interesting and possibly quite relevant to your investigation."

"What type of information are you referring?" the officer asked.

"I think I have the remaining piece of a bracelet belonging to the victim, Maureen Hensley," I told him.

"You do realize that we take our job here quite seriously and don't have time to listen to speculative or hypothetical situations. Have you any foundation to base this evidence?"

"Yes. I found it inside a gavel."

"You found a bracelet inside a gavel and you want to conclude that it belongs to a murder victim? he asked, in an effort to mock or convey contempt with respect to my allegation.

"Sir, with all due respect, the bracelet found in my possession is missing several links. Nonetheless, the name on the back of the bracelet states "Maureen." I also discovered it inadvertently. The person who put this bracelet inside the gavel did so with the intent of concealing its contents."

"May I ask where you found it?" he said.

"I found it at the Middlesex County Court House."

"Come again?"

"I said I found it – "

"I heard you the first time. Listen, our department has worked day and night on this investigation for the last two years. There are officers who have become so stressed out over it, they ended up getting divorced. There are guys who haven't slept in weeks. And you come in here with a bracelet telling me you have evidence to link this entire case to a murderer. Let me ask you then, who is your suspect?"

"Timothy Crawford or should I say Judge Timothy Crawford."

"Timothy Crawford of Landsdale Superior Court?" the officer inquired with a look of surprise.

"That's correct."

"Are you out of your mind? Do you know what you're saying here? This is a man of great integrity. He isn't a killer. He's one of the nicest people you would ever meet."

"I understand. Believe me, I was just as shocked as you were when I found out."

"Do you have this bracelet on you today?" he asked.

"Yes, I do."

"May I see it?" he pleaded.

"Here you go."

He removed the top of the box and placed the bracelet in his hand. He examined it thoroughly and called upon some of the other officers present in the building to come and inspect it.

"Wow, this definitely looks like the bracelet we discovered," said one of the other men.

"All of the evidence derived from the 2001 murder is kept in storage. We need to retrieve that part of the bracelet before determining if the piece I'm holding is the exact match," replied the commanding officer.

"How long before you get those results?" Meg asked.

"I don't know, two or three days, maybe."

"But all you need to do is see if the piece I found fits the other part," I responded.

"I can see that. But we'll also be running tests for prints and other forensics. It's not as easy as you describe."

"We don't have much time. Right now, two women are in danger," Meg answered frantically.

"I promise you, we will do everything we can to find them, ma'am."

"What about questioning the judge?" I asked.

"In order to do that we need reasonable suspicion. Until we get the results back, we don't have anything to go on. We can't arrest the judge before we calculate the outcome of the evidence you provided and determine if it is even sufficient to establish probable cause justifying such an arrest," the officer related.

With that in mind, Meg and I left the building relying on the promise of the police to look further into this ordeal. They had my phone number and reassured me they would call with any new information by the end of the week. On Thursday afternoon, I received a call from one of the police officers involved in the investigation. He had informed me that the bracelet was a perfect match.

The police were now convinced they had the killer. They contacted Maureen's parents and informed them of their intent to make an arrest. By two-thirty, they obtained a warrant issued by a magistrate to be served at the residence of Timothy Crawford. Police cruisers pulled up in front of the judge's home around six o'clock. The judge had arrived home only moments before and was beginning to make dinner when the door bell rang.

"Yes, officers. What can I do for you?" he asked.

"Mister Crawford, we have a warrant for your arrest for the murder of Maureen Hensley."

CHAPTER TWENTY-EIGHT

THE JUDGE APPEARED dismayed at their unexpected arrival and raised his voice to the officer about to place him in handcuffs.

"What are you fools doing here!" he yelled.

"We found evidence that directly links you to murder," replied a State Trooper called upon by the local police to assist in the judge's apprehension.

"What murder? What are you talking about?"

"Maureen Hensley."

"I presided over that case, you idiot. How could I be responsible for her death!" he shouted.

"We found the bracelet belonging to the victim. It was inside the handle of your gavel, sir."

"What does that mean? Isn't it possible someone else put it there to frame me?"

"Where are the women you kidnaped?" an officer demanded.

""I'm going to tell you this for the last time. I didn't kidnap anyone nor was I any accomplice to murder. You are all making a terrible mistake. If you fools bring me downtown and embarrass me, I can assure you, I will see that none of you return to the force."

"I'm sorry Mister Crawford, but it is our job to bring you to the station house for booking."

"This is ridiculous. Search my home if you think I'm the killer. Go ahead, you morons won't find anything."

"We will make a cursory inspection as soon as we place you in the cruiser."

"This arrest is not valid. You have no probable cause. I am a judge, God damn it." The police searched the upper level of the home first and found nothing. Then they carefully scrutinized the first floor and the basement hoping to encounter any sign of foul play. When nothing turned up, they drove to the station.

When they arrived inside the precinct, they took fingerprints and had the judge fill out some preliminary forms.

"I want you to call Brendan Schneider, a high profile defense lawyer," the judge instructed.

"Sir, we want to ask you a few questions."

"I have said all I need to say. I will not respond to any more inquiries until Brendan Schneider arrives."

The police honored his request and refrained from interrogating the judge until counsel was present. Judge Crawford was led back to his cell where he waited until Brendan arrived several hours later. Around ten o'clock, Brendan arrived and signed in at the front desk. He was led to Judge Crawford's cell and found him sitting on the floor.

"Judge, I'm so sorry I'm late. I got the message that you called. What happened?"

"These idiots think I had something to do with your wife's disappearance. Now they think I'm the serial killer."

"This is ridiculous, Judge. Let me talk to them."

"Brendan, they found a bracelet in my chambers. How do you suppose it got there?"

"I don't know, but we'll find out."

"I think somebody wants to incriminate me."

"Just stay right there. Officer! I need to speak with the arresting party. This is an outrage. This man has done nothing wrong. You had no probable cause to bring him here," Brendan protested.

"With all due respect, sir," replied the captain, "probable cause to arrest was manifested by virtue of a discovery made by a private person. Therefore, the evidence is not tainted as you might believe since it was not gathered through government means."

"You keep speaking about evidence, what evidence?" asked Brendan who was growing impatient with the entire police department and accusing them of violating the defendant's 4th Amendment rights.

"The evidence of a murder. It is direct evidence. An instrumentality of a crime related to the victim. The bracelet is an exact match."

"Here, look for yourself," the captain told him, as he handed Brendan the piece of jewelry. "This piece was discovered near the river and this piece was found inside the defendant's chambers. You can clearly see the pieces fit perfectly and the names on the back state "Maureen Hensley."

"All that proves is the bracelet had been placed there. You have nothing to link this to any murderer. Anyone could have put this inside the judge's chambers when he was away. Why would the judge put it there? Do you really think if someone wanted to escape culpability for murder they would conceal evidence in an area where it is more probable than not that this evidence would be discovered?"

"Sir, records indicate that when Maureen Hensley was murdered the judge was away for two weeks, supposedly in California."

"Are you telling me that you are going to charge this highly respected officer of the court with a capital offense?"

"That is what I am saying at this time."

"Who is the person who discovered this evidence?"

"I am not at liberty to disclose that information."

"Like hell you are," Brendan argued. "This wasn't an informant. He found something and brought it to your attention. He was not working for the government so there is no right to anonymity."

"Fine, Mister Schneider, let me get the file and give you that important piece of information," the captain said with a sarcastic tone. "Ah yes, here it is. The name's Dillon . . . Dillon Fletcher."

Brendan looked amazed knowing he recognized the name, but couldn't believe it was me who went to the police.

"Dillon Fletcher? That son of a bitch dropped by to see me last week because he thought my wife was abducted by a serial killer. Then he tells me his ex-girlfriend was missing and now he has convinced all of you that Judge Crawford is a serial killer. You can't be that serious. Look – this Dillon guy – he's a law school student. You know how they are. They think because they're in school they can solve any crime because they've read over fifty thousand pages of case law. This guy is off his rocker. That's probably the reason his girlfriend broke it off. I'll be paying him a visit shortly."

"Now, don't do anything crazy, Mister Schneider."

"Relax, fellas. I'm going to sit down and have a reasonable conversation with this young, curious, future esquire. He has made a big mistake and I have already been a party to a wrongful conviction. I will not allow this to happen again," Brendan told them before returning to the judge's cell.

If Crawford were any more belligerent toward the officers he would have been charged with obstruction of justice. Losing his composure wouldn't be advantageous to his health. Though middle-aged, he had elevated blood pressure and high cholesterol. He didn't need to acquire additional factors of heart disease. I'm sure presiding over thousands of cases stressed him out over the years. It definitely contributed to his hair loss. He tried to hide it by combing it over, but everybody knew. He was balding and it was obvious. You would think with his money he would make an attempt to alter his appearance, but his rapid receding hairline never phased him. If that was me, I would have made an appointment with the plastic surgeon to have a follicular transplant.

"Judge, I have to leave now. I will be in touch with you tomorrow. I want to speak with the person responsible for putting you here."

"Who is he, Brendan? I'll see to it that he pays for this. He has ruined my career. I've built my reputation on integrity within the judicial forum and I will not allow some idiot to tarnish it."

"I understand, Judge. This guy who accused you – well – he's a law student."

"What? Who is he? Which school does he attend? I want him removed. Call the Dean and let me speak with him," the judge commanded with a look of fury in his eyes.

"I can't do that, Judge, but I promise to straighten this whole thing out," Brendan said.

The next day Meg and I were hanging out near the pool munching on Tostitos and pretzels when Brendan appeared with another lawyer. His facial expression did not put me at ease. Even though, I too, was a graduate of law school, I remained intimidated by experienced members of the legal profession.

Simply put, I was a rookie waiting to be sworn in following my successful Bar results. Even if I passed, I didn't know anything. Here, I was accusing formidable men in robes with murder. I was anticipating a lecture from the defense attorney chastising me for my outrageous conduct and unreasonable allegations, but instead, he surprised me with questions, as though he really took an interest in what I had to say. He opened the gate surrounding the pool and closed it behind him. Then he advanced carrying his legal pad and a leather brief case. "Mister Fletcher, Good morning."

"Hello, Brendan. What brings you here?"

"Oh, I think you know why I dropped by."

"Does it have something to do with Kerri?"

"No. We'll talk about her later. Now, I want to know why you and your friend here took it upon yourself to go to the police and accuse a judge of a murder you knew nothing about. I handled this case. I know the killer is still out there. You have no business in this."

"Excuse me for interrupting, Brendan," said Meg, "but Dillon was concerned about Kerri. He came to see you and stumbled upon the bracelet by accident. He obviously jumped to conclusions and was afraid. He didn't know what to do and panicked. I don't honestly believe the judge is a killer."

"But the police do. Thanks to you, I have to bail him out and prove he didn't commit these murders. I want this guy captured as much as you. I want my wife back. I think about her every day. But going after innocent people is not how to handle this. Please, from now on, stay out of this. If I need your assistance, I will call you," Brendan said.

"Who do you think did this?" asked Meg.

"Right now, anyone is a suspect, but you would think someone with access to the courts would be first on the list."

"What are you going to do?" Dillon inquired.

"I'm going to question a lot of people."

"Do you think the judge was set up?"

"It's quite possible, Meg."

"Then it has to be somebody who either works for him or was a party appearing before him in some proceeding," Meg replied.

"Exactly. And I plan to find out just who this person is."

"Before Kerri went missing, she mentioned that all of the victims abducted had abortions. Is it possible for you to find out if the judge presided over cases involving abortions?" asked Dillon.

"Yes, but what about my wife? She didn't terminate her pregnancy?" Brendan said.

"I know but I think this person hates anyone who had an abortion or allowed the proceeding to occur. Maybe the judge handled such a matter and now this person is seeking revenge," Dillon stated.

"I appreciate your input, both of you. I will look into your assertions and promise to call you if anything related to the killings or Kerri's disappearance surfaces. Promise me you will let the police handle this. Under no circumstances are you to investigate this further. Understood?"

"Yes, we understand."

"Good. Enjoy the rest of your day."

Brendan drove off and returned to the office where he made a few phone calls, one being the Prosecutor's Office.

A week later, he appeared with Judge Crawford at the arraignment. The trial court judge looked over the affidavits along with the charges and found that there was insufficient evidence to bring any accusations against the defendant. Therefore, Judge Crawford was released and all charges against him were dropped.

CHAPTER TWENTY-NINE

I MAY HAVE given Brendan my promise to keep my distance from the serial killing investigation, but I have been known to lie on occasion. This would be one such time where my absence of allegiance would be justified. Besides, no one would take notice that I was hanging around the court house asking questions. It was about four-thirty in the afternoon, and I stood outside one of the court rooms until the trial adjourned. I noticed after the judge dismissed the jury and departed toward his chambers, the court officer came out and locked the door. I had to ask him a few questions for curiosity sake.

"Does every room get locked at four-thirty?"

"Yes, the court house closes at four-thirty and all rooms are sealed off," he said.

"Do you lock all the rooms?"

"No, every court room has an officer who locks each door."

"Does anyone else have access to the court room?"

"Not from the outside. Administrative staff have keys and can gain access from the judge's chambers," he replied.

"Thanks for your help."

My job was going to be a lot harder than I expected. If the killer was an employee in the administrative building of the court house, I had a long journey ahead of me. There were over seven hundred employees in the building. Any one of them could have been the culprit. As I was walking toward the elevator to make my exit, I noticed my friend, Denise, walking in the opposite direction. I shouted out to her.

"Hey, what are you doing here?" she asked, with a look of surprise.

"Just visiting. Did you have jury duty or something?"

"No. I work here now. I was hired as the law librarian on the second floor."

"Good for you," I said.

"Yeah, at least I'll get some experience and exposure."

"Hey, Denise, do you think you can get into the computer and obtain employee information?"

"Dillon, that's illegal. I can't fool around with personal information."

"Look, I need to find out if the serial killer works here."

"What are you talking about?" she asked with a confused look.

"The person who abducted and killed those women over the last two years. I think this same person kidnaped Kerri and I think he works here."

"How are you so sure?" she asked with enormous incredulity.

"Because before Kerri went missing, she provided me with a lot of information. I didn't listen to her at first, but as time went on it all made sense. It started to fit together. You have to just trust me on this."

"Dillon, I could lose my job. Worse, I could be disbarred."

"Don't worry, nobody will find out. Besides, these are exigent circumstances and your actions would be justified."

"What do you want me to do?" she asked, shrugging her shoulders, as we were making our way outside the building toward the rear of the parking lot.

"Look up the names of all court personnel including law clerks and check to see who was missing from work on these dates. I handed her a piece of paper with the relevant dates on which these women were murdered.

"How long do you think it will take?"

"Oh, Dillon, there are at least one hundred law clerks and over fifty officers. Give me about a week."

"I really appreciate this, Denise. Call me as soon as you are finished."

Almost a week had gone by, and Summer was just about over with the arrival of Labor Day. I was invited to a friend's barbeque, but declined to attend. I spent the day watching the Jerry Lewis telethon and surfing the web. My life became an absolute bore. The only thing that changed was my drinking habit. I finished off a six pack within an hour. I stayed up late watching sitcoms from the 70's on *TV Land*.

Life was great back then. No responsibilities, no deadlines to meet, no broken hearts from bad relationships. I wouldn't mind being a teenager again. At least I felt like one when I met Kerri. I guess this was how love was supposed to feel. You date for awhile, then before you know it, you're sleeping with the enemy. I just couldn't figure some women out. The harder I tried, the more I realized just how unsuccessful I had become. Maybe the next woman I happen to go out with will come with an instructions manual.

Denise kept her promise and called me on September 16th. The information she provided would soon prove to be the smoking gun missing from this perplexing case that had sent police departments in New England on a wild goose chase for the last three years. I didn't want to get Denise in trouble, nor risk having someone overhear our confidential communication, so we both agreed to meet at an undisclosed location. I couldn't wait to obtain the information.

Denise assured me that she had discovered a plausible suspect and I was willing to hear what she had to say. She pulled into the parking lot and climbed out of her Hyundai Elantra. She stood in her three-inch platform sandals which put her at about five-foot-two. She was rather petite, but nonetheless, had a spectacular figure. I ran to help her after noticing she had difficulty carrying her back pack. I soon realized that she had brought numerous copies of employees' personal information including names, addresses, telephone numbers, hours worked, and length of employment.

"I brought everything I could get off the computer," she said.

"I really appreciate everything you did. You don't know how grateful I am."

"No problem, Dillon."

"How long did this take you?"

"Oh, just a few days to print everything out. I couldn't do much while I was working, but I waited until lunch hour or when everybody went home for the day."

"I understand. This is great. If the killer works here, these papers will definitely incriminate him." I said.

"Well, I have to go Dillon. I promised I would meet up with a friend."

"Okay, Denise. I'll keep in touch. Thanks, again. Really, you're a life saver."

If I had to stay up throughout the night without any sleep it was well worth it. As I glanced through the papers while sitting on the bedroom floor, I couldn't help but question why the killer would place culpable evidence inside the judge's chambers. The only thing that made sense was this had to be a set-up.

But how would the killer know someone would stumble upon the hidden piece of jewelry? Why the judge? What did he do to make somebody want to destroy his reputation? This person obviously had some personal vendetta against Judge Crawford but for what reason? By eleven-thirty in the evening, I was almost finished reviewing half of the pages. I was tempted to call it a night, but persevered and luckily, got my second wind around midnight.

I came upon something that I found quite interesting. Judge Crawford had two law clerks who worked simultaneously on his cases. They reported to him on a daily basis. One was a female, age twenty-five, named Stacy, who graduated from the University of Michigan Law School and one male law clerk, age forty-two, who graduated from Boston U. His name was Kyle Davenport. It just so happened that Kyle was absent from work around the time of all the murders. Granted, this information wouldn't be enough to go to the authorities, but I had good reason to follow through with my instincts.

I did some research on my own and found that in 1994, Judge Crawford recused himself from presiding over a case involving a minor who wanted to seek a judicial bypass and terminate her pregnancy. Her parents objected to her decision to abort the child and the case was brought before the judge. It turned out that he had personal views about the subject matter of litigation and deemed it necessary to allow another administrative body to adjudicate the controversy.

In 1973, just six months into their marriage, Judge Crawford's wife became pregnant. Fearing ridicule and embarrassment from both sides of the family, the two parties agreed that abortion was the overall best available option. Neither of them wanted a child so early, but like most teenagers, they were in love and sexually active. Ironically, they'd always used protection except this one time when they were alone in a hotel and things sort of got out of control.

There was heavy drinking involved and before they knew it, neither of them had a clue what they were doing. Two months later, they received the shocking news and had to weigh their decision to keep the baby and face being disowned or choose abortion and hopefully avoid having to resolve the issue. Their parents were both devout Irish-Catholics who swore by the Bible and could quote Scripture verbatim. Had the abortion been disclosed during this time, the family would have been a total outcast and likely excommunicated from the church for committing such an immoral and malign act.

It all made sense now. The killer despised the judge for what he did over three decades ago. He was administering retribution for what he perceived to be murder. Now the tables were turned and he got to play the authoritative role in administering justice. Kyle was usually around when Brendan met in the judge's chambers so he overheard conversations between Brendan and the judge regarding Brendan's wife and their future plans to purchase a new home. Kyle was extremely jealous and despised Brendan. He followed him home several times intending to kill Brendan so he could be with Alison, but the opportunity was never available. Then he sought revenge against the judge, but Kyle's systematic plan fizzled out when the charges against Judge Crawford were dropped. Now for the first time, the killer had to face reality and acknowledge the fact that his plan to punish one of Middlesex County's most beloved and respected justices, would be foiled.

The next day, I waited outside the court house until Kyle left for the day. I followed him home keeping far enough away so as to not draw attention to myself. He turned off the freeway and headed toward a long narrow road in a southerly direction.

At that moment, I turned off my headlights and kept up the pace. It felt like I was driving for hours; then he made another exit. I lost him. I had him in my line of sight. Then suddenly, he was gone. I turned the car around and realized I had missed a right turn up ahead. You wouldn't know where the street was unless you lived in that area because it was surrounded by large trees and a lot of the land was used strictly for agricultural purposes. Then, I saw all I needed to see. A one mile stretch of cornfields and farming equipment. I started to hyperventilate. I was now on the same road where he took his victims before killing them. The same road where Debbie Meyers was fortunate to have escaped, and now the same road where Kerri and Alison had been kept hostage.

Part of me wanted to end this ordeal right then and drive up to the ancient house and rescue both women. But I knew that was too risky. I wasn't armed and I had no experience in handling this type of situation. After getting lost a few times, I finally returned on to the main road and got back on the expressway. I floored the accelerator and drove to a state police barracks where I was greeted by one of the troopers inside.

"Can I help you, sir?" he asked worriedly.

I was shaking and barely could get the words out. After a few breaths, I responded, "I know who the killer is. I know where he lives."

"What killer?" he replied.

"The serial killer. I think I discovered his identity."

"Who is he?" he asked, while handing me a cup of water.

"His name is Kyle Davenport. He was a law clerk in Middlesex County Superior Court."

"How do you know he's the one?"

"I have exact dates which show he was missing from work on the days those women were kidnaped."

"What else do you have?"

"I followed him. I drove all the way to his house. I took the same route that Debbie Meyers traveled and saw everything as she described it to police."

"I'll tell you what. We'll run his name and see if we get an address. I'll have a few officers drive out to the scene and if he's there we'll definitely question him."

"How long will that take?"

"Shouldn't be but a few minutes. Okay – Kyle Davenport – that's funny," he said, entering the data in the computer.

"What. What is it?" I urged.

"The only Kyle Davenport resides at 245 Hookset Road in Manchester, New Hampshire. I don't have a Massachusetts address for that name."

"I don't understand. I just followed him home less than thirty minutes ago."

"Oh, I believe you. Something is very weird here."

"What are you going to do?"

"I'm going to call the Manchester Township Tax Assessor's Office."

"What for?"

"I want to know who the owner of that house is."

"It's Kyle Davenport, sir."

"I don't like to gamble, young man," the officer replied, "but how would you like to wager that this Kyle Davenport does not own this house?"

"How do you know?"

"Because I just got a message sent to me that says Kyle Davenport died seven years ago and he was ninety-two-years-old."

"What? Then who is this person who resides at 245 Hookset Road?"

"That's the $64,000 question."

Within an hour, the FBI had arrived on the scene and basically took over the investigation. I was questioned and provided as much information as possible then was told they would handle everything from here on out. The first thing the Federal Bureau did was obtain Kyle's records at the court house.

Because he was a federal employee, Kyle had to provide fingerprints before he was placed on the payroll. The prints were taken to the lab and the results came back about twenty minutes later. Kyle Davenport was really Chad Bourne.

In 1986, Chad was a substitute teacher for the Dracut County Public School District. He had to be fingerprinted before receiving his certificate. Unbeknownst to Chad at that time, the information was sent to Boston where it remained on his file. Two years before entering law school, he volunteered at an abortion clinic where he obtained all of his victim's personal information.

The FBI began to plot how they were going to capture him. Should they arrest him at work the next day or immediately go directly to his house and apprehend him. I stood there with a confused look on my face wondering how this guy faked his way through law school without being caught. Then, he managed to secure a job as a judicial law clerk and nobody had any idea who he really was.

It was approaching ten o'clock in the evening, and agents rushed to the alleged perpetrator's residence based on the description I provided. I traveled behind in case they took a wrong turn, but I was really hoping to see Kerri alive and unharmed. Once they realized I was on their tail, they ordered me to desist and return home. I reluctantly obeyed, turning my vehicle around and headed in the opposite direction.

FBI representatives ascertained the location and began to surround the curtilage of the dwelling. As they approached the front of the house, they soon discovered there wasn't any entrance. They quietly walked to the side where they came upon a pick-up truck parked out back. After everyone obtained their weapons and assigned positions, one of the men yelled out "Chad Bourne, come out with your hands up! The entire area is surrounded with FBI agents who are armed and ready to shoot."

As soon as he said this, shots were fired from the basement window. One of the bullets struck an officer in the leg. An ambulance was summoned within a few minutes and he was taken to the emergency room where he was released a few hours later.

The killer was not going to surrender. Instead, he chose a stand off. He threatened the men that if they did not drop down their weapons he would kill the women he held as hostages. Agents were dubious as to whether the women inside were really alive and therefore, could not take Chad's imminent threat to inflict harm with great import.

"Chad, we know you killed those women. The best thing you can do is give yourself up."

"Never."

"You leave us no choice but to come inside."

"If you try, I will kill these women. Don't test me."

"How do I know they are alive? Let me here them speak."

"No. You will have to trust me."

"How can we trust you? You have lied practically your whole life."

"I'm telling you they are alive. Now get off my property before I shoot another officer."

"Why are you doing this? What did these women do to you?"

"I said get off my property."

Again, he fired shots in their direction forcing the men to temporarily retreat. There was only one entrance into the home and that was through the basement door that was bolted down. Their only opportunity to kill him would be to shoot him through the house. But they weren't sure who else was inside. As they approached the right side of the house, one of the agents who went by the name *Hawk* yelled out, "I hear a woman's voice!"

The men ran toward that section of the house and heard someone scream, "help us!"

Hawk then spotted a small window which was too small for anyone to fit through. He squatted down and looked inside but saw nothing. Then he shouted, "is anyone in there?"

"Yes! Oh, my God. Please help us," Alison pleaded.

"How many of you are in there?"

"Just two of us. Please hurry."

"What are your names?"

"I'm Alison."

"And my name is Kerri."

There wasn't any way for the officers to invade the house without putting the lives of the two women at risk. Their only alternative was to get hold of a sharp shooter to take him out. Finding someone on short notice was going to be rather difficult, but the Feds knew they had limited time to act if they wanted to avoid another murder.

CHAPTER THIRTY

CHAD WASN'T GOING to give the FBI and local authorities any opportunity to enter his house without responding with deadly force. Once he realized that the Feds ascertained the location of Kerri and Alison, he went downstairs to remove the chains from their ankles in order to bring the women upstairs.

"So you bitches can't keep your mouths shut. Which one of you called out to the police?" Chad demanded urgently.

Both of them remained silent and so he questioned them further.

"I want to know who disobeyed my orders and spoke to police when I specifically stated not to say a single fucking word."

Neither of the women looked up at Chad and continued to avoid answering him. He walked up to Alison and slapped her across the face. Then he did the same to Kerri but he wasn't finished with her yet. He unbuttoned her blouse and began to massage her breasts while masturbating. After pleasuring himself, he forced the women upstairs into the living room where he tied them up and blindfolded them. Then he slid the furniture to one side of the room to act as a shield in the event the Feds decided to fire. Now if the authorities were dumb enough to shoot at him, they might miss their intended target and kill one of the innocent hostages. They would be foolish to attempt a rescue without knowing the killer's exact location.

It was already approaching two-thirty in the morning, and authorities did not develop any concoction for overtaking the killer. There were at least fifty law enforcement officers who were armed with artillery, wearing bullet proof vests, and carrying tear gas. Amazingly, the press got hold of what was going on and before you knew it, helicopters were flying over at low altitudes.

"Get these choppers the hell out of here," said one of the commanding officers. "They're disrupting our proposed sequence of action!"

Lines of vehicles from local and cable television stations rolled in and started setting up in order to broadcast the live action. No sooner did nearby residents appear to see first-hand who was responsible for the atrocities that plagued their counties and disrupted their lifestyle for over thirty-six months.

Less than two hours earlier, no one would have known this place even existed. Now, thousands of residents poured in to get a glimpse of the events. Many were outspoken and chatted with the media stating they would accept nothing less than to see his dead body carried away. Others wished they could kill him themselves. By three-thirty in the morning, it turned into a wild demonstration.

The FBI did its part in roping off the area, yet that didn't deter a bunch of extremists carrying weaponry, who still believed they had a right to exercise vigilantism. As justified as they might have been, the Feds did not have time to babysit the general public. Exigent circumstances required immediate action. Anyone who crossed that line would be prosecuted.

Brendan received a phone call from family members informing him that the news media announced Alison was still alive and being held hostage. He arrived at the incident shortly thereafter and approached one of the agents demanding answers.

"Is Alison Schneider inside the house?"

"Sir, I'm going to have to ask you to step back," an agent replied.

"I'm her husband, I have a right to know what's happening in there."

"Right now, we know that two women are alive inside. One of them is indeed your wife."

"I'm going in there," Brendan told him.

"Like hell, you are. Do you want to get yourself killed? Besides, your wife probably has a gun pointed at her right now. If you try anything stupid, the killer won't hesitate to take out his first hostage." Minutes later, shots again were fired and police retaliated. They had to get Chad to respond to their demands. Finally, after speaking with a representative of the phone company, they were able to obtain his phone number. One of the men dialed and the phone rang over twenty times before Chad answered it out of frustration. "What the hell do you want you son of a bitch?"

"Chad, we want to talk this out."

"I'm not coming out."

"What can we do for you? Do you need anything?"

"Yeah. I need all of you to get the hell off my property right now."

"You know that's not possible, Chad. You are responsible for murdering over five people that we know about. I'm sure there are more victims out there that are unaccounted for."

"I didn't kill anybody."

"I'm afraid we have proof, Chad. If you give yourself up the prosecutor might make you a deal and spare you the death penalty."

"You think I'm stupid? I know Massachusetts doesn't have a death penalty, you dumb ass. I went to law school, remember?"

"Okay, Chad. You leave us no choice but to enter the house. We have over one hundred armed men and women out here. Once I give them authorization, they will proceed to come inside."

"And I will proceed to shoot their heads off. Remember, there are two women inside this house and I don't think you want to sacrifice their lives to be a hero."

"No one wants to be a hero, Chad. Why are you doing this?"

"I told you to leave my property."

As one of the commanding officers was speaking to Chad on the phone, Hawk, in a furtive manner, approached the side of the house and attempted to shoot tear gas through one of the small windows.

He soon discovered that his scheme was thwarted due to the fact that no one was near that part of the room. Hawk quickly realized he was down to just a handful of options. Either shoot the killer through the house and hope to make contact without injuring any victims or somehow obtain entry through other means.

The top story in all of New England was the recent discovery of the serial killer, but another item of news that many found shocking was the unexpected death of a renowned and illustrious attorney named Raymond Sciarpa. He was the highly acclaimed prosecutor in the Derek Martin trial. His wife discovered his body inside their home. The cause of death was labeled a suicide.

Hospital records from the emergency physician provided a detailed description of medications found in his blood. Apparently, Sciarpa had simultaneously ingested a variety of antidepressants and washed them down with a few shots of hard liquor. I guess he wanted to make sure he didn't wake up. His wife of seventeen years told police he had been suffering from depression since the release of Derek Martin from prison. Prosecuting the wrong guy and having to face responsibility for his erroneous conviction brought Sciarpa to the edge.

He was a respected man who believed in justice. One thing he didn't tolerate were excuses. And the thing that brought him the most disappointment was watching a defendant try to fit the role of a victim. In over two decades of doing prosecutorial work for the D.A.'s office, he helped put away over five hundred hardened criminals. He wasn't the guy you would invite to a party because he didn't socialize much outside of court. And if you ever received a motor vehicle violation and had to appear before him, you weren't afforded any breaks. You paid the ticket and got the points.

Sciarpa honestly believed the best method for improving the criminal justice system was through deterrence and harsh punishment. If a person knew that committing a specific crime would result in imprisonment, he might think twice before engaging in that course of conduct. I strongly disagree with his philosophy. I think people commit crimes today because they want to see the inside of a prison cell. Modern day prisons do not portray living conditions as viewed through television programs and movies. They don't remind you of Alcatraz.

Today, prisons look more like hotels and country club facilities. I like working out, but I have to pay a monthly fee as part of my membership. A prisoner just has to rob a bank and now he gets to use the pool, the weight room, play basketball, racquetball, and it's all complimentary. In addition to that, if the inmate is on his best behavior, he might be permitted to use the library so by the time he's released, he can work towards attaining his law degree. What about three square meals per day? I bet the average American family doesn't even get that.

I honestly believe in rehabilitation and though I am probably the minority on this issue, I still remain firm in my conviction that people can conform their behavior to the appropriate societal standard. Chad, however, was impervious to punishment so the best thing that could happen to him would be the death sentence. But that would only occur if the State could show Chad killed some of his victims outside the Commonwealth, thereby establishing jurisdiction of another sovereign which holds a liberal view with respect to capital punishment. This theory will likely fail because all the victims whose bodies were discovered were murdered in Massachusetts.

Chad was becoming impatient and pacing back and forth considering other available alternatives, if any, did in fact exist. Kerri had an idea and when Chad left the room momentarily, she whispered her proposal to Alison.

"Hey, listen. Maybe I can get him to let me use the bathroom. I might find something in there to use as a weapon."

"Kerri, don't be foolish. He'll kill you," Alison replied.

"Not if I kill him first."

"It's too risky. Let the police handle this."

"Alison, we could be in here for days. This guy is not giving up and there's no way the police will attempt a rescue knowing we're in here with him."

"I know, but if something goes wrong, we're as good as dead."

"Nothing will happen. I promise. Just go along with what I do. Okay?"

"All right. Just make sure you know what you're doing."

Kerri yelled out to Chad while he was inside another room.

"Excuse me? Hello? I was wondering if I could use the bathroom. I really have to go and I can't hold it anymore," said Kerri.

"Why didn't you tell me before I brought you upstairs?" he asked with fury.

"I didn't have to go then."

"All right. I'll untie you and if you try anything stupid your body parts will end up in the freezer."

"I understand," she responded.

Chad gradually removed the chain around Kerri's ankles and escorted her inside the bathroom.

"Are you gonna stand here and watch me?" she asked.

"You have two minutes," he told her, before shutting the door.

Kerri knew she had little time but searched the entire room as fast as she could, looking for anything to facilitate an attack against the killer. She stumbled upon some pills in the medicine cabinet and thought about poisoning him.

"Too risky," she murmured.

She turned on the faucet, hoping to stall for time.

"What are you doing in there?" he asked.

"I'm washing my hands. Do you mind?"

She returned moments later and sat back down on the floor next to Alison. Chad then tied her hands behind her back and then strolled toward the kitchen window peering outside at FBI agents.

"Did you find anything?" Alison asked.

"Shhh . . . I'll tell you later," replied Kerri, who was quite reluctant about exposing her scheme, knowing Chad was within an earshot of both of them. After a few minutes, Chad went downstairs in order to obtain more ammunition.

Once Kerri discovered what he was doing, she removed the small razor she held in her hand and began cutting the rope fastened around her hands.

"What are you doing?" Alison asked.

"Trying to get us both out of here," Kerri said.

"What if he comes back and sees you?"

"Don't worry, I'll make it."

"Where did you get that?" Alison asked, with great curiosity.

"I found it inside one of the bathroom cabinets."

"Hurry up, I think he's walking back toward us," Alison responded apprehensively.

Kerri immediately refrained from slicing the rope and concealed the razor underneath the carpet where she was sitting. She had managed to cut halfway through without giving the appearance that an escape was contemplated. Instead, her mobility was purported to be restricted and with great difficulty, as manifested by her facial expression. But she needed to buy more time.

I've got it, she thought. *I'll ask if I can smoke.*

"Chad, do you have a cigarette?"

"How are you going to smoke with your hands tied behind your back?"

"I was hoping you would hold it for me."

"I'm not your baby sitter."

"I know Chad. I'm just getting a little restless. When I don't smoke I get anxious. I'm sorry."

"Wait here and let me see if I have any lying around."

"Where am I gonna go Chad? I'm tied up at the moment."

Chad went into the bedroom to look for a pack of cigarettes. This was Kerri's opportunity to remove the rope fastened around her. She picked up the razor and cut through the rope faster than a surgeon about to make his incision. Within seconds, she was free and ran over to Alison hoping to untie her as well. But by this time, Chad was walking out of the room, so Kerri left the razor by Alison and resumed her position in the corner.

"Here, I found these lying around. That's all I have," he told her.

There was just one problem. Kerri didn't smoke. In fact, she never lit up a cigarette in her entire life.

Chad placed the cigarette in her mouth and lit it for her. No sooner did Kerri's face turn bright red and gasping for air, she replied, "what brand is that? They're horrible."

Luckily, Chad didn't catch on and realize Kerri was setting him up. He threw the cigarettes on the floor and proceeded toward the bedroom.

"Alison, start slicing through the rope," Kerri said.

"I can't reach it. The razor is behind me."

"Get up and get it."

"What if he sees me?"

"Never mind. I'll do it."

Kerri, trying to be as quiet as possible, got up and sat beside Alison and began cutting the rope. She was just about finished loosening it when Chad walked into the room.

"What the hell are you doing?" he yelled.

"Alison just go along with me," she whispered.

Kerri moved in toward Alison and gave her a kiss on the lips.

"I'm sorry," Kerri said. "I just couldn't help myself."

"So you're a lesbian?" Chad asked jokingly.

"I guess I am," she answered.

Kerri was no more a lesbian than Chad was sane, but she had to be quick on her feet if any attempt at eluding danger was within reach.

The FBI was growing restless, as all they could do was sit outside and discuss their options which unfortunately, were diminishing by the second.

"Where's that damn sharp shooter?" demanded Hawk.

"He should be here soon," replied another agent. "Soon may be too late," Hawk said, aware that he was running on empty.

"That's the best we can do for now."

"No. The best we can do is take this guy out without causing any other fatalities," said Hawk.

Hawk proceeded to his car where he made a few phone calls; one being his family telling them he didn't know when he was going to return home.

The hostage situation was approaching seven hours. The sharpshooter was supposed to be flown in from a small town in New

Mexico. Apparently, this guy was damn good. He could hit a target smaller than a bottle cap from a half mile away. The only thing he couldn't do was touch down in Boston due to a severe tornado that was hovering over the Four Corners of the Western United States. All airports had shut down and no planes were permitted to take off until hours later. The FBI was counting on his anticipated arrival.

Within an hour, a small plane carrying ammunition and food landed in a nearby cornfield about three hundred yards from the site of the alleged standoff. The door opened and a man of exceptional size, with deep, thick skin and a visible scar under his right eye, stepped down from the aircraft. He was escorted by two other men wearing bullet proof vests and carrying Super Maxx 5000's. The sharpshooter introduced himself to Hawk and the other men bordering the immediate area.

"I thought you would never get here," Hawk said.

"I apologize for the delay, but all planes were temporarily grounded from the storm," he replied.

"That's okay. The important thing is you are here now and we can get back to business," Hawk answered.

"I have with me a highly technological electromagnetic device far superior to that of infrared which will provide us with a clearly defined location of the individuals inside the house," the man said.

His birth name was Siloh but he changed it to Zack when he became of majority age. He used it for a few years until he earned the reputation of one of the finest sharpshooters in all the west. Then he was known as simply "Sharpie." Sharpie had a fear of guns when he was a young boy. He lived with his father after his mother died from a rare kidney disease. She was only thirty-two.

Sharpie grew up fast and learned the tricks of survival. His father purchased a gun when Sharpie was just eleven-years-old and taught him how to use it. It was called the Thunder Ranch, a model 22 revolver manufactured by Smith and Wesson. His father instructed him never to touch the gun unless his father gave him permission and was present when Sharpie handled it.

It was locked away in a large cabinet in the pantry where his father also stored bottles of wine which he made himself from the grapes that were grown on his three-acre ranch. His father had raised cattle and sold them off if the price was right. The gun wasn't for recreation. It was to protect his family's economic future by preventing unwanted trespassers from entering the land and absconding with livestock.

Each day Sharpie's father would take him outside and let him practice hitting targets at close range, until Sharpie developed enough confidence to shoot from greater distances. By the time Sharpie became a teenager, he wasn't just entering target shooting contests, he was winning them hands down. Today, he is quite popular in New Mexico, living with his wife and two children in a small town called Los Primos.

"How many people are inside?" Sharpie asked.

"I think two women."

"Well, I can pick up any movement with my scope. It detects any heat that is emitted within the house."

Sharpie assembled all of his equipment and got within close range of the killer's whereabouts.

"Right now, I am looking at someone pacing back and forth," he said.

"Can you tell if it's the killer?" Hawk inquired.

"No. I can't make out any facial identification because it is very dark inside that room."

"Can you shoot him through the house?"

"Yes. But I must be damn certain before I pull the trigger."

Sharpie only had to pull the trigger once to take out the enemy. He was just that consistent.

"Don't worry, though. Once the morning arrives, I'll have a clean shot at him."

"So we have to wait another three or four hours before anything gets done?" asked Hawk.

"Unfortunately, that's the safest approach."

Chad could see that the agents were up to something when he saw the plane landing in the far distance. He didn't take any chances and moved both women back downstairs. He was hoping that it would be dark enough to prevent the officers or the sharpshooter from taking him out if they couldn't see inside the house.

The sun came up at 5:36 a.m., just as predicted by the weather bureau. Agents moved in and Sharpie went to work. He could see all three of them huddled on the floor in the basement. Chad was intelligent enough to place himself in the middle of the two women making it more complex to get off a clean hit. He also put on a long wig to confuse the men. But Sharpie was too experienced to fall for any trickery. His machinery put him right inside the house as though he were rubbing noses with the killer.

"If you have a clear shot, take it," shouted one of the commanding officers.

A shot rang through and ricocheted off the floor within close proximity of where they were seated. Sharpie missed on purpose in order to see if the killer would increase his mobility and separate himself far enough from the women. This was Kerri's opportunity to make a run at an escape.

"Where the hell are you going?" Chad yelled.

"I'm not staying here and getting shot," she said, standing up from the floor.

"Sit your ass down before I put a bullet in your head!"

"You're gonna have to shoot me cause I'm not staying here."

Before he could say anything, another shot ripped through the siding on the house and struck Chad in his right knee. The force of the shot knocked the gun out of his hand and Kerri scrambled to the floor in an extreme attempt at retrieving it. Her hands were nervously examining the floor trying to feel the deadly weapon which was only inches away.

She picked it up and was immediately wrestled to the ground when Chad struck her from behind. Kerri held on to the gun as though it were a child clinging to life. He tried to pull it from her, but she kicked him between his legs and he fell to the ground in excruciating pain.

Alison then intervened and they managed to subdue the killer. Kerri could have ended his life at that moment by pulling the trigger. But she resisted, because she didn't believe in taking life and most of all, she wanted him to pay. Death would be too easy, much like a reward. She wasn't going to let him depart this world without retribution.

When they realized he wasn't responding in a threatening manner, they both ran across the room and opened the latch on the trap door. Within seconds, the two women were outside and breathing fresh air. It was the first time in months for Alison. The FBI moved in and apprehended the killer. Others remained behind and removed all of the evidence found in the basement.

There were a total of four bodies recovered from the home. It was possible that Chad had killed in excess of a dozen women. Police also found newspaper articles, telephone numbers and addresses of other women Chad had intended to abduct and kill in the future.

Chad's luck had finally run out. He could have been a successful man. He possessed the requisite intellect but his reasoning was substantially impaired. He was an artist with tremendous talent and painted several murals while studying in college. Yet, he was blinded by his own desire for revenge and he could never release his feelings of vengeance.

Chad was certain he would never see the inside of a prison. He already figured out what his defense was going to be. What else could he raise? Insanity. Of course, unlike all other crimes where the burden, of production rests with the State, insanity must initially be proven by the defendant by a showing of a preponderance of evidence. Once the defendant meets that burden, the State must show he is sane beyond a reasonable doubt. A good defense attorney could easily establish that Chad lacked some substantial capacity to either appreciate the criminality of his conduct, or conform his conduct to the requirements of law. All that mattered was whether Chad was competent at the time he committed the murders.

Chad was escorted into one of the vehicles and taken into custody. He was now the property of the FBI. People cheered as he drove away and Chad demonstrated his disapproval by making an inappropriate gesture with his finger. After two years of tension and living in fear, the residents of Massachusetts could breath a sigh of relief. The evil monster that lurked their neighborhoods was finally captured.

Chad was tried in federal court. This meant the burden of proof standard for insanity was slightly higher than in state court. In other words, Chad had to demonstrate he was insane by clear and convincing evidence, not the preponderance of evidence requirement he would have had to prove in state court.

The jury didn't buy the insanity defense for one moment, despite numerous psychiatrists who testified in his behalf. He was convicted of five counts of first degree murder and two counts of kidnaping. He was sentenced to 240 years in prison with no possibility of parole. The judge referred to him as inhumanly cruel, diabolical, and wicked. He chastised Chad for over fifteen minutes, then ended with compelling statements attacking Chad's character.

"You are nothing short of a despicable and abhorrent piece of garbage. You could have gone far in this world with your legal background. You were blessed with intelligence but you wasted that gift. Now you will waste the rest of your life rotting inside a prison cell for your devilish ways. Remove this piece of trash from the courtroom." Chad was led away and placed inside a van specifically designed to transport prison inmates. He was sent upstate to Concord, New Hampshire, where he would live out the rest of his days.

CHAPTER THIRTY-ONE

ALISON RUSHED OUT of the house and ran into Brendan's arms. With tears swiftly gliding down her face, she was ever so appreciative that Brendan was standing by to take her home. He wrapped his over coat around her and they engaged in a kiss.

"I never thought I would see you again," she told him.

"I know. I had those same thoughts," he replied.

They walked back toward the car and were approached by a female news reporter who was hoping for a last minute interview. Alison stopped momentarily and then gazed into the camera and made the following statement: "I'm just so happy to be alive and I am so glad this nightmare is over. I want to put it all behind me and move on with my family. My children are what kept me going throughout this whole ordeal." With that said, she was helped into the family car and driven home.

Kerri remained with the officers, providing them with additional information to help wrap up the investigation. I watched everything from the television in my apartment. They questioned her for about an hour and constantly referred to her as the heroine in this tragedy. She deserved all of the attention. She was courageous throughout the ordeal and never backed down. I was so relieved to see her walk out of that house alive. But I also knew she would eventually be walking out of my life forever.

Soon after, Kerri was promised a position with the Federal Bureau of Investigations at their home office in Washington, D.C. She gave up the practice of law and decided to pursue criminals in a different fashion. Her responsibilities would involve communicating with law enforcement and other federal agencies about widespread potential threats of terrorism, and hunting down inherently dangerous felons.

She left her two-bedroom apartment in Massachusetts and moved into a lavishly elegant condominium in Alexandria, Virginia. She concealed her new identity and no longer communicated with family or friends, while on assignment. Three years later, she would marry an ex-marine and have two beautiful girls, Kellie and Anne.

It was the beginning of November, and I was expecting an early Christmas gift. The postman placed the mail inside the mailbox and I rushed outside hoping to obtain my results from the Massachusetts Bar Exam. They had finally arrived after four long months of waiting and torturing myself to death.

Afraid to open it at first, I held it up to the light to view its contents, but I couldn't see anything inside. My heart was racing and I felt like I was back in law school. This was it. My whole career was stuffed inside a white envelope. If I failed, I would let my entire family down. Not to mention having to take it again which would cost an additional $800 bucks. I slid my finger through the top portion and took out the three pages found inside. I unfolded them and glanced at the top. To my surprise, I had passed; just barely I'm certain, but nonetheless.

Later the following year, I would join a law firm in New York City as a first-year associate earning $55,000. I couldn't complain. The commute wasn't bad and the hours were good. I could have done without the subway, but that's the way to travel in New York City. If you want to work there, you have to get used to traveling with large crowds of people. Some days I felt as though I couldn't breath with my face against the subway doors. And if you were unfortunate enough to travel on the hottest day of the year and you happened to be adjacent to someone who forgot to shower that morning, it could have been a long ride.

Lunch was satisfying, especially when it was free. Most of the time, I ate in the cafeteria, but on this particular day, I was in municipal court so I thought about dining in Little Italy. It was just a few stops on the subway from the administration building.

It was a gorgeous afternoon—and pleasantly warm—so I decided to eat outside. I found a table in the corner facing the street. Foot traffic was heavy, as employees rushed to their favorite restaurants hoping to avoid long lines. Cabs were dropping off passengers on the corner of Mulberry Street, while Italian music was playing in the background. A waiter approached the table and informed me of the daily specials. But I chose to order something off the menu.

Then I glanced at the wine list before making my selection. I decided to go with a glass of Chardonnay. For lunch, I had my favorite Italian dish: cavatelli with meat sauce, and a garden salad with balsamic vinaigrette.

As I was about to signal to the waiter that I was ready to order, a woman advanced in my direction.

"Is this table taken?" she asked.

"No, no one is sitting there," I said.

I then introduced myself and engaged in conversation.

"So what do you do?" she asked.

"Oh, I'm an attorney," I replied.

"Really? So am I?" she stated, humorously.

"You're kidding?" I responded.

"No, I'm a public defender," she said.

"Where did you go to school?" I asked.

"New York Law."

"Impressive," I replied.

"I was lucky to get in," she stated. "My LSAT score wasn't so great. And I hated those horrible logical games."

"I know what you mean," I told her. "I bombed the LSAT. In fact, I took it twice. Got the same score both times."

"Oh, I'm so sorry. I didn't introduce myself. I feel like such an idiot. My name is Alexis," she declared, extending her hand in my direction.

"Nice to meet you, Alexis."

"Do you come down to Little Italy often?" she asked.

"Not really. I was just in the mood for Italian. I've been eating a lot of crap lately," I answered.

"Oh, my God. That's so funny. I can tell you what my diet has been for the last few weeks. Salad, yogurt and *Slim Fast*," she acknowledged. I thought she was being sarcastic.

"You? On a diet?" I asked with bewilderment. The woman was barely over one hundred and ten pounds.

"Yes. I have been following a strict regimen. I haven't always been this weight," she explained, telling me about her past experiences and the difficulty involved in shedding those undesirable pounds.

"Well, you look fine," I told her, hoping that she would agree to see me in the future.

"Thanks. I'll take whatever compliment I can get."

"Shall we order?" I suggested.

"I think that would be great."

The waiter approached and took our orders. Alexis had the chicken marsala and a diet soda. I went with my first choice. Minutes later, the best homemade bread was brought to our table. We both had made a meal on that alone. Alexis was so hungry she requested a second basket be brought with lots of warm butter.

Now this was too good to be true. What were the odds of finding two attorneys who share similar interests sitting at the same table? I had to open the middle section of the newspaper and read my horoscope. For the last few months I felt like a bowling pin. Each time I got back up, I was immediately knocked down again.

When I glanced at my sign, it didn't mention anything about meeting someone with similar interests. In fact, it said I was too depressed to find romance. So much for trusting the Zodiac.

I managed to get Alexis's number before leaving the restaurant. We would date for five months before becoming engaged. I decided to propose to her on her birthday for two reasons, actually. One, she would never forget the date, and two, I would only have to buy her one gift, an expensive engagement ring. It was an elegant 14 karat, diamond Solitaire that sparkled like a perpetual fireworks exhibition.

The splendid dimension of the ring accentuated her beautiful and well-groomed fingers. I found her to be more beautiful each passing day.

We moved into our first home, after renting an apartment for three years. The four bedroom, modern colonial, with a huge backyard and an in-ground swimming pool constructed in the shape of a figure eight, was located in a quiet, suburban community. The backyard had a swing set, which was one of the reasons why we purchased the house. Alexis would practice law, until our first child was born that following April.

At that moment, I realized that opportunity is what you make of it. Sometimes you had to search for it in the most difficult places. I thought that running away and starting over was the answer. Leaving behind family and friends and pursuing a career in another state obviously didn't work. Alexis made that perfectly clear. When I saw a conflict, I ran from it. It was easier to deal with if left alone. Alexis never ran from anything. She never met a challenge she couldn't handle.

When things got rough financially and we were strapped, I thought about changing careers, maybe getting out of the law field. But we hung tough and persevered, and somehow we made it. Looking back I wouldn't have changed anything. In spite of all the hardship and misfortune, I could start to smell success. I realized that success had to be earned. You had to pay your dues along the way. If it was achieved too easily then it wasn't success, but just plain luck. Success isn't based on one's occupation, earning capacity or how far of a climb it is up the corporate ladder, but how many times you fall off the ladder and have the courage to climb back up.

I like to judge success by the sum of one's failures in life. For if you haven't failed, then you truly have never succeeded. It took me years to figure it out, but it was definitely worth it in the end. As someone once said, "Now, instead of agonizing over the storm, I dance in the rain."

Breinigsville, PA USA
23 August 2010
244108BV00003B/69/P